What readers think of *The Opportunity*

Well-written fictional expose' on government contracting
...provides an insightful look at government contracting seamy underbelly, with sharp and cunning characters and themes of corruption, morality, and accountability. From the political front offices, backrooms, and bedrooms of Washington D.C. to the flashy satellite singles scene of Rehoboth Beach, *The Opportunity* gives the reader an insider's look into a money-and-sex driven world that, sometimes simultaneously, operates both in the shadows and in the public eye. *Brent Lewis on January 30, 2016*

The Opportunity: A Must Read
I recently had the pleasure of reading Frank Hopkins' latest novel, *The Opportunity*, which I highly recommend to those interested in a novel which documents how government corruption could occur in Federal Government contracting. The novel faithfully explores how government contractors approach winning a major contract and the single life scene in the Rehoboth, Delaware area. *Carl Pergler November 14, 2014*

Hard to put down. Hopkins has a sense of ...
the Washington scene and its corruption. His heroes are those persons who wade through the paperwork to find the culprits. Journey along with the author ... and find out more than you ever imagined about how our government works and doesn't work. The issues of women using sex to get information are all too common in our government. *Tom the Baker December 26, 2014*

I really enjoyed the book *The Opportunity*.
..fast paced and exciting. Someone once asked me what I read for, I responded "I love local color". The book certainly contains it with realistic descriptions of scenes set in the Washington, DC and Rehoboth Beach, Delaware areas. I recommend *The Opportunity* to all readers interested in a read which holds your attention about the government contacting industry. *Nancy Oppenheim December 22, 2014*

This fictitious example is entertaining and fun to read
A description of a federal procurement life cycle. Fictitious?

Maybe not! Well done story about marketing, competition, personal goals, and Government review of a competitive. *The Opportunity* by Frank Hopkins was one of those stories for me even though I have lived in the Washington, D.C. area and have been close to government life in many ways. The competitive and sometimes grim real world of the contracting game was an unknown. This book, exciting and readable and is written with enough intrigue to keep the interest going until the very end.. *Amazon Customer July26, 2016*

Contract work with a twist of intrigue

A rare book that takes you into the details of government contract bidding, but adds a twist of intrigue. *Jack Coppley June 28, 2016*

Read it!

Once you pick it up it's hard to put down! Frank Hopkins did an excellent job in bringing the characters to life and creating a fabulous storyline! a real must read! *Lisa on August 12, 2016*

Another Winner by Frank Hopkins

...it seems to be the goal the principal characters in *The Opportunity* to retire rich as early as possible; nothing much is acknowledged of the intrinsic value of their work. Rather it is a means to the end of acquiring wealth, and to the extent it does not do that, it has no value. Frank Hopkins' experience as an economist and as a consultant in both government and business shows in his precise descriptions of the contracting process. Along with everything else, readers gain a good understanding of how things work (and don't work) in Washington. That may or may not be a good thing. ...if you get the opportunity to read Frank E. Hopkins' newest novel, *The Opportunity*, do not fail to do so. It is another winner... *Robert J. Anderson November 15, 2014*

Intriguing Fictional read....Hopkins nails it!

Excellent, *The Opportunity* by Frank E. Hopkins keeps you reading, anticipating how the book's discussion of corruption between the US government, its contractors and Congress is brought to justice. The stories of sexual misconduct, spying on the Government and its competition, favors to enhance careers, create entwining twists and turns that excite the reader from the beginning until its tragic ending...I highly recommend this book a great Summer beach read. *Judith L. Kirlan July 4, 2016.*

Seductive and Engrossing!
Once again Hopkins' delivers ...."The Opportunity" is a compelling story, exposing unscrupulous characters who are employed in the business of Federal Government Contracting. Hopkins' addresses the breach of trust, immorality and irresponsible attitude while attempting to win a contract. As a reader unfamiliar with the intricacies of government contracting Hopkins brings his characters to life by detailing the strategies involved for winning a contract: starting with an RFP (request for proposal),capturing the contract, identifying a capture program manager, producing a team prior to the "bid" and writing the proposal. His experience as a consultant in Government and Business lends credibility to the narrative. The book continues to draw you in from beginning to end. An unforgettable read! *Linda D on July 28, 2017*

Definitely read this book
There are still surprises left in life! The Opportunity by Frank Hopkins was one of those stories for me even though. I have lived in the Washington, D.C. area and have been close to government life in many ways. The competitive and sometimes grim real world of the contracting game was an unknown. This book, exciting and readable, is written with enough intrigue to keep the interest going until the very end. Of course this is fiction ....or is it? *S. Steinberg on July 26, 2016*

Great read.
i just finished Hopkins "Opportunity". What a great read! Hopkins has a great story line that exposes the reader to the inside of what goes on in contractors seeking lucrative government bids. Sex, government, corruption and the beach. What a great combination. *W. Kennedy on February 4, 2017*

All that you love and hate about Washington D. C.
In "The Opportunity" author Frank Hopkins gives the reader a close look at corruption in Washington, both the political and corporate variety and exposes the age-old practice of beautiful, sexy women wielding their physical assets to seduce weak willed

men into giving them what they want and occasionally, need.
Amazon Customer on June 8, 2016

Enjoyable
I enjoyed the book very much. It put into writing a lot of what really does go on in securing contracts. Plus, being from Delaware it's fun to read something with a local flair. Going to read more of Frank's writing! *Stephanie Downey on April 24, 2017*

Thank you for reading *The Opportunity*. If you liked the book, or my other books, please write an Amazon review to inform other potential readers they would enjoy the book. Please open my Amazon author page to access the forms to write your review.

https://www.amazon.com/Frank-E.-Hopkins/e/B0028AR904

Chick on the book cover of the book you want to review and the review option will appear toward the bottom of the page.

The

Opportunity

Frank E. Hopkins

Books by Frank E Hopkins

Fiction:
>*Abandoned Homes: Vietnam Revenge Killings*
>*First Time*
>*The Opportunity*
>*Unplanned Choices*

Non-fiction:
>*Locational Analysis: An Interregional Econometric Model of Agriculture, Mining, Manufacturing and Services,* with Curtis Harris.

ISBN: 1500838438
ISBN 13: 978-1500838430

Ocean View Publishing
Ocean View, Delaware

DEDICATION

Dedicated to the honest government employees and contractors who keep our country running.

ACKNOWLEDGMENTS

Several chapters of *The Opportunity* were written in the Friday Free Writes meetings of the Rehoboth Beach Writers Guild. I would like to thank Frank Minni and the members of the Free Writes group who commented and improved early chapter drafts. I would like to thank the Salisbury Critique Group of the Eastern Shore Writers Association for reading and advising me on how to improve several of the chapters of the book. Numerous individuals provided invaluable help by reading and commenting on a prepublication version of the book, including Mary Lou Butler and Carl Pergler. Bob Anderson, Ph.D. and Walt Curran provided invaluable insight and recommendations for correcting errors and improving the readability of *The Opportunity*. I want to thank CreateSpace, who performed the final copy editing, identifying errors and suggesting improvements in the novel. Damon of www.Damonza.com produced the cover which captures the main theme of *The Opportunity*.

Chapter 1 July 4 Weekend (Saturday, July 2, 2011)

"Amy, you look like a hooker," said Pete Taylor.

"I'd rather show cleavage and turn men on than have an extra forty pounds in my stomach pressing against my cummerbund."

"It's only thirty pounds which isn't much if you're six-two. I hope you don't dress that way when you meet our clients."

"You know I wear formal business attire."

"Amy, don't pretend you dress matronly. You dress to make your male clients helpless," Art replied.

"You both never object when we sign contracts or task orders. Pete, if you're going to complain quit staring at my boobs."

"Pete can't. He never outgrew his teenage fixation," Art said.

"Have some respect. I'm still your boss," replied Pete.

"We all agreed three years ago when I joined the beach house that as soon as we crossed the Chesapeake Bay Bridge we left CIN Inc. behind," Art said.

"True, but then respect me as a friend—and don't exaggerate my extra weight."

Pete, Amy, and Art worked together at Computer Information Networks Inc. They referred to their company as CIN Inc.

Pete Taylor, a fifty-six-year-old teenager and the general manager of IT services for CIN Inc. sat on the front porch of their Dewey Beach summer rental house sipping his second martini at 4:00 p.m. Amy Ericson, a thirty-eight-year-old, blue-eyed, voluptuous, five-foot six-inch, blonde business development and marketing executive, sipped her second glass of wine. The contrast between Amy and Pete resembled the differences between a male and female walrus. Art Mitchell, a thin fifty-five-year-old returned from his daily five-mile afternoon run and climbed the steps to the porch.

The three retired into the house to shower and dress in formal attire for the party, returning to the porch at five thirty. Art, sipping his first beer said, "Amy, can you help me with my tie? I still can't believe we wear tuxedos on a ninety-plus-degree July Fourth weekend."

"It's tradition, the thirty-fifth anniversary of the formal July Fourth party. Besides, you look great. You'll attract every woman at the party," Amy replied.

"I doubt it. Everyone there knows I'm dating Joan and that she's out of town."

"Art, don't underestimate the deviousness of the female sex drive," Pete said. "You're attractive because you're handsome and don't hit on them. But we know Amy, not Art, is the sex magnet. She'll leave the party with an entourage."

"I'm faithful. I'll leave with both of you. Art, your tie looks good. It's almost six. Let's catch the Jolly Trolley," Amy replied.

"I agree. I'm in no shape to drive," Pete said.

The three left their St. Louis Street A-frame, walked to Route 1 and boarded the trolley towed by a pickup truck. Their formal clothing received minor stares from the other bikini- and bathing-suit-attired passengers, who knew any behavior could be expected at the beach.

They arrived at the Henlopen Avenue beach house party in Rehoboth Beach a few minutes after it started.

"Three champagnes?" Art asked, sweating through his white, starched shirt. He stood next to Amy and Pete at a long table under a white canvas canopy next to the entrance walkway to the party house. Twenty other guests jostled for the attention of the bartenders who offered beer, soda, wine, and champagne. Art and Amy sipped the champagne while Pete guzzled his.

"Pete, you'd better slow down or you'll end the night early," Amy said.

"Maybe you're right."

The threesome split up and mingled. They agreed to meet in front of the house and walk into Rehoboth for dinner at eight.

Amy spent the next two hours talking to her friends, who also worked in marketing for federal government contracting firms, sharing the latest gossip about their clients and anticipated contracts. Art wandered around the party, sipping champagne, talking to his friends, and not approaching the available, attractive, sensual, and financially secure women surrounding him, thinking he'd rather be home with Joan watching a golf or a tennis match on TV.

Pete did not have another glass of champagne. He walked into the kitchen, and asked one of the hostesses, dressed in a sexy French maid outfit, "Can I have a martini?"

"Sure. Isn't champagne good enough for you? Vodka or gin?"

"I'm getting bloated from the bubbles and just want something to sip. Vodka's fine."

"I understand."

Pete had the reputation at the beach and in Washington of being a heavy drinker. He sipped his drink and talked to anyone he met about business, the rise in the stock market, and who was dating whom.

At 8:00 p.m. the three met and walked to the Summer House. Pete had a martini and a glass of wine to wash down a sixteen-ounce steak dinner. Art and Amy ate rockfish and grilled tuna, respectively, and drank two glasses of wine during the ninety-minute dinner.

"I'm going for a walk on the boardwalk. Anyone want to join me?" Pete asked when they finished dinner.

They agreed, left the coolness of the restaurant, and began walking the two and a half blocks to the boardwalk. Even though the afternoon heat had cooled to eighty-five degrees by early evening, it hit them as they strolled, still adorned in their formal clothes. Happy adults with their young children, groups of teenagers, and young single adults packed the sidewalks searching for summer fun. Rehoboth Avenue had congested and stalled traffic. The drivers searched for nonexistent parking spaces.

Pete strolled with Art and Amy pointing out the bikini-clad young women he would like to meet. His size normally hid the effects of drinking, but he wove as he identified the bikini displaying the next nearest object of his desire. Art noticed Pete sweated profusely. After walking for five minutes, they passed a stately, barely clothed blonde in her early twenties.

Pete turned to Art and said, "Did you see…"

He clutched his chest and fell to the ground shaking.

Art bent over Pete who could not talk, but uttered gurgling sounds. A crowd formed as Art called 911. Several of them speculated that he was drunk, had a heart attack, a stroke, or experienced other fatal disorders. Art concurred with the crowd's suggestions related to health problems, having seen Pete consume twice as much alcohol without slurring his words or passing out.

The 911 operators dispatched an ambulance from Beebe Medical Center in Lewes, a short seven miles from Pete's shaking body. The traffic on Route 1 between Lewes and Rehoboth was as congested as that on Rehoboth Avenue.

While waiting for the ambulance, Amy and Art worried about Pete's health. Amy reminisced about her first adult beach summer, her first meeting with Pete, and her career at CIN Inc. Art, seeing the pain in Pete's face, wondered if he would survive.

Amy looked at Art. "Men let their weaknesses control their lives."

Chapter 2 Amy's Story (July 2003)

Amy had been an easygoing education major who married her college sweetheart, Tony Aliberti after graduation. She supported him for seven years, teaching third grade, while he went to the University of Maryland, School of Medicine in Baltimore and served his internship and completed his residency at Johns Hopkins. His education exposed him to endless hours of work and willing women at the hospital. While faithful to the work, he succumbed to temptation. Amy had no clue to his behavior. She expected to quit work and have children when he started his medical practice. Instead, he announced he wanted a divorce. Her perfect life ended at twenty-eight in 2002. She became cold and calculating vowing never to trust a man to control her economic life.

Amy's friends supported her after her husband left while she was legally separated. While waiting for her divorce, they gave her suggestions on attracting men. Amy initially rejected the advice since she vowed to abstain from men. She eventually followed part of their counsel to regain her pre-married body: losing twenty pounds, toning her muscles, and transforming herself from a frumpy married woman to one with an irresistible body. She never became skinny, but regained her late-teenage voluptuous curves that raised the blood pressure and hastened the breathing of any testosterone-producing man.

While Amy loved teaching, she realized her salary would never support her aspirations. On a very hot July Tuesday afternoon her best friend and college roommate, Joan Watkins, met her for lunch. "You look fabulous," Joan said as she sat at Amy's table.

"Thanks. I feel better when I don't think of Tony."

"You have to forget him. With your new body you'll have no trouble attracting men."

"Not really. Most of the men in Columbia are married and there are few single men at work. All the teachers and administrators are either women or married."

They both ordered a glass of Chardonnay and the salmon salad. Amy would have had a cheeseburger topped with bacon, and fries if she was still married.

"There are other ways to meet men and Columbia isn't the greatest location. You should move to DC."

"I can't afford to live in DC on a teacher's salary. I'd have to get another job."

"Do what I do. My degree's in English literature, but I work in marketing for an IT firm and make twice as much as you."

"I'm not qualified."

"Amy, all you need is a smile, a tight-fitting dress, a good personality, and the ability to talk and listen to clients."

"I don't want to be a hooker."

"You don't have to sleep with anyone. Older men unconsciously want to please young, attractive women. Awarding your company a contract or task order assures your clients they will keep seeing you."

"It still sounds like prostitution."

"Amy, look at any ad on TV or in magazines. Sexy models, both men and women, are the basis for all marketing. It's human nature. Use your natural charms to get rich."

"I don't want to stay poor and I'm still pissed at Tony. I had a great life planned. He'd make a lot of money to support our family while I became the perfect mother."

"Don't stay bitter. Do something about it. Use your femininity to get rich. When you're ready for a man, your looks and a high income will attract whoever you want."

"Men want women with a good income? I thought all

they're interested in is breasts."

"They don't want someone who is poor and needy even if they have large boobs. You'll earn more in a successful career in business development than your ex-husband will as a doctor. If you save your bonus money, in fifteen years he couldn't touch your lifestyle," Joan said.

"Really! How much could I make?"

"It's all based on commission. I'm marketing an opportunity at one agency, and if we win the contract I expect to get an annual bonus of $100,000 for five years. The bonus is above my base salary plus commissions I'm owed for previous wins. Incidentally, my base salary is higher than your teacher's salary."

"I never knew. You don't have a rich lifestyle."

"True, but I save my bonus money so I can retire early. A whole new world awaits you if you have the courage to grab it."

"Fabulous money and no teaching plans to prepare daily. How do I get a marketing job?"

"I'll introduce you to people in government contracting. It's up to you to convince them you're qualified to switch from teaching to marketing. If they have a need they'll offer you an entry level position. In addition to a new job, I have a solution that could solve your man problem."

"I don't have a man problem."

"You do. You just don't realize it. The Delaware beaches are a perfect place for meeting men. Join me this weekend at my beach house and you can start your new life."

"It's hot here. The beach would be cooler than Columbia. I've heard drunken singles in their twenties go to the beach and attend wild parties—not people like us."

"Young adults do have fun at the beach. The population from Lewes, Delaware, to Ocean City, Maryland, swells to over a half a million during a busy summer weekend. There should be one man for you."

"I'm not looking for a man, but I'll still go."

"You'll like the beach house. While most people rent or own condos or hotel rooms, the beach house has its own culture. We associate with more than thirty beach houses with professional singles from their late twenties to their sixties. There's at least one party every weekend. It's the perfect place for professional networking or to meet men."

"I'll concentrate on networking."

"Good. Please upgrade your wardrobe to fit in with the beach crowd and attract a new employer."

"Sounds like you want me to sell myself sexually."

"No, but your dress hangs off you and could fit a woman twenty pounds heavier. It's not very flattering. I imagine most of your clothes are too large for your new body."

"They are."

"Do you have any plans this afternoon?"

"No."

"Let's go shopping at Columbia Mall."

Amy had separated from her husband six months earlier and was still legally married. She did not anticipate the impact of her first beach weekend. Joan, who took Friday afternoon off, arrived at Amy's Columbia townhouse at 1:00 p.m. and honked the car's horn.

Amy bounded out her door, dressed in shorts and a loose-fitting blouse, as instructed by Joan, carrying two pieces of luggage containing her new beach wardrobe. Joan, seeing her enthusiasm, said, "You look ready for the beach."

"I am. Do you always leave so early?"

"Yes. If we leave later it will take us four hours. There are bottlenecks on the Chesapeake Bay Bridge before Annapolis and on Route 1 in Lewes, Delaware. We'd have to leave later than seven to complete the trip within three hours, and we'd miss Friday evening's fun."

"How do you get off work every Friday afternoon?"

"I'm in marketing. I don't punch a clock and I set my own schedule."

"What will we do during the weekend?"

"The first thing we'll do is choose a room and have a drink."

"The rooms aren't already assigned?"

"No, whoever arrives first has their choice. The second arrival has the next choice and so forth. It's another reason for leaving early."

"How are the rooms?"

"Small. There are four rooms upstairs with twin beds and three downstairs with single beds. We'll pick an upstairs room."

"Sounds like a big house."

"Not really. It's not a mansion, but it's very functional."

"Do the members own the beach house?"

"No, we lease the home as a group for the summer from May 1 through the end of September. Our group has held an annual lease for ten years."

"Wow. It's a permanent summer vacation home."

"Yes, many single professionals move their social life to the Delaware beaches in the summer. Our house is great since there's no TV blaring depressing world news that could destroy the weekend."

"I'm getting excited and nervous. I hope your friends will like me."

"The men will love you or at least try to."

Amy, who had been celibate since her husband left, said "What! I'm not ready for that."

"Don't worry. They're all gentlemen, but watch out for Pete," Joan said.

"Why?"

"He comes on strong, likes voluptuous blondes, and doesn't know how to build a long-term relationship. He drinks too much and is divorced. Pete's old, in his late forties. But he is very charming and rich."

"I heard old people went to Rehoboth, and the young stayed in Dewey."

"That's what the Washington Post wants its readers to believe. All age groups mingle at both beaches."

"I'm not into old men who are unfaithful. I just ended a relationship with a young adulterous man."

"Good. There's another reason I want you to meet Pete."

"Why?"

"He works at my company, CIN Inc., managing their IT contracts. He told me he's looking for a marketing rep for the Department of Education. I told him you'd be perfect."

"Joan, did you plan this meeting before you invited me to lunch?"

"Of course. Long-range planning is the key to successful marketing."

"Thanks, now I'll be nervous when I meet him."

"Don't worry, his charm will relax you. But it's important not to consummate any attraction that might occur with a potential boss."

"Joan, I'm not so lonely that I'll throw myself at the first man I meet at the beach."

"We'll see. Pete should be no problem to you sexually. I told him that if he came on to you, I'd either kill him or ruin his reputation at the beach."

"Joan, I can take care of myself."

"Amy, you've never been to a single-scene Delaware beach weekend. It's not a grammar school playground. It could be out of your league especially after you've had a few drinks. He'll behave. Pete feared the last threat of ruining his reputation more than death."

"I won't drink."

"Sure."

"Who else should I worry about?"

"All the men you meet."

"I'm beginning to be concerned."

"Don't be. I'll watch out for you."

The remainder of their drive was uneventful. Amy enjoyed the scenery of old farm houses, growing corn and soybeans, and wheat stubble from its recent harvest. As they drove, Joan described the proper, but flirtatious behavior for a soon-to-be divorced woman on her first beach house weekend. They arrived in two and a half hours.

"What do think of the house?" Joan asked.

"It's quaint?"

"It's not Southampton, but it works. The front porch is the center of the house. We throw great dinner parties there on Saturday night, invite guests, and discuss world events, business, and our social life."

Amy looked at the three picnic tables on the screened-in porch and assumed the dinner parties would be very informal. "That should be fun."

"I'm going to have a glass of wine, but I agree you should have soda."

"OK. I don't drink much. I don't want to meet your friends slurring my words. Can we go see the beach?" Amy asked.

"Not until I finish my wine. You'll be arrested if a cop catches you drinking alcohol outside your home or on the beach."

"You're kidding."

"No. They walk you to the police station. If you're belligerent, they take you to the Georgetown jail and keep you overnight, unless you can make bail."

"Good to know."

Twenty minutes later they walked along Route 1, with Joan pointing out the major single bars: Starboard, Jimmy's Grille, Bottle and Cork, Whiskey Beach, Nalu Hawaiian, and the Rusty Rudder. They turned left at Duke Street and headed toward the beach. Upon seeing the ocean, Amy turned to Joan and said, "Thanks for inviting me. I needed this. I might have been slightly depressed for the last six months."

"You're more than slightly depressed. This weekend should solve that problem."

"I hope so. What's next?"

"We'll go back to the house after we finish our walk and meet other members."

They returned at six to an empty house. Joan said, "I'm going to have another glass of wine and get ready for the evening. I'll show you Rehoboth."

"I'll stay sober. Where is the shower?"

"Outside. Let me show you."

"How do you dress for an evening in Rehoboth?"

"Casual, I'm going to wear blue shorts and a white blouse."

"I'll dress the same as you."

They were both ready to leave at seven but had to stay for another fifteen minutes as Joan introduced Amy to the only couple in the house who had just arrived.

"Hi, Carol, Ted. I'd like you to meet Amy. It's her first time at the beach."

"Hope you enjoy it." Ted responded.

"I plan to. Joan's my tour guide. We're going to Rehoboth for dinner. Would you like to join us?" Amy asked.

"No, we're staying in tonight. We plan to go fishing on a six-hour head boat trip out of Indian River Inlet. We have to be there at seven thirty. We plan to catch dinner for the house," Carol said.

"Good luck."

"Let's go." Joan said.

As they walked toward Joan's car, a blond overweight man pulled behind them in a gray Mustang convertible, waved with a beer in his hand, and yelled, "Joan."

He stared at Amy, dressed in white shorts and a loose-fitting low-cut pink blouse, glanced at her hand, and smiled as he observed no ring. "Who's your friend?"

"Ben, meet Amy. She's here for a quiet weekend."

"Nice to meet you. I'll see you later. I have to claim a room," he said as he bounded into a house across the street.

"Joan, I noticed you didn't ask him to join us for dinner."

"He's not my type. He's an overgrown child who divorced a few years ago. Still searching for the ideal woman, but settling for anyone who will sleep with him," Joan said

"He won't be successful until he loses weight. Does he always drink when he drives?"

"Ben always drinks. That's a problem at the beach."

"Really?"

"Let's take the Jolly Trolley to Rehoboth and eat at Dogfish Head," Joan proposed.

"Dogfish Head doesn't sound appetizing, but I'll eat wherever you want. What's the Jolly Trolley?"

"A dogfish is a sand shark, which is common here. It's a moderately priced seafood restaurant. The Jolly Trolley has saved more lives from drunk drivers than the lifeguards have rescued drowning swimmers. It's a truck that pulls an open van that looks like an old-fashioned trolley."

After dinner, Joan guided Amy through the cultural sites of Rehoboth including the art galleries and gift shops while strolling toward the boardwalk along Rehoboth Avenue.

After nine thirty and the fourth art gallery, Amy said, "Rehoboth reminds me of the village of La Jolla, north of San Diego."

"It's similar except for the flat terrain."

"I'm getting tired. I'm not used to walking for an hour after dinner."

"Let's go to O'Reilly's. It has tables where we can sit and rest and a DJ. They play music from the seventies, eighties, and nineties. Most of my beach friends wind up there on a Friday night."

"I love it here. The ocean's so beautiful at night," Amy said as she gazed at the breaking waves illuminated by the early moonlight.

"The night's still early. I hope you can repeat that sentiment on the drive home."

"So do I. It's hard to be lonely here."

They walked to O'Reilly's, joining the short line at the front door.

"Is there always a line?" Amy asked.

"Yes, it's very popular."

After a minute the line moved and the bouncer asked, "Proof of age?"

The question thrilled Amy who had not been asked that question for several years. After they entered the bar, she turned to Joan and said, "I guess my new clothes work. I'm not a matron anymore."

"True. Let's find a table."

They walked the short hallway, flanked by entrances to the men's and women's rooms, and toward an open area facing a long bar half filled with patrons. Joan turned right toward the twenty-by-fifteen-foot dance floor, and found a four-person table bordering it. Slow moving adults ranging in age from the late twenties to the sixties danced to the sounds of *Life in the Fast Lane* by the Eagles.

A waitress asked, "What would you like?"

"Chardonnay for her and Diet Coke for me," Amy replied. "Joan, the drinks are my treat. Thanks for bringing me here."

"You're welcome."

They talked for a half hour with Joan pointing out her friends and introducing Amy to several who stopped by the table. Joan ended the conversation when a thin man in his midforties approached them as *Hot Stuff* by Donna Summer started, and asked, "Joan, would you like to dance?"

"Sure, Bill, this is Amy. She is new to the beach."

"Hi. You'll love it here."

Bill eased Joan onto the dance floor and they executed a perfectly choreographed hustle. When they finished, she returned to the table.

"Joan, I didn't know you could dance."

"If you're going to be a successful single, you'll have to learn."

"How?"

"There are plenty of dance halls in DC, several near you. You can enroll for lessons and they always have open dances you can attend. I go to the Chevy Chase Ballroom. We can go next week."

"Great," Amy responded, thinking this single life may not be so bad. She fantasized how her new life would be different from the years when she dedicated herself to Tony. Several of the male dancers revived her sexual yearnings. Over the next hour she accepted invitations to dance from two men. After eleven, sitting alone at the table, a drunken Ben interrupted her dreams. Ben, leaning over the table, asked her to dance to a slow song, *Let's Get it On* by Marvin Gaye.

Amy rose and followed him to the dance floor. He took her in his arms and drew her close to him. She revolted at his beer and garlic breath and tried to move away, pushing her arms against him. He responded by trying to hold her tighter.

"I don't want to dance this close."

"I do." He pulled her tighter, hurting her.

"I don't." She stomped the heel of her sneaker on his open-toed flip flop.

"You bitch." He released his grip.

She fled to the table, noticing movement on the dance floor had ceased and that everyone stared at them.

"What's wrong with you?" he screamed as he followed her.

"You. Go look in the mirror. You're a joke."

Ben lost control. He raised his open hand above his head to slap Amy. She saw his intent, covered her face with her hands and closed her eyes. As soon as Ben raised his hand a large middle-aged man standing next to Amy's table, grabbed Ben's hand, and clocked him on the jaw with his right fist. Ben went down fast.

Amy, waiting for the impact on her face heard a loud noise and a banging sound as Ben landed on the floor. She opened her eyes and saw a man standing over Ben saying, "You should leave. I don't just mean the bar, but the beach. No one threatens a guest in our beach house."

The barroom crowd cheered at the quickness and finality of the rescue as Ben rose with his shattered ego and limped out of O'Reilly's.

Amy looked over at the man, who said, "Hi, I'm Pete. I hoped to meet you later this evening."

"What happened?"

"Joan described you over the phone so I recognized you and walked over to the table waiting for Joan to return to introduce me. I saw the struggle on the dance floor. My Marine Corps training kicked in when I saw him follow you to the table screaming and in the process of slapping you. He's gone now."

"Thanks. Does this happen a lot here?"

"No, it's the first time I've seen a fight or a woman accosted in the ten years I've been coming here."

Joan, who had rushed over, said, "I'm glad Pete saved you. It was tense."

"Yes, I was lucky. I should have just refused to dance with him but I'm too polite."

"Don't be. Make sure that you're always in control with men," Joan replied.

"Even me," Pete said.

"Yes, especially with the smooth ones."

"Amy, follow Joan's advice. We'll talk about your future later. How about lunch at one on Sunday?" Pete asked.

"I'll look forward to that."

"See you later," Pete said as he walked off to the bar.

Amy and Joan rode the Jolly Trolley home at midnight accompanied by several of Joan's male friends for protection from Ben. They walked to their beach house from the Jolly Trolley stop and noticed Ben's car was missing.

Amy, Joan, Ted, and Carol enjoyed a wine-and-cheese party at a beach house in Rehoboth from six to eight on Saturday. They returned to the Dewey beach house and Ted and Carol hosted a dinner for seven of grilled sea bass they'd caught, salad, and corn on the cob. Amy continued her abstinence from alcohol during the wine-and-cheese party, dinner, and later dancing at O'Reilly's. Her Friday evening meeting with uncontrolled testosterone and alcohol did not reoccur Saturday. She did not see Pete that night.

Amy became concerned when she returned from tennis at eleven-thirty Sunday morning, and Pete had still not returned. Ted greeted her in the kitchen. "Pete called and asked you to meet him at Victoria's Restaurant in Rehoboth for lunch at one."

"Did he leave a number for me to call to confirm? I have no idea where it is."

"No. He promised to be there."

"Trust him. Pete won't miss a business appointment. I'll drive you," Joan said.

Joan dropped Amy off at the end of Olive Avenue and directed her to the restaurant. "Give me a call when you finish, and we'll drive home."

"Sorry I ignored you this weekend, but I fell in love and spent my time with my new friend," Pete said after Amy entered the crowded restaurant and sat at his table.

"Do you do that often?"

"Too often, but I hope it's my last time. We're not here to talk about my childish behavior but your future."

"Good, I like the weekend beach lifestyle better than my current life in Columbia. A new job would help. However, I know nothing about marketing."

"Don't worry, we'll teach you. You'd begin working on a contract at the Department of Education so you can meet the clients before you switch to marketing in a year."

"How do you know I'm qualified?"

"Joan briefed me on your background and I trust her. I made a few independent checks. I liked your behavior on Friday night when Ben tried to take advantage of your innocence. It showed me that you wouldn't let anyone push you around, including a client."

"Can you tell me more about the job, the pay, and when I'd start?"

"CIN Inc. has a policy support contract in the Congressional Liaison Office at the Department of Education. We conduct research in response to congressional questions and to satisfy congressional reporting requirements. We prepare documents and PowerPoint presentations they use to brief Congress or other agencies. How are your computer skills?"

"Excellent. I took several courses in college and have kept up as part of my teaching. I'm proficient in Microsoft Office, PowerPoint, and Project. I can create diagrams using VISIO."

"That's more than enough. The starting pay is sixty-five thousand which is more than your teaching salary. Can you start this week?"

"I accept and can start this week, but why the rush?"

Amy calculated that the new salary exceeded her teaching salary by 20 percent.

"Everything is rushed in government contracting. We just received a new task order we have to staff. One measurement of our performance is how quickly we fill open positions. Our company's profit and our personal bonuses are dependent on our performance."

"What will happen if I don't switch to marketing?"

"Nothing but your potential income won't be as great. If you meet your goals in the marketing bonus plan, you could double your income."

"I hope the Education staff like me. Is Tuesday OK?"

"Wednesday is better."

He handed her an employee application package. "Fill out the forms before you report to HR. The company's address and a map are included in the package. Joan tells me you're going through a divorce and don't have a favorable view of men."

"I wonder how much Joan told you about me. Yes, I'm getting divorced. This is my first singles weekend. My view of men became negative because of Tony, my soon-to-be ex-husband, and became worse with Friday night's experience. However, your behavior's created a thaw."

"Joan, as a great marketer, only told me enough to sell you and nothing else. You'll get over your attitude toward men. You'll have to since you'll be working with men every day. Don't worry about men liking you. You're a very personable woman. The female clients will like you since many of them share the same divorce experience."

Joan picked up Amy after lunch. They drove to Columbia.

"Well!"

"I start work on Wednesday."

"Congratulations. You'll love it. Don't worry about the sexual pressure. You'll learn how to handle it."

"I'm not worried. My parents were born in Sweden, and we have a different outlook on sex than most Americans. This weekend made me realize I'm lonely and shouldn't deny myself its pleasure. I plan to move to DC as you suggested and enjoy my new single life. I don't look Italian. I'm too blonde and light skinned, so as soon as I'm divorced, I'm going back to my maiden name."

"Great. It's better to make a complete break with your old married life. Many women never recover from their divorce and live the same life for the next thirty years, except they never get a man to replace their ex-husband."

"That won't happen to me. I plan to get my share of men on my terms."

"I like changing your name. There are millions of attractive Italian women, but blonde Scandinavians, with their sexual reputation are much more exotic."

Amy followed Joan's guidance and learned to recognize and use the power of her body and personality to manipulate hapless men to win contracts and task orders. She observed that Joan, with her beautiful raven hair, thin five-foot-six athletic body, used her sexual appeal to get men to notice her before she started talking at marketing meetings, the beach, and client presentations. A few months after viewing Joan's behavior, the more voluptuous Amy thought, I can do that.

Amy's performance as a government contractor validated Joan and Pete's confidence in her. Amy's clients loved her open approach. She transferred to marketing within a year and applied their advice in developing her marketing skills.

Amy began to enjoy single life in the fall of 2003, after her divorce as the focus of her life changed from Columbia, Maryland, to the Washington, DC, area. She purchased a two-bedroom apartment in the Elizabeth Condo in Friendship Heights, Maryland, financed by her divorce settlement. Amy began dating, but refused to develop serious relationships.

At Joan's invitation, she joined the Dewey Beach house in the summer of 2004. Amy planned to retire early at forty.

Chapter 3 Amy's New Career

Pete, in his role as CIN Inc.'s vice president for IT services had the responsibility for managing daily operations and identifying, winning, and developing long-term contracts.

In a January 2008 review of Amy's previous year's marketing efforts, Pete complimented her on the Department of Education's contract opportunities she had identified and won, and he handed her an envelope. "This is your bonus for last year."

Amy had worked hard, winning over $100 million in contracts and expected a large check and stock options. She opened the envelope and smiled as she glanced at the check for $50,000 and read the letter providing her with options for five thousand shares of CIN Inc. stock which could be exercised at a strike price of $20 in three years. The current price of CIN stock was $18. Amy did not know Pete had options for four hundred thousand shares with an average strike price of $12. Amy's cash bonus equaled one-fifth of a percent of the $25 million in revenue generated in 2006 from earlier contract wins over the last three years, not the $100 million she had won that year.

"Thanks, I look forward to these bonus checks."

"They should be nothing compared to the stock options."

"Only if the stock price increases."

"I expect it to triple in five years if CIN Inc. continues to grow. You're going to be a rich woman."

While Amy may be rich, Pete thought, he would be wealthy when he cashed in over $10 million in profits from his options. He had unbounded confidence in CIN Inc.'s future growth.

"Education's potential contracts are great but you'd do better if we transferred you to the Department of Energy. Your salary has grown from sixty-five thousand to ninety thousand since you joined us, and you earned a bonus of $50,000 last year. While your bonuses will grow at Education, they're limited, but the Department of Energy has large contracts where your bonuses will dwarf your Education earnings."

Amy, knowing Pete did not joke about money, but not wanting to lose her potential future bonuses from the Education work, said, "How much?"

He handed a document to Amy.

"I'm glad you asked. It's written in this contract. If you move to marketing the Department of Energy or DOE, you'll receive a promotion from a marketing specialist to a marketing director, with a salary of one hundred and ten thousand and a bonus related to your performance. The bonuses from your original Department of Education contracts would carry over to your new position. Read the contract. You don't have to answer me right away. Turn to page three and read paragraph five, Bonus Plan."

Amy complied and smiled as she finished reading calculating the value of her potential bonus.

"At one-fifth of one percent of the total value of the contract, your bonus for a five-year, one-billion-dollar contract is two million or four hundred thousand per year," Pete volunteered.

"I'll change but does DOE have contracts that large and can we win them?"

"Yes, there're several large DOE contracts up for competition in the next few years. We have the technical experience and DOE knows us, but we need a strong project manager, with DOE experience, to bid on a one-billion-dollar contract. You'll have to find someone we can hire and bid. That will be your first task in marketing

DOE." Pete followed the industry practice of hiring client agency staff to help win contracts.

Amy diligently marketed DOE for the first six months of her new assignment. She began by contacting the DOE managers of CIN Inc.'s two existing headquarters contracts: help desk support and database support. Both managers stated they approved of CIN Inc.'s performance.

During the second month Amy examined the potential DOE large opportunities, using several of the publicly available federal opportunity search databases— Input, FedSources—and recommended that Pete pursue the DOE IT Consolidated Support Contract, held by Global Computer Services. The contract's goal was to remove IT redundancies and lower the cost of DOE IT support. The current contract scheduled to end in December 2010, was the first large contract CIN Inc. could bid. She refrained from marketing the opportunity until Pete approved committing the company to the bid.

In her third month she scheduled appointments with the DOE technical managers to introduce herself and CIN Inc. to those unfamiliar with the company. The managers did not realize she phrased several of her questions to identify their qualifications for employment at CIN Inc.

When Amy walked into Art's office, they both recognized they had met before.

"Hi, I'm Amy Ericson. We danced a few times at the Cosmopolitan dances."

"Hi, true. But you never told me your last name and I didn't recognize you when you called."

"You're a good dancer, but since our appointment is for a half hour rather than talking about dancing I'd want to describe CIN Inc. and ask you a few questions related to your future potential programs."

"You're a good dancer too. I agree, tell me about your firm."

A group of successful middle-aged Washington, DC,

area professionals organized the Cosmopolitan dances, held at exclusive locations, such as the Austrian Embassy.

Amy handed Art a bound PowerPoint presentation and spent fifteen minutes describing CIN Inc., its two current DOE headquarters contracts, and their general IT qualifications to support DOE. She answered Art's questions as she talked, and when finished, asked, "Any further questions?"

"No. CIN Inc. appears qualified compared to other firms at DOE. I talked to Jim Dillard on the help desk support contract and June Bassett on the database support contract at the Energy Information Administration (EIA) and both said CIN Inc. had delivered superior performance."

"Can you summarize your division's work in management applications and any potential opportunities we could bid?" Amy asked.

"Sure."

Art explained how DOE used standard commercial software, including the Oracle relational database management system, to develop their management applications: human resources, finance, property management, et cetera.

"We manage the applications and the servers used, monitoring IT performance and user responses. The help desk and applications design and development are managed by other groups."

Amy listened, fascinated with Art's description.

"Several contractors support us. However, their functions will be transferred to the DOE IT Consolidated Support Contract when it's re-competed in a few years. So my office will not have many contracts to compete in the next few years."

"How will the DOE IT Consolidated Support Contract affect your office?"

"No impact. We'll manage the same task orders from the existing or new contractors under the IT Support

Contract. The consolidation is expected to save DOE contract management money."

"When did you start going to the Cosmopolitan dances?"

"Only six months ago. My wife died two and half years ago and I felt it was time to begin a new social life."

"Sorry to hear about your wife. You're right; it's a great way to meet other singles. Do you expect to work at DOE until you retire?"

"I'm not sure. With my kids graduated from college and having jobs, and my wife's death I don't need to work so hard or even stay in Washington, and I've been working at DOE for almost thirty years. I'm close to receiving a full pension. I may quit and get a less-stressful job with a government contracting firm."

"Thanks for your time. Perhaps I'll see you at the next dance."

"Maybe. Thanks for describing CIN Inc. Your firm is very qualified to support DOE."

Amy thought Art would be ideal for CIN Inc. after he left federal service. At the regular weekly meeting with Pete, she said, "I've identified a potential candidate from DOE to help us manage a large contract."

"Great. Who?"

"Art Mitchell, a GS-15, IT specialist, who runs the Management Applications Division. He'll have thirty years in federal government service soon, and told me he'll retire and hopes to become a government contractor. I checked around DOE and everyone loves him. He has a great management reputation."

"How well do you know him?"

"Not very well, I've met him marketing, and we both attended Cosmopolitan dances. I'll approach him about a job."

"Good, use all your marketing skills to get him interested. I'm putting his recruitment on your action item list. Keep me posted on your progress monthly. Get a commitment before another firm offers him a job."

"I will."

Pete's pursuit strategy for the DOE IT contract included hiring Art Mitchell.

Chapter 4 Recruiting Art (December 2008)

Art first met Pete at a Christmas party sponsored by CIN Inc. in 2008 two and a half years before Pete's collapse in Rehoboth in 2011.

Art married his college sweetheart, Bev, after graduating with an electrical engineering degree from the University of Maryland in 1977. They had two children, lived in a small home in Cleveland Park in Washington, DC and were happy for all twenty-six years of their marriage. His wife died from pancreatic cancer in 2005 when he was forty-eight. When his children left for college, his loneliness soared, plunging him into a depression for one year which he conquered by renewing his commitment to work. He moved from his house, with its old memories, to the fifth floor in a stately art-deco two-bedroom condo, built in 1931, at 4000 Cathedral Avenue, off Massachusetts Avenue in the Wesley Heights area of Washington, DC.

The Information Technology Department in the Department of Energy hired Art after his college graduation. He earned a master's degree in information technology, at night from George Washington University, worked hard, avoided political entanglements when presidential administrations changed and rose to a GS-15 grade. Art managed twenty-six staff and all DOE management application contracts. With an increasingly secure income, job security, and thirty-year government pension, he looked forward to retirement.

Art adjusted to living without his wife, but did not have stirrings for other women until two years after her death. He had little sexual desire and no skill at navigating the single female world in the Washington, DC, area.

Following Pete's instruction, Amy made an appointment with Art to begin the formal recruitment process. She arrived at the DOE Forrestal Building office at 1:00 on Friday, April 11, 2008, dressed conservatively in a loose-fitting business suit armed with material extolling the attributes of working at CIN Inc.

Art met her at the main entrance with a briefcase and suggested, "Let's cross the street and have coffee at the DOE cafeteria. It'll be easier to talk there at this time of day without being overheard. I don't want to get fired before I reach thirty years of service."

He recognized Amy's long-term game. He was flattered by CIN Inc's. pursuit of him and expected others to follow. Art decided to work with people he liked rather than to maximize his salary. While he could survive financially on his thirty-year GS-15 retirement, he could live lavishly with the addition of a contractor's salary.

"I could use coffee," Amy said, after they entered the restaurant.

They sat in a far corner with Amy placing her CIN Inc. recruiting material on the table.

"While I've briefed you on CIN Inc. capabilities related to DOE, today I want to discuss the entire company, its potential growth, and how we treat our senior employees," Amy said.

"I'm mainly interested in the latter topic although I guess your potential growth directly affects salaries."

"It does. Much of what I'll tell you is company proprietary and I want your assurance you won't repeat it outside this meeting."

"I agree."

"Since we're recruiting you, we won't bid on any new contracts you have responsibility for to ensure there is no conflict of interest."

"Thanks, I appreciate that."

"When is your thirty-year anniversary and when are you available to work for CIN Inc.?"

"January 2009."

"Good that gives us nine months to court you."

Amy spent fifteen minutes describing the company's financial status, market penetration within agencies, lines of business, and growth plans for the next five years from its current annual revenue of $1.25 billion to $2 billion in 2013.

"Our current contract backlog is over two billion dollars, which, if spent when scheduled will bring us to one billion, seven hundred and fifty million by 2013. Our business development procedures have been successful and we count on them to close the gap between backlog projections and our two-billion-dollar revenue goal."

"Very impressive, what type of work would I be assigned?"

"We don't know. That's why we're beginning the discussions early."

At Art's invitation, Amy started playing on the summer DOE IT Department softball team, on the fields near the Washington Monument. She knew Art was a widower but was surprised he never took a woman to the softball games. As a handsome and available man, he could be expected to be preyed upon by the many educated, upper-income, single women in DC.

Amy noticed Art liked women, but had no idea on how to approach them and missed most of their overtures. In early September as part of her recruitment effort, Amy invited Art to a Monday evening dinner party at Café Deluxe, on Wisconsin Avenue in Cleveland Park. Her goals were to discourage Art from considering other firms and to introduce him to Joan Watkins. She hoped a relationship that both needed would develop.

Amy and Joan arrived a few minutes before 7:00 p.m.

Jim Russo and Art both arrived a few minutes later. Amy made introductions. Art trailed Amy and Joan on the short walk through the noisy crowded restaurant to the table, with his eyes comparing the differences in their sensuality. Amy's attire, as always, showed her curves, displaying an invitation of adventure to all men while Joan dressed in an attractive green professional business suit, outlining her athletic body, and setting off her raven hair. Art liked the subtleness of her Red Door perfume compared to the loudness of that worn by Amy. After they were seated they exchanged business cards.

Amy ordered a bottle of red wine as they read the menu and started the conversation. "Art, you have something in common with both Joan and Jim. Joan runs and plays tennis and, like me, is in marketing at CIN Inc., while Jim works for us, managing our DOE contracts at the National Labs."

The waiter came, poured the wine, and took their orders.

Art, wanting to talk to Joan, but being shy, asked, "Jim, what do you do for DOE?"

Jim recited what he and Amy had practiced earlier in the afternoon, stressing the IT content of his contracts located in the exotic regions of Berkley, California; central Washington State; Los Alamos, New Mexico; and Oakridge, Tennessee.

"If you worked at CIN Inc., and like to travel, you could work on these contracts."

"Perhaps, but I'm not ready to leave DOE for at least four months."

"Art's waiting for his thirtieth-year anniversary so he can have the full pension of a GS-15. We can wait, but we want you to be excited about CIN Inc.," Amy responded.

Art, who felt more excited talking to Joan than changing jobs, said, "I'll give CIN Inc. the first right of refusal when I am ready to leave. Joan, where do you run?"

"On the C&O canal on weekends but during the

week I run in my neighborhood in the morning before work."

"I have the same routine. It's surprising I haven't seen you on the weekends. How far do you run?"

"Five to ten miles, depending on how I feel. The canal's very long. I usually run in the Great Falls area."

"That explains why we never crossed paths. I run the same distances in Georgetown."

Their conversation continued throughout the evening.

"I enjoyed our dinner. Joan, if it's OK, I may call you with questions concerning CIN Inc. to check what Amy tells me."

"Don't you trust me?" Amy said.

"Of course I trust you, but it's prudent to have a second opinion."

Art left thinking working for CIN Inc. may be the perfect way to finish his career.

On Wednesday morning Art called Joan's cell phone.

"Joan Watkins, CIN Inc., can I help you?"

"Hi, Joan. It's Art Mitchell. We met at dinner on Monday evening."

"Hi. Are you calling to check up on Amy's recruitment pitch?"

"No, I used that as a ploy to let you know I might call."

"Amy told me you're shy."

"I am. I thought it might be fun to run together on the C&O canal this weekend."

"It would. How about meeting me Saturday morning around ten?"

"Perfect. Where?"

"Since I live in northern Virginia is Great Falls OK?"

"Yes, I'll meet you at the lock in front of the canal house."

"See you then. Thanks for calling."

Both hung up smiling.

Joan arrived a few minutes early dressed in red running shorts, and a loose pink sweat shirt, with her long raven hair tied in a ponytail. Art arrived a few minutes later wearing blue shorts and a blue sweat shirt. He noticed her strong muscular legs not visible at their Monday evening dinner.

"Hi, Joan. You look different in running clothes than in a business suit. Good but different."

"I'd rather dress this way."

"You look more athletic today than on Monday."

"I feel more athletic. Where do you want to run?" Joan said.

"How about running west? It's less crowded."

"Sure. How far do you want to run?"

"Is eight miles, OK?"

"Perfect."

They started running with Joan setting the pace. Art noticed at the end of the first mile Joan breathed without difficulty while he became winded. Seeing Art's problem, Joan slowed from a seven to an eight minute mile pace without commenting on Art's shortness of breath. He recovered within a half mile and engaged in a normal conversation for the rest of the run.

"You're a great runner," Art said after they finished.

"Thanks. I've been running for years. I love getting runner's high. It's better than drinking wine."

"I agree. Thanks for slowing down after the first mile. I don't think I could have continued at that pace."

"I hoped you didn't notice. You're a good runner. Distance is more important than pace. I always run in the Marine Corps marathon so I have been developing a faster pace each year. After I run I always sit on the grass and have a light lunch. Would you like to join me? I've brought enough for two."

"Yes, thanks."

They walked to her car and she retrieved a thermos, a small cooler, and a blanket.

Joan spread the blanket on the grass between the parking lot and the canal.

"Would you like coffee and juice?"

"Yes, black."

"I've several chocolate croissants. Would you like one?"

"Yes. I'm glad I run so I don't feel guilty eating pastry."

"If I didn't run, I'd look like a blimp."

As they ate they discussed their backgrounds, careful to include any information they thought would advance their relationship.

"We should play tennis sometime," Art said when they were walking to their cars.

"Sure, let's play tomorrow afternoon at my place in McLean."

"What time?"

"Two." Joan took out a business card and wrote her address on the back.

"See you tomorrow," Art said as he platonically kissed her on the cheek.

"I look forward to tennis," she said returning the kiss on his cheek with a warm embrace.

"Shall we meet for brunch after your run tomorrow?" Amy asked Joan on the phone on Saturday afternoon.

"I like to but I'm busy. I'm playing tennis with Art Mitchell."

"What? That was fast. I thought Art was shy."

"So did I. He called on Wednesday and we went running on the canal this morning. It's nice to find an athletic man instead of the players I normally meet."

"I'm surprised."

"Amy, I'm trying to help you and CIN Inc. recruit him, nothing more."

"That I don't believe."

Amy smiled. Her plan was working better than she expected.

The tennis game on Sunday boosted Art's ego since unlike running he discovered he played tennis better than Joan.

At the end of their second set Joan said, "I give up. I'll show you my apartment and serve you a glass of wine as a reward for your excellent tennis."

"Thanks."

"I'm going to ask you for tennis lessons."

"I'm not that good. Besides, if I'm a successful teacher, you'll start winning."

"Not likely. But if that happens we'll play doubles and I'll be your partner."

"Sounds good," Art said.

Art realized she talked as if they would develop a long-term relationship even though the words only mentioned playing tennis together.

He stayed for dinner and woke up for an early breakfast. Their tennis match marked the beginning of an exclusive relationship.

Art pulled out the gold-embossed invitation to the 2008 CIN Inc. Christmas party from his briefcase while sitting in his car in front of his Cathedral Avenue DC condo smiling because Amy had told him to expect a job offer at the party which began at 5:00 p.m. He drove to the twenty-two story Monument Building. CIN Inc. headquarters occupied the most expensive top floors.

This was Art's first visit. The opulence of the glass-walled foyer entrance, with its yellow-marble floor, gray-granite wall, and twenty-five-foot-high ceiling, punctuated by a ten-foot-wide crystal chandelier, overwhelmed him. He walked to the elevators and rode to the twenty-second floor, and entered the CIN Inc. receptionist area and asked for Amy who appeared within fifteen seconds. She wore three-inch-high heels and a tight-fitting short-hemmed lavender cocktail dress. Art thought the outfit tasteful but sensual enough, with a slight view of her cleavage. She dressed to attract men and to entice potential clients at the party.

"Art thanks for coming early. You look great."

"Thanks, so do you."

"Let me show you around the office. We have four floors, but I'm restricted to showing you this one, since we have classified or proprietary work on the other floors. They contain offices and proposal areas. This floor has been designed to impress our visitors."

Art noticed high-ranking officials from other firms with contracts he managed attended the party. The CIN Inc. staff wore name tags, but at least half the guests, who Art assumed were contractors, did not.

Art walked beside Amy as she opened a door to a large conference room, with a full wall of windows overseeing the early evening of Tysons Corner offices and traffic-filled roads. Food covered the large conference table. A tuxedo-dressed bartender prepared drinks for the guests at a bar located in the far right corner of the room.

"Art, the floor will be open for the party. But most of the guests will congregate in this room. Private client conversations will be conducted in our executive offices during the party. Let's go to Pete's office."

Art looked in each office as he followed Amy. He compared their size and tasteful wooden furniture to the small offices and gray metal furniture provided to the management at DOE. Pete's office by design seduced Art's view of the future with its large corner size and windows that provided a view north to McLean and Potomac Falls, Virginia and west to the Blue Ridge Mountains. The panoramic scene reminded Art of the views from office buildings in Denver.

"Art Mitchell, I'd like you to meet, my boss, Pete Taylor."

They shook hands.

"I'll leave and get a glass of wine and mingle with our clients," Amy said.

After Amy left, Pete said, "Amy has spoken of you often. She thinks you'd be a great hire for CIN Inc. I've reviewed your resume and I'm impressed with your managerial and technical skills. I've talked to individuals who know you—none from DOE—and I have decided to offer you a job."

"What type of work would I do?"

"You'd spend the first month learning our company's procedures. We'll then assign you to manage an IT contract. Later we'll bid you as the lead manager on a large contract," Pete said as he handed him an envelope.

"The offer letter's on the top. It includes your salary and an outline of your responsibilities. The rest of the packet includes HR information, medical, and retirement benefits. Take the package with you and call me as soon as you make a decision," Pete advised.

Art skimmed the offer letter and noticed the base salary exceeded his expectations. It was 20 percent higher than his current GS-15 salary. He heard from friends to expect a lower salary. After reading the letter he replace the documents in the envelope and placed it in his inside jacket pocket. He shook Pete's hand, saying, "Thanks for the offer. I'll call you as soon as I make a decision."

"I'll wait to hear from you. Enjoy the party."

Art left Pete and walked to one of the food stations and filled a plate with shrimp, roast beef, and coleslaw. He recognized Jim Russo and walked over to him and started a conversation. After talking for thirty minutes, Jim excused himself, saying he had to talk to a client.

Pete walked up to Art with a single malt scotch in one hand and Joan by his side.

"Art, I'd like you to meet Joan Watkins. She's a friend of Amy's and markets Health and Human Services."

Art extended his hand, shaking hers, "It's nice to

meet you."

"Likewise. Do you like our party?"

Before he could answer, Pete said, "There's someone I have to talk to. Enjoy yourself."

After Pete walked away they started laughing.

"Pete gave me an offer letter."

"I hope it's acceptable."

"I only read the cover letter, but I'm going to read the complete package before I decide."

"Good move."

They spent the next two hours in conversation.

Art left the party at eight.

Pete cornered Amy, "I introduced Joan to Art. They talked together until he left. I wonder if they'll start an office romance."

"Pete, for a player, you're very naïve. They've been dating for four months. I introduced him to Joan and Jim Russo as part of my recruitment effort."

"Why wasn't I told?"

"I believed you'd screw up their relationship trying to recruit Art."

"You're right."

Art opened the offer envelope after he entered his apartment and reread the letter, examining the meaning of each sentence. He would start as a director which he knew was one level below being a vice president. His bonus plan depended on the company's profit, Pete's division profits, and his contract management performance, plus the additional revenue he earned for CIN Inc. The health plan was better than DOE's. He planned to call Pete on Monday afternoon, accept the position and give his two-week notice to DOE, the day of his thirtieth anniversary.

Art's first month of work exhausted him. His first day on Monday included an all-day CIN Inc. orientation session. Art reported to the HR department at 8:30 a.m. He attached his CIN Inc. ID badge to his suit coat collar, opened his orientation packet and found a note from Pete, asking him to meet in his office at the end of the day.

Pete said, "You know Jim Russo. How did you like orientation?"

"Long, but filled with CIN Inc. facts and procedures I am glad I learned."

"As you know, Jim manages our DOE National Labs contracts. We plan to assign you to manage the Brookhaven National Lab IT support contract. You'll report to Jim with respect to this contract and to me on other matters."

"I've prepared a set of reference material on the contract, including the Request for Proposal (RFP), CIN Inc proposal, our contract with DOE, our monthly status reports, and all our deliverables," Jim said.

He handed Art a USB drive containing the documents.

"Read this material and we can meet next week to discuss the contract. I won't make the assignment and notify DOE until you're sure you're ready."

"I've enrolled you in our management training course which meets daily at nine o'clock, starting tomorrow, for two hours for the next two weeks. Let me show you your office," Pete said.

They followed Pete, who turned right from his corner office and passed six closed doors, before Art noticed a sign on a door with his name and position.

Pete opened the door and ushered Art and Jim in and said, "Art, I hope you like it."

Art noticed the beautiful view of western Tysons Corner and the Blue Ridge Mountains. "I like it."

In the management course Art learned the CIN Inc. procedures for hiring and firing staff, how to handle problem staff situations, the firm's time card and financial reporting procedures, and an introduction to its computer-based knowledge management procedures. The course included homework assignments and tests. Art did not have enough time in the day to complete his homework assignments. He took the DOE documents home.

On Friday morning, Art received an e-mail message from Pete inviting him to his office at 5:00 p.m. for a staff meeting. When he entered the room Pete, Amy, Jim, and several others he did not know sat at the conference table.

"I hold these happy hours on a semi-regular basis. You know most of the people here," Pete said, and introduced Art to those he had not met.

"We just have a few drinks to dodge the Friday evening Beltway, Dulles toll road, Route 7 and 66 rush hours. We have no set agenda and don't have to talk about business. You have been so busy learning about CIN Inc. that I haven't had time to see how you're doing and give you a few new assignments."

Pete took Art aside from the others, gave him his favorite drink, a Dogfish Head Pale Ale, while he sipped a single malt scotch.

"I'm doing fine. There's a lot to learn. CIN Inc. is better organized than DOE."

"Good to hear. If DOE was as well organized as us they wouldn't need contractors and we'd be out of business. In addition to your management duties, we plan to use you in business development because of your great reputation at DOE."

"I'm prohibited from bidding on any project I was involved in at DOE for two years."

"We know that. However, there are other opportunities we can bid. You'll be helpful in marketing and working on proposals, given your IT background. Next week, take the interactive marketing skills class. It lasts five days for four hours a day. The week after enroll in our interactive capture management class. It's two days, four hours per day. It'll show you how CIN Inc. identifies opportunities to bid and how we develop a strategy to capture or win a contract. The remaining three days you'll take the bid and proposal class which shows you how to develop a PowerPoint presentation to get a bid approved and funded from upper management and how to prepare a winning proposal."

"This is like going to school again."

"That it is. But after you learn our procedures you can begin earning revenue which pays your salary."

"I've talked to Jim and we've decided to postpone your assuming control of the DOE Brookhaven contract until the end of the month when you finish your required course work."

Chapter 5 Pete Taylor's Dreams

Pete Taylor earned an electrical engineering degree at the University of Maryland, and married his college sweetheart immediately after graduation. He served as a Marine officer in the late 1970s. Pete retired from the Marines realizing he could not become rich as a career officer, and used his Marine Corps savings to finance an MBA at the University of Maryland. He and his wife divorced after ten years of marriage. They had two children, a daughter and a son.

Pete had two major dreams after his divorce: retiring rich early and enjoying unencumbered sex. Pete's dreams were no different than those of millions of men his age living in major cities, growing up during the sexual revolution, before AIDS tempered unlimited promiscuous behavior. The personal computer, communication and Internet booms, easy money, favorable tax rates, 401k and IRA retirement plans during the eighties and nineties, promised a steady growth in net worth for aggressive individuals. Unfortunately, those planning for early retirement were not students of history, forgetting the stock market crashes of 1973 and 1987. The IT-based crash of the late '90s postponed their planned early retirement for ten years with declines of over 50 percent in the stock market's value.

In 1986, Pete, single and thirty-one years old, owned a 401k fund worth $100,000 before joining an employee-owned firm, Information Management Associates, where he worked from 1986 to 1998. IMA, a successful database development firm deposit 10 percent of his salary in IMA stock in an IRA annually. The stock did not trade in the market, but was privately held by the employee-owned firm. An independent accounting firm assigned a value to the stock based upon earnings and sales of similar publicly held firms. The value of IMA stock and Pete's portfolio increased 25 percent annually. Pete estimated his IMA IRA would exceed two million by 2005, when he planned to retire at fifty. In addition, Pete estimated his older 401k, after recovering from the crash in 1987, would exceed a third of a million by 2000.

Pete was content in his early forties in the mid-nineties having had a successful career at IMA. He owned a heavily mortgaged French chateau-style home on three acres in Great Falls, Virginia and had recovered financially from his divorce.

Pete pursued a young database analyst, Lucille, at IMA to satisfy his second goal. Like most executives he worked more than forty hours a week and when not working, spent time in the embrace of the curvaceous redhead Lucille, twenty years his junior. He used to love watching Lucille's eyes bulge as he told her of his plans to become a multimillionaire and retire early.

In 1998, IMA decided to expand into the computer and network facilities management area by purchasing Computer Equipment Management, using a $100 million loan. CEM held a facility operations contract with the Department of the Treasury. Pete supported this action hoping it would significantly increase the value of IRA stock. However, with Pete unaware, CEM's competitors undercut the IMA-CEM bid price for the re-competition. The bank held IMA assets and contracts as collateral for the loan which they recalled after IMA-CEM lost. IMA declared bankruptcy and the value of their employee IRA-based IMA stock vanished postponing Pete's first goal of early retirement. He and Lucille became unemployed.

Pete's IMA's IRA retirement fund decreased from $630,000 to zero. Fortunately, Pete's original 401k was worth $200,000 in 1998, and the value of his house still provided him a base to pursue his now delayed first goal.

With his dreams of early retirement postponed, Pete fell into a mild depression and increased his moderate drinking to reduce the pain. Another firm rapidly hired Lucille because of her technical and interview skills while Pete remained unemployed for several months. His short-term financial planning resembled that of many middle managers of his generation. He lived paycheck to paycheck, without extra funds in his checking account to continue spending on Lucille, who did not appreciate this change in her lifestyle.

Two weeks after her reemployment she called Pete. "Hi, it's Lucille. Let's meet at the Café Deluxe in Tysons Corner for a drink after I get off from work."

"Sure. What time?"

"Five thirty."

Pete, surprised at her call, since she had been withdrawing from him looked forward to the drink and the remainder of the evening sleeping with her. When he arrived at the bar he noticed her standing alone with a stern look.

"Hi, Lucille. How's work?"

"Work's great. I like my new job. Pete, we have to talk. I feel cheated by you. You'd always told me how wealthy you're going to be and your plans for an early retirement. I believed you told me all those stories to assure me that when we married, we'd have a great time traveling and playing together."

Pete, horrified at the prospect, said, "I never said anything about marriage."

"I know but girls always think that way when they're in a long-term relationship. Now you can't even afford to take me to a nice restaurant for dinner. You're no longer marriage material. Who knows how long it will take you to get a new job and recover financially, at your age—perhaps never."

Pete, not believing what he heard, winced at her

reference to his age.

"I can't count on you for a future. I've met a nice guy at work, and I want to develop that relationship. We should stop seeing each other," Lucille said.

Pete, not expecting the evening or their relationship to end, could not talk. He thought she went with him because of his looks, sense of humor, and his excellence in bed. Now he realized her interests were primarily financial. After several minutes with Lucille staring at him, he finally spoke.

"It's good to know how you feel. Well, we did enjoy each other. I guess I can't argue with you or convince you to change your mind."

"No. I want to end it."

Pete walked away, vowing never to get involved with a woman whose long-term interest was a retirement ticket. He decided to restrict his dates to financially secure non-coworker women.

Joe Raymond, Pete's boss, an old drinking buddy, also lost his job. One day when both had nothing to do, they met for happy hour at the Café Deluxe in Tysons Corner. On his second martini, Pete stated, "I can't believe we lost on cost."

"At first neither could I, but I've heard rumors our competition had help," Joe said.

"What do you mean?"

"A friend told me he saw the winner's, brown-haired, thirty-something, marketing rep at dinner with the government's fifty-year-old technical officer of the contract several times, starting six months before Treasury awarded the contract. From the way they talked, he assumed she was screwing him in exchange for information. That's why we lost."

"Christ, can't we expose them and have the work stopped and the contract re-competed?"

"No, we don't have proof and they're not going to

admit their guilt."

"IMA's management was too honest to survive in the government contracting world. If I'm in this situation in the future, I'll use different marketing procedures."

Pete did not comment, but thought so will I. IMA's honesty postponed my retirement by at least ten years and I'm not going to let that happen again. I'll do whatever is necessary to win my next contract.

Pete joined CIN Inc. in 1998, as a vice-president in charge of IT contracts, receiving a $50,000 signing bonus which he invested in non-IT stocks. He survived the IT stock crash in the late 1990s and worked hard so that by 2007 his annual salary plus cash bonuses not counting stock options exceeded a quarter of a million. He enjoyed his job and now planned to retire at sixty in 2012 with an estate valued at over ten million.

On Wednesday, October 3, 2008, Pete's office phone rang. Noticing his Smith-Barney stockbroker's name on Caller ID, he hesitantly picked up the phone.

"Sorry to bring you bad news but the NASD index is crashing. It has dropped 10 percent since Friday. Your portfolio is down 12 percent to eight hundred and fifty thousand. You may want to think about selling your NASD index and IT firm stocks. We honestly, don't know if the market will continue to fall or if the market will rise next week."

Pete, not wanting to be burned twice thought the real estate and financial industry crises would be long-term and replied, "Sell everything."

"Are you sure? We don't know if it's a small correction or a major decline."

"Yes. At my age I don't want to take the risk. I want to retire soon. Sell it all."

His broker did as directed and Pete only lost 15 percent of his portfolio, compared with market declines of 50 percent between 2008 and 2009.

THE OPPORTUNITY

Pete, pleased with his reaction to the latest stock market crash, felt buoyed by the potential growth in CIN Inc., and confident of success at DOE since hiring Art and appointing Amy as the marketing lead. He had developed plans to win similar-sized contracts at three other agencies. If CIN Inc. won two out of the four opportunities its stock price would rise over 300 percent to $60 in the next three years increasing the net value of his potential CIN Inc. stock options to $8 million. Not wanting to leave winning to pure chance, he intended to use electronic information-gathering procedures to give CIN Inc. an edge over its competition.

Pete's sex life satisfied him. He never repeated the mistake he made with Lucille, falling in love with a younger woman, confusing her reason for being with him as love.

Pete anticipated the future.

Chapter 6 The Opportunity

Pete followed Amy's advice to pursue the $1 billion five-year DOE IT Consolidated Support Contract. Pete's long-term strategy for winning the contract began when he summoned Amy to his office on March 17, 2009.

Amy always impressed Pete when he saw her thinking Amy could not hide her figure no matter how loose the sweater. While proud of his decision not to date CIN Inc. employees, he realized that as a divorcee with two children in college he had no chance with Amy. Pete knew she had no respect for a man, like her ex-husband, who only wanted short-term flings with women.

"Hi, you wanted to see me," Amy said.

"We've decided to market the DOE IT Consolidated Support opportunity."

"Good. DOE won't publish the Request for Proposal for six months to a year."

"That should give us enough time. I'll get with Art and see what he knows about the contract and put together a draft plan for capturing it."

"Have you decided on a capture manager I should work with?" Amy asked.

"Yes, I'll be the capture manager," Pete said, "since this bid is so important to us. I want you as a marketing lead to do the initial analysis of whether we're qualified to bid, and if we can beat the incumbent, General Computing Support, and the other competition before we start the formal capture process."

While Amy as the marketing lead was the outside contact with the client, Pete as the capture manager, served as the inside corporate strategist who took Amy's findings and developed a strategy and team, composed of CIN Inc. and subcontractors, to capture or win the contract.

"Talking to Art is a good move, since we hired him for his DOE intelligence. Are you going to bid him as the program manager?" Amy asked.

"We need to vet him at DOE to see if he's acceptable and doesn't have any enemies among the contract evaluation team."

"Understood."

"Both of us will attend the bidder's conference where they're supposed to release a draft RFP."

On April, 2009 Pete and Amy took the subway to DOE headquarters. After they passed DOE security, they walked to the auditorium, registered at the welcome desk, and picked up the PowerPoint presentation. They took aisle seats halfway from the front of the speaker's dais of the three-quarter filled room.

"Write down the name of any company from the attendees you recognize, and I'll do the same. I want to know our competition and identify potential subcontractors," Pete said.

Amy searched the room looking for marketers and corporate management and developed a list of twenty-two contractors. Pete identified thirty-four including nineteen on Amy's list. At 10:00 a.m., the DOE Chief Information Officer welcomed the attendees and thanked them for their interest.

He concluded, "I am now turning over the formal presentation of the meeting to the DOE IT Consolidated Support Contracting officer, Ben Kaiser."

Amy, having forgotten Ben's name, stared in shock as he approached the podium. Pete, watching Amy realized she had recognized him. Amy turned toward Pete, "That's…"

"We'll talk later."

"I forgot his name when I was researching the

opportunity," whispered Amy.

Ben presented DOE's view of the Contact's requirements. He informed the audience that they could download a draft RFP from the DOE website. Ben stressed contractors must deliver all comments to DOE by May 20. They would be used to improve the draft RFP. The meeting adjourned at 11:45 a.m. Amy and Pete caught the subway back to West Falls Church, not discussing the meeting until they sat in the privacy of a half-empty subway car.

"The Contracting Officer was the guy at the beach who you knocked down and told to leave the beach."

"I know."

"Did you know before the meeting?"

"Yes, but I didn't want to upset you and affect your work on the opportunity."

"I understand, but now what do we do? If he remembers us we'll never win the contract."

"I'm not so sure. He doesn't make the final decision, the Chief Information Officer does. He can attack us but does he want to run the risk of the beach story being repeated. It would show his criticism of CIN Inc. was biased, ruining his credibility. Let me develop an approach for handling Ben Kaiser while you continue your work at creating a winning strategy. Read and distribute the draft RFP to our contracts office, Art, and our DOE program managers. Ask them to develop questions by May 15 so we can review and consolidate them before submitting them."

Chapter 7 Courting Ben

CIN Inc.'s Human Resources Department hires private investigators to examine the background of potential critical hires as they did with Amy and Art. Since Pete did not plan to hire Ben, he could not use this approach, but contacted his own private detective to conduct a more detailed investigation to discover Ben's weaknesses that Amy could use in her marketing plan. Pete paid for the private investigator's time with his and not corporate funds so his actions could not be traced to CIN Inc.

Pete first met George Steen, a retired Washington, DC police detective when they served in the Marines. George lived in the Chevy Chase area of DC, west of Connecticut Avenue, in a small brick colonial home, and supplemented his police income by providing private personal information to selected friends in the last ten years of his thirty-year service. George continued this practice after retiring making more money than his highest salary as a cop. His ethics transcended the constitutional constraints imposed upon normal citizens. He thought the Constitution as interpreted by the Supreme Court placed the public at a disadvantage to criminals by requiring the mandatory use of warrants for searching vehicles or homes.

Pete had a passion for secrecy, fearing discovery of a connection between himself and George. He did not want to be implicated by the police if they caught him. Pete always purchased an untraceable cell phone at different 7-Elevens to contact him.

"George Steen here."

"It's your friend. Let's meet for lunch tomorrow at

noon in Rock Creek Park near the Lincoln Memorial. I'll be sitting on a bench."

"OK." George hung up the phone.

Pete kept walking and threw the untraceable phone down a sewer.

Pete arrived first and began eating a corned beef on rye on Tuesday, May 19, 2009. He glanced left watching George approach. George sat on the bench, unwrapped a chicken salad on pumpernickel sandwich, and spoke first, "Hey, Pete, I'm surprised that you're not at the beach since it's so warm."

"Unfortunately, I still work and I'm not retired. I can't enjoy the weather the way you can. Besides, the women are here in the spring and not at the beach. How's your family?"

"Great. Emily and I are expecting our third grandchild in June."

"I called because I need to learn about Ben Kaiser, a DOE employee, who we may hire as a contract officer. I want to know about his strengths and weaknesses and what motivates him. We can't afford to have a contracting officer with questionable morals."

Pete's lie gave him plausible deniability on his motives for investigating Ben if DOE caught George. Pete handed George a slip of paper with Ben's contact information.

George glanced at the paper and said, "When do you want my report?"

"In ten days. I'll pay you the normal fee of ten thousand in cash."

"Understood—that should be no problem." George did not believe Pete's stated motivation, and didn't care, since Pete hired him for at least four assignments a year. Ben and George stopped discussing the job and began talking about their families.

George drove home and began his investigation. He

started his PC, and opened his investigative report template, filled in Ben's contact information and saved it under a fictitious name. George opened the Facebook icon on his second screen and executed a search for Ben Kaiser's name, hoping Ben had a Facebook account. Seventeen listings of Ben's name appeared. He reviewed the names and profiles and clicked on the picture that had the closest description to Ben's. The screen displayed Ben's Facebook home page. George clicked on the Info option on the left of the screen, which opened a new screen containing Ben's education, a short description of his interests and activities, his professional life, and a list of forty-three friends, and most of his e-mail addresses. George learned Ben earned a law degree from George Washington and liked to dance. He entered the information from Facebook into Ben's investigative report.

George analyzed Ben's friends, grouping them into family, professional, and social contacts. He noticed female social contacts predominated. He opened Ben's professional and social friends' icons, reviewed and summarized their information in his report. This phase of the investigation took four hours. Pete realized ten years earlier it would have taken several detectives at least a week to discover as much information as he had completed in one afternoon.

He quit reviewing Ben's files when Emily called him to dinner. She served baked salmon, green beans, and a salad. Emily loved her husband and decided to serve him life-extending food to postpone becoming a widow. She kept the dinner conversation stress free, never questioning him about his work, concentrating on their family and their next planned vacation.

She did not mind when he said, "I'm going back to work. Please call me when the Big Bang Theory starts."

While the first phase of the investigation involved collecting general information, the second phase concentrated on private personal data aimed at revealing Ben's moral, ethical, and legal behavior. George began by accessing the Intelius website and entering George's contact information. He chose the most expensive Intelius alternative for a detailed background report covering personal history, addresses, and property owned; past criminal and legal activity; and marital and divorce statistics. George learned Ben had two children in an eleven-year marriage that ended in divorce in 1999 and had not remarried. Ben had been arrested and convicted twice for driving while intoxicated - DWI, in 1995 and 2002. He assumed Ben must have a drinking problem. George wondered if drinking ruined his marriage. While Ben might be an alcoholic, he could find no reports of criminal activity. He entered the background information into Ben's report, and returned to his wife in the family room to watch the Big Bang Theory and enjoy the rest of evening.

George went to bed early since he had to wake up at dawn to begin the third phase of the investigation, personal observation. He arrived at Ben's Cleveland Park row house at 7:00 on Friday morning, parking a block away with an unobstructed view of the door of Ben's house. George waited thirty minutes for Ben to leave. Ben walked toward Connecticut Avenue. George left his car. He followed Ben at a discreet distance to the Cleveland Park Metro station. He returned to his car, drove home, informed Emily he had to work that evening, and invited her to accompany him to the Smithsonian that morning.

After several hours of walking the halls of the west building of the National Gallery of Art, George and Emily had lunch in the museum restaurant, and walked to the East Gallery. Emily considered these museum visits as part of their physical fitness program. They took the Metro home.

George left the house at 4:30 p.m. and drove to the Cleveland Park Metro station, parking halfway between the station and George's home. He walked to the subway exit that George entered in the morning and sat on a bench reading the Washington Post, hoping Ben did not stop for a drink on Friday evening. Ben appeared at 5:30 p.m. and walked straight home. George moved his car closer to Ben's house and waited assuming Ben would leave and either walk or drive to his favorite bar to support his drinking habit.

Ben left the house at 7:15 driving a 2007 Silver Toyota convertible and headed toward Connecticut Avenue. George jotted down the license number and followed him north on Connecticut Avenue driving through Chevy Chase, Maryland. He entered the Beltway and drove east. George hoped Ben had not embarked on a weekend trip. His fear subsided when Ben exited on Colesville Road, heading north. George thought Ben was driving to a date with one of his female Facebook friends. He abandoned his theory when Ben turned right on Industrial Parkway into an office and warehouse park. He followed Ben as he took the first left and drove by several low-rise buildings. He parked in front of a nondescript building with a small sign identifying it as the Hollywood Ballroom.

George parked several spaces past Ben and watched him enter the Ballroom, followed by several middle-aged, well-dressed, attractive women. George waited several minutes before he left his car to avoid Ben. He walked toward Ben's car and as he reached it, bent down to tie his shoe and attach a magnetic GPS tracking device inside the wheel fender.

After returning to his car George drove several hundred feet to a lot and parked. He activated his laptop and search for the Hollywood Ballroom. The ballroom's home page identified the facility as having 7200 square feet devoted to dancing. A review of other pages on the website showed happy dancers and provided a schedule of dancing activities which showed that Friday's schedule included a samba lesson led by Steve followed by three and a half hours of dancing for $15. Intrigued by the website but not wanting to learn to samba, George waited forty-five minutes in his car. After watching at least one hundred people enter the ballroom, he paid the entrance fee.

He entered the building, noticing a bar to his right, without customers, and a dance floor on his left, filled with couples performing the samba with various skill levels. Ben danced the samba perfectly with a well-endowed blonde. George stayed for an hour and a half, witnessing dancers interchanging partners and performing waltzes, swing, the cha-cha, fox-trots, disco, and avoiding the bar. George drove home to the arms of willing Emily, who he did not have to dance with to hold. He knew his late nights on this case had ended, since the tracking device always reported the location of Ben's car.

George slept well, getting up early smiling as he dressed, thinking he should take Emily, who was still sleeping, to the Hollywood Ballroom and integrate dancing into Emily's quest to stay healthy and live to be one hundred. He smelled the freshly brewed coffee as he left the bedroom and walked downstairs to the kitchen, marveling at the technology that started the coffee at 7:15 a.m. He poured a cup and went to his study and turned on his PC.

George accessed his e-mail, scanned the list of incoming messages, noting it had no business-critical e-mails; most e-mails were ads or spam. He left the e-mail and accessed his tracking icon. The home page map showed Ben's car at his home. He then opened the historical playback option, inserting the time when he placed the tracking device on Ben's car to the present. The report showed the car did not move until 11:15 p.m. while the map playback traced a route from the Hollywood Ballroom to Ben's home. George noted with satisfaction that the car spent only forty-five minutes moving. George's tracking device operated only when the car moved; thus, the less Ben drove the car, the longer the battery with an operating life of sixty hours would last. Since Ben took the Metro to work, George felt confident he should not have to replace the tracking device before receiving the ten thousand in cash.

George loved the new technology—from automatic coffee makers and personal search databases to car-tracking devices since they allowed him to conduct a credible investigation, without interviews, walking, or driving. He next used his favorite e-mail phishing application which allowed him to obtain confidential information normally kept on a home computer and not in the personal search databases, without illegally breaking and entering a residence. George opened Ben's report and retrieved his e-mail address. This action ended the first phase of George's electronic breaking-and-entering activity.

George's sent a phishing e-mail to Ben that when opened would transmit a Trojan horse to Ben's hard disk, to allow George to download Ben's data files, including passwords and credit card information, track Ben's keystrokes, and watch Ben's PC screen in real time on George's second screen, while his first screen displayed his PC activity. An unscrupulous hacker could use a Trojan horse to erase files, crash a computer, or steal. Since George had an interest in obtaining information, without malicious intent, Ben's PC was safe from destruction.

George developed his phishing e-mail by drafting an e-mail from the Hollywood Ballroom, thanking Ben for his support, with a statement requesting Ben click on the Hollywood Ballroom's website to review the Ballroom's calendar and the latest planned activities. George sent the e-mail through an anonymous website from a PC that George had earlier captured using a Trojan horse. This process ensured the phishing e-mail could not be traced to his PC.

George smelled the bacon cooking and left the study to join Emily in the kitchen. He planned to enjoy breakfast and help his wife in the garden until Ben opened his e-mail which triggered a cell phone e-mail notification to George.

His cell phone beeped in mid-morning. He stopped working in the garden and opened the e-mail from Ben's PC which established an Internet link between both PCs. George began downloading passwords from Ben's PC, e-mail, social and financial accounts.

As George viewed Ben's PC screen, he became curious when he saw a web page of the www.match.com site, displaying a full page of pictures and summaries of attractive and plain women. He watched as Ben clicked on an attractive woman's photo, initiating a display of her detailed social resume and a description of the type of man she hoped to be her match. George had heard of match.com, but being happily married for over thirty years, had never accessed the website. George looked in fascination as Ben chose the option to send an e-mail to the woman. Ben copied and edited a prewritten e-mail to be consistent with the woman's requirements. The e-mail suggested they meet for dinner to get to know each other. Ben selected two more women and sent them similar e-mails. George followed Ben's every keystroke, and was surprised when Ben accessed a site called Plenty of Fish and sent two more e-mails. Ben's next Internet adventure shocked George. Ben opened adultfriendfinder.com, displaying semi- or fully-nude women who substituted a sexual for a social resume, indicating the sexual practices their desired partners—men, women, or both—should perform if they wanted to meet. Ben didn't send e-mails at this site. George realized Ben was a sex addict. He knew Pete would be interested for whatever reason he had ordered the investigation.

George quit work before lunch which he prepared and brought to the deck, surprising Emily when he handed her a tray with a salad for both of them. He thanked her for being a great wife. He did not tell her since she kept him emotionally and physically satisfied he had no desire to search dating sites and porn on the web, which he found pitiful.

After lunch George returned to his PC and reviewed Ben's files, noting the large number of image files. He downloaded several directories and opened the first image, being rewarded with a photo of a fully dressed large-breasted woman in a provocative pose. George opened several more files and realized Ben preferred well-endowed women. He added this information to Ben's report but neglected to upload the photos. George wondered if normal single men engaged in Ben's behavior.

George left the sex-related files and concentrated on Ben's financial status. He used his previously obtained passwords to review Ben's checking account, noting its constant positive value never falling below $5,000. Ben's stockbroker files revealed Ben had financial assets of over $500,000.

George started to examine Ben's e-mail traffic when he received a notice on his phone at 3:00 p.m. that Ben was driving, indicating he had not turned off his PC. He opened the car tracking website and followed Ben's progress until he parked on P Street in Georgetown. George turned the tracking website off after Ben had not moved the car for fifteen minutes. George opened Ben's e-mail inbox and began categorizing the e-mails into three groups: business, family, and social. He classified the potential spam that bypassed the spam filter as business e-mail. He did not classify the phishing e-mail he sent earlier in the morning. Business accounted for over 70 percent, while family, including parents, sister, and children, only accounted for 5 percent. The remaining e-mails were social and included appointments for tennis and golf, e-mails from women on his Facebook friend list, or responses to his sexual social network inquires.

George opened the tracking website after being notified that Ben's car moved late in the afternoon. He followed the car on his PC screen as it drove up Wisconsin

Avenue, turned right at Nebraska Avenue and then left at Connecticut Avenue in Chevy Chase. He parked on Legation Street across from a condo at 5410 Connecticut Avenue. When the car didn't move for thirty minutes, George turned off his computer and took Emily out to dinner. George thought Ben must have a girlfriend when he found the car had not moved early the next morning. He planned to identify her and summarize her relationship with Ben.

George wrote his sleeping wife a note saying he would return in a few hours, filled a thermos with coffee, took several donuts and a camera and drove his wife's car to 5410 Connecticut Avenue. He found Ben's car and parked halfway between his car and the front entrance to the condo, hoping Ben would take his girlfriend for a walk or to brunch. He drank coffee, ate donuts and waited an hour, before he saw Ben leaving the apartment entrance, accompanied by a stylish middle-aged blonde. George turned on his digital camera and took photos at the rate of one every ten seconds, lowering his camera, when they both crossed the street.

Satisfied with the pictures, George drove home, went to church with his wife, and took her to Clyde's on Wisconsin Avenue in Maryland for brunch. After eating he returned home and accessed Ben's Facebook account. He compared the pictures on Ben's friend list with those in his camera, stopping at Laura Clark, a perfect match. George opened Laura's Facebook page and copied her basic information to Ben's report. He learned that Laura owned a federal contracting firm, L. Clark Associates, and complimented Ben on his choice of a wealthy woman. George accessed L. Clark Associates' web page. He smiled when he learned Laura's company specialized in high-level IT support and had four contracts with DOE. He realized Ben mixed business with pleasure. George discovered Ben was the contracting officer on two of Laura's contracts. He knew Pete would be interested in Ben's sexual ethics.

THE OPPORTUNITY

George felt Pete would appreciate his report but didn't turn it in early knowing that new information could appear and impact the major elements of the report. George followed the movement of Ben's car and spied on Ben's e-mails. By Thursday, he discovered Ben dated other women. Most of these dates were one- or two-time events. George could not tell from the e-mails why they ended, but he assumed Ben had a serious relationship with Laura, while the others were sexual diversions, since the tracking of Ben's car showed he visited Laura twice a week. Ben went to the Hollywood Ballroom without Laura on Friday and Sunday evenings.

Using an untraceable cell phone, Pete called George to arrange a lunch meeting in front of the West Building of the National Gallery of Art at noon on Friday, May 29, the tenth day of the study. George arrived first, impressed by federal employees, spending their lunch hour running on the Mall. When Pete ambled by and sat on the bench, George said, "Pete, you and I should join the runners and lose weight."

"I would if I could just to watch the women, but I'm afraid I'd have a heart attack."

"Emily makes me walk so I'm safe. I may take up dancing to stay in shape." George opened his plastic container, filled with a chicken Caesar salad.

"You're lucky to have a woman to take care of you. I see she even has you trained to eat healthy food. What did you find out about Ben Kaiser?" Pete opened the wrapping on his foot-long steak-and-cheese sub.

George handed Pete a thumb drive, saying "It's in here. Ben gave me the idea to take up dancing. I discovered he's financially secure, has a girlfriend, his PC hard drive is full of porn, and he uses three sexual social networks to meet women. He dances at the Hollywood Ballroom, an adult singles dance hall, on Fridays and Sundays. Ben goes alone to meet women. He's a sex addict."

"I guess we have something in common. I can't hold that against him as a potential employee."

"Be careful with the thumb drive; it's password protected. The password is Ben1500. If it's incorrectly accessed three times in succession, the data will be erased from the drive. Ben's girlfriend, Laura Clark, is the sole owner of a business holding contracts with DOE. Ben is the contracting officer on two of the contracts. I don't know any of the details, but it doesn't sound ethical."

"Interesting—you may be right. Anything else?"

"Nothing important; the details are on the thumb drive."

George and Pete continued eating lunch and talking about their Marine Corps memories.

George stopped in Ben's neighborhood on the way home and parked two blocks from Ben's car. He put on a light cotton parka and left the car, walking with a cane. He continued to Ben's car, shaking his body, appearing ready to fall to anybody noticing him. When he was next to Ben's car he fell against it, using it to stop his fall, while at the same time reaching in and removing the tracking device. He straightened himself and continued to wobble around the block until he reached his car.

George waited until later in the evening and checked his PC, finding Ben's active. George entered Ben's PC and removed the Trojan horse he had planted nine days earlier, eliminating the electronic ties between himself and Ben.

Pete and Amy spent the weekend at their group's beach house. Not wanting to talk business at the beach he asked her to meet in his office on Monday at 11:00 a.m.

After she arrived, he said, "I've researched the background of Ben Kaiser, the DOE Contracting Officer."

"What did you find out? I hope he's not the same jerk

I met at the beach."

"Could be worse?"

Pete did not give her a copy of the thumb drive but summarized what he wanted Amy to know. He concentrated on Ben's sex addiction for well-endowed blondes, his current girlfriend with DOE contracts, and his dancing at the Hollywood Ballroom.

"He does sound worse."

"Yes, but his faults give you an opening to get close to him. It's the only way you're going to get DOE confidential information."

"You want me to become his friend?"

"Whatever it takes. Remember your bonus—two million dollars."

"I understand. I guess I go dancing this weekend and skip the beach. I wonder if he'll remember our first meeting."

"Are there any impediments to bidding the proposal?" Pete asked Amy.

"No. Everyone who read the draft RFP is positive. We have excellent qualifications for most of the work."

"Good. The next step is to solve the Ben problem."

In her third year at CIN Inc., Amy enjoyed her sexual freedom. She dated the technical manager of one of the contracts she marketed. As their relationship developed, Amy noticed the task orders awarded to her firm doubled. She questioned her lover who said CIN Inc. deserved the work since they performed better than other firms. When the relationship ended, the number of task orders fell. Amy understood the direct connection between sex and revenue.

Amy began dating the contracting officer of a different contract and observed the same phenomena. Amy rationalized that since CIN Inc. performed well, they deserved the work and because she had genuine affection for her lover there were no ethical problems in the relationship. Her income doubled in three years and she counted on CIN Inc. stock options to become rich.

Amy went to her office and opened the Hollywood Ballroom website to help plan her June 5 Friday evening. While she had elementary dancing skills, she looked forward to the waltz lesson thinking the Hollywood Ballroom could be fun. She reviewed the photos of the dancing couples which did not include Ben. The women either wore evening gowns or dressed conservatively. Amy chose the conservative approach planning to wear a tight dark blue skirt and a light loose sweater, tight enough to show off her breasts. She chose the blue color so as not to appear too aggressive to Ben who she hoped would take the lead in their relationship. In addition to learning about the contract, she intended to enjoy herself, realizing she had come a long way when her husband dumped her and she believed sex was only for love. She wondered how to seduce him; from what Pete told her it would not be hard.

Amy arrived at the Hollywood Ballroom at 7:45 p.m. and found she was almost alone with a few men and women on the left and right of the dance floor sitting scattered at the tables with plastic cups. Since she always remained sober when working, she walked to the bar and ordered a Diet Coke and sat at an unoccupied table. Other dancers filled the ballroom.

At 8:00 p.m. Steve, the dance instructor, strolled to the front of the bandstand and said, "Let's start. Women, please stand to my right; men, to my left. We're waltzing tonight. I'll demonstrate the men's initial steps first, followed by the women's steps, and then you'll dance as couples."

Steve demonstrated the box steps, having the men and women separately repeat the steps. When he finished he said, "Both women and men walk to the center of the dance floor pick a partner, and be sure to introduce yourself. Since the women outnumber the men, change partners throughout the hour so everyone will get a chance to dance. Those without partners dance the steps as if you had a partner."

Amy searched for but could not find Ben as she moved toward the center pairing herself with an older man. They introduced themselves and danced the basic steps without music. Steve walked between the couples, offering advice, and after several minutes, he went to the bandstand and said, "We'll try it with music," and played the *Tennessee Waltz.*

"Please return to the sides of the dance floor." Steve said when the music ended.

Steve then selected a partner from among the women dancers and demonstrated how to move counterclockwise around the dance floor. He repeated his call for everyone to move to the center of the dance floor and choose a partner.

A tall thin man in his early fifties, rushed toward her, cutting off other potential partners, and introduced himself. "I'm Jim. Is this your first time here? I haven't seen you before."

"Yes. I'm Amy."

"Do you like it?"

"So far."

"Have you waltzed before?"

"Yes, years ago, and I seem to be remembering how."

Amy had decided not to show off her dancing skills that evening, believing men were more interested in women they could help rather those who danced better than them.

The music started and Jim glided her expertly around the dance floor. He complimented her. "You're a natural dancer. I'm wondering you keep looking over the dance floor. Are you looking for your date?"

"No, I don't have a date. I'm just trying to observe everything."

"Good. I enjoyed dancing with you."

His comments surprised her since she did not realize she broadcast her search for Ben and began to worry he would not show up. Thinking about Jim's last statement and his aggressive behavior in selecting her, she wondered if she might have another problem, Jim scaring Ben away.

When the music ended, Steve asked the dancers to return to the sides of the dance floor and he demonstrated how to dance the waltz around the dance floor without turning. When his demonstration ended he said, "Move to the center, and pick a different partner, so that you can learn to dance with more than one partner."

Amy breathed easier, thinking Steve had solved her problem with Jim. Apparently, Jim did not listen. He walked toward Amy, asking, "Would you like to try it again?"

Amy smiled, saying, "I'm going to follow Steve's advice." She walked toward a surprised overweight man in his early sixties, saying, "Hi, I'm Amy."

"I'm Joe."

Jim, who had experienced this behavior before did not worry. As a great dancer, he knew most woman loved to have him as a partner.

Amy walked to her side of the dance floor after the dance ended and broke into a smile as she saw Ben walk to the men's side and stand available for the next phase of the lesson. She moved across from him, focused on his face, noting that it was 8:40 and the dance lesson would soon be over so she had to make a bold move.

Ben did not understand her behavior. He had been going to the Hollywood Ballroom in Silver Spring, Maryland, for years, but had never seen a woman with such a curvaceous body staring at him. Steve began introducing the promenade step waltz.

"Pick a partner and we'll practice the new step with music."

"Hi, I'm Amy." Ben heard her say after watching her walk straight up to him, holding out her arms in a dance posture.

"I'm Ben."

Ben was happy to hear the music start since he had nothing intelligent to say as they began to waltz. He was initially tense but Amy started talking as they danced, relaxing him, moving closer to him than was normal at the Hollywood Ballroom.

"Ben, you're a good dancer, very easy to follow. You must have been dancing forever. Do you come here often? This is my first time."

"I've been coming here for years."

They parted when the dance ended.

Steve next taught the dancers how to partially separate and dance the promenade waltz steps, walking forward, with an overhand turn. Amy knew she had not mastered these new steps. When the music started, Amy looked at Ben and walked toward him, but when five feet away from Ben, a tall thin redhead brushed in front of her, smiling at Ben, who returned her smile.

Amy chose another partner who introduced himself as Stan. She wondered how many dances it would take to reconnect with Ben. As she was trying to master the new steps, her understanding partner, provided guidance so that when the music ended she felt competent in dancing the waltz and the variations she learned. She saw that Ben looked at her several times during the dance.

At the end of the lesson the dancers returned to their tables. Steve thanked the students and began playing a fox-trot, announcing the name of the dance which caused the dancers to leave their tables and choose partners. No one asked her to dance. Amy observed men asking women, and women asking men to dance which made sense since women outnumbered men. This gave her an option if Ben did not approach her.

Amy had problems with the tango, the next dance announced by Steve. Rather than risk being embarrassed by showing her ignorance of the dance, she walked to the bar and ordered another Diet Coke. As she was returning to her table, Jim approached and asked, "Would you like to dance?"

"I don't know how to tango."

"Don't worry it's easy. I'll teach you."

Jim took her Coke and set it down on the table and held out his hand. Amy hesitated, but thought, I may as well enjoy myself and took his hand. Jim's instructions were easy to follow and by the end of the dance, Amy had remembered what she had forgotten of the tango's elementary steps. He sat down next to her appearing ready to stay for the rest of the evening.

"Jim, you're a great dancer, and I thank you for the tango lesson, but since it's my first time here, I'd like to dance with more than one partner."

"I understand. I still want to dance with you later."

Amy returned the smile, saying, "OK." She did not want to spend the evening sitting out the dances, if she didn't dance with Ben again. She glanced around the dance floor and saw Ben sitting alone, across from her without the redhead. Steve began a cha-cha. Stan asked her to dance. She accepted.

The evening wore on and while Amy had no shortage of dance partners, by 9:45 she still had not talked to Ben after their only dance. She decided to become more aggressive and earn her bonus. She saw Ben leave the dance floor and walk toward the bar. Stan asked her to dance but she declined, saying, "Maybe later. I'm thirsty." She followed Ben who stood in line ahead of her. He surprised Amy, given her remembrance of him at the beach, by ordering a Diet Coke.

A second waitress addressed Amy, "What can I get you?"

"Diet Coke?"

She paid and turned, facing Ben. "Hi."

"Hi."

"Why does everyone drink soda, rather than beer or

wine."

"I don't think you'd enjoy dancing with a guy with a six-pack of beer breath."

"I never thought of that," Amy said.

"Alcohol also affects a dancer's rhythm."

"The next dance is a swing." Amy heard Steve announce.

"Would you like to dance?" Amy asked.

"Sure. East or West Coast?"

"Triple step."

"That's the East Coast. Show me where you're sitting. We can put our drinks there," Ben said.

Amy, not speaking, but feeling great, led him to her table and placed her drink next to her seat, noticing approvingly that Ben stared at her breasts. Ben put his glass next to hers, took her hand and walked to the dance floor.

They both danced without talking until the dance ended.

"Thank you," Amy said.

"You're a great dancer."

"I know how to swing, but I'm not sure about the other dances they play here."

Steve started a cha-cha.

"Everybody knows how to cha-cha. Let's dance," Ben said.

They spent the rest of the evening together, either dancing or talking at Amy's table. She did not ask Ben where he worked, but he asked her, "What do you do?"

"I work at a government contracting firm. But, I'd rather not talk about work."

Ben, not wanting to ruin his chances, didn't mention the topic again.

Amy strove to brush her breast against him during every slow dance and felt her prey shudder.

Amy observed the dancers began to leave around 11:00 and said, "It looks like it's time to go."

"Yes, I'm glad I met you. Can I have your phone number?"

They exchanged phone numbers, and Ben asked, "Are you planning to come here on Sunday?"

"I might. Will you be here?"

"Yes."

"Then, I'll come. Where do you live?" Amy already knew the answer, but it allowed her to start her impromptu plan for getting close to Ben.

"Cleveland Park in DC."

"That's convenient. I live right up Wisconsin Avenue in Friendship Heights north of the DC-Maryland border. Why don't we meet at Clyde's in the Giant shopping center for a salad before we go dancing and we can drive together?"

Ben, thinking his good looks and dancing skills had enticed Amy, said, "OK, we should meet at five since the lessons start at seven on Sunday."

Amy prepared for the kill on Sunday afternoon, dressing in a low-cut white sweater, showing off the top quarter of her tanned breasts and a pleated blue skirt that would emphasize the sensuality of her hips during the scheduled samba dance lesson. She walked to Clyde's from her condo on Sunday afternoon, arriving a few minutes early and smiled at Ben who had already arrived.

Amy ordered an ice tea. Ben did the same, saying, "I'm glad you suggested Clyde's. It has great seafood and gives us a chance to talk."

"That's true. We danced and didn't talk much on Friday night."

"That's what I wanted to talk about. We've met before, but I guess you don't remember."

The waiter walked over with their drinks, and asked if they had decided on what to order. Amy selected a garden salad and one jumbo lump crab cake, and Ben, the pan-seared Atlantic salmon.

THE OPPORTUNITY

After the waiter left, Amy said, "Go ahead."

"We first met in Dewey Beach. You were walking with a friend and I asked your friend who you were. She introduced us. Later, I had too many drinks at a party, and not enough to eat for dinner. I couldn't stop thinking of you. After dinner I searched the bars to find you. I met you a few hours and many drinks later in O'Reilly's. I asked you to dance which you did. But I was a stupid drunk and tried to molest you on the dance floor. You stepped on my foot and broke away. I freaked and tried to slap you when Pete Taylor punched me on the jaw. I went down and out for a few seconds.

When I came to, Pete stood over me and told me to leave the beach and never come back again. I was pissed but what could I do? Blood poured from my mouth and my head hurt. I walked back to Dewey. I didn't want to meet anyone I knew. Some of my beach house members were in the bar but did nothing to help me. I reached my car, decided not to go into my beach house, drove north on Route 1 and stopped at the first motel that had a vacancy. I got a room and cleaned myself up. I was lucky I didn't kill someone or myself driving. My original drunken thought was to kill Pete for punching me, believing it was your fault for being a tease and that I had done nothing wrong.

"I woke up the next morning with a hangover and a missing tooth wondering why I had acted the way I did. I walked to McDonald's ordered an orange juice, large coffee, pancakes, and sausages. After I chugged the juice I became sick after I ate half of the breakfast and ran to the bathroom to vomit. A member of my beach house who was in the restaurant came into the bathroom. He saw me on my knees, my head over the toilet, and said, 'You've got to stop drinking. It's going to kill you with a destroyed liver, a car accident, or another fight. You were out of line last night. I'd take Pete's advice and leave the beach. It may save your life.'

"I continued throwing up as he talked. When I finished, I turned around and looked at him. He looked shocked, and said, 'You look like shit, like you're almost dead.'

"'Why didn't anyone help me?' I asked.

"He replied, 'Because it was your fault. You get drunk every weekend and embarrass our beach house. Other houses have told us they don't invite us to parties anymore, because they don't want you there. We met last night when we returned home and took a vote. You're out of the beach house. We'll refund the prorated amount of your share for the rest of the season but you can't come back.'

"I didn't say a thing. He left the bathroom and I left the restaurant, never to return to the beach. It was the best advice Pete and my old beach house could have given me."

The waiter arrived and served them dinner.

"I didn't realize that was your normal behavior, I just figured you were drunk and I didn't know how to handle the situation because I was new at the beach."

Ben, grateful for a break in his confession began eating and after several minutes, he resumed talking, "No, I had a chronic problem. Go ahead and eat. I don't want your salad to spoil and give you another reason not to like me."

Amy began eating, saying, "What was your chronic problem?"

"I'm an alcoholic. People had been telling me for years since my divorce that I drank too much. Several of my girlfriends asked me if I was an alcoholic. I laughed and denied the obvious. Even my daughters said my drinking embarrassed them in front of their relatives and friends. I stayed in the motel until eleven that morning, when I felt steady enough to drive home. On the way I reminisced about the night before, what my friends had been telling me, and how they expelled me from the beach house. I realized I had to change. When I felt like stopping at the

Red Eye Dock Bar as I approached the Kent Narrows Bridge, I recognized I might be an alcoholic. The only way to test that was to try to stop drinking. I succeeded in driving home without stopping. However, abstinence ended at eight fifteen that evening when I could not stand being without a drink. I finished half an opened bottle of Chardonnay and when that was empty, my mood changed, and I opened and finished another bottle. The next morning, I woke up late and found myself vomiting over the toilet again. When the sickness passed after drinking a quart of orange juice, I realized I had to change, joined AA and never had another drink."

"You're so different now from the Friday when we met. I wondered how you had become thin and why you had changed. Thanks for telling me. If you hadn't, this would have been our first and last date." Amy lied. She realized Ben felt indebted to her for changing his life and she would use his feelings to her benefit over the next year.

"Stopping drinking and starting dancing made me thin. I wonder if I had behaved the way I do now, instead of being a drunk, would have changed your opinion of me at the beach."

"Obviously."

"OK, it's your turn to talk."

"I've nothing as exciting to tell. I was a third grade teacher happily married to a husband who wasn't. He left me for another woman and not expecting it I was heartbroken. He convinced me all men were pigs and I didn't go out for over six months. My friend Joan invited me to the beach to reintroduce me into the single world. Then I met you. It was a setback."

"Sorry."

"It didn't last long. I resumed dating and recovered from my marriage. I now enjoy single life. How is your relationship with your children?"

"Completely turned around. Whereas before they

never called me, and made excuses to avoid me when I had visitation rights. After I reformed they began to call and tell me about their lives and never missed a chance for me to visit them. They're older now. One is married and the other is in college so I don't spend much time with them, but if I hadn't met you and changed my life, I'm sure we'd be estranged."

"I'm happy for you." Throughout the remainder of dinner and the drive to the Hollywood Ballroom, Amy directed the conversation toward Ben and his family and how events in his life had developed since he quit drinking.

As with dinner, Amy insisted on paying her share of the entrance fee into the Hollywood Ballroom. They both followed protocol and exchanged partners during the lesson. The physical demands of the samba shocked Amy.

When the lesson ended she said, "Christ, my feet hurt. Is the samba always painful?"

"No, just learn to relax your feet as you move back and forth to the rhythm. I'll show you how when Steve plays a samba."

They did not exchange partners throughout the remainder of the evening. Ben always helped Amy learn steps for dances where she lacked proficiency. At 9:30 p.m. Amy suggested, "I've had enough of dancing this weekend. Why don't you drive me home and I'll serve you ice cream and coffee."

Ben, sensing that his changed lifestyle, charms, and good looks had already mentally seduced Amy, said, "I'd like coffee and ice cream."

On the trip home, Ben started to talk about his work. "I work for the Department of Energy. Does your firm have contracts with DOE?"

"Yes, I work at Computer Information Networks Inc. We have a few DOE contracts in networking, desktop maintenance, and help desk support."

"CIN Inc. has a great reputation. What do you do

there?"

"I help out in business development and proposals."

"Are you going after the DOE IT Consolidated Support Contract?"

"I don't know. Even if I did I couldn't tell you or anybody else, it's proprietary information."

"For what it's worth, I recommend you bid. We're very unhappy with the incumbent."

"It's not that easy. When management makes a bid decision they have to be sure they can beat the competition as well as the incumbent. They have to evaluate the cost of the proposal with the probability of winning."

"I'm not that analytical, I'm only a lawyer. I'm the contracting officer for the DOE IT Consolidated Support Contract. I hope the numbers work out so CIN Inc. bids. We don't want the incumbent to win on cost."

Ben hoped to replicate the sexual success he'd had with Laura, using the same procedures with Amy.

Amy thought, he must be hungry, already providing me with confidential information and we haven't had sex. Well, that will change tonight, as a quid pro quo payback.

After Ben parked a half block from Amy's building, they walked to her apartment. The marble floor of the Elizabeth Condo impressed him. He rode up to the twelfth floor in the east elevator tower. He became nervous as Amy opened the door.

"Here's home. Let me give you a tour. The kitchen is on the left, the room through the kitchen is the dining room. The living room is to your left and the hall is on the right side of the living room. I have two baths and bedrooms back there which I can show you later."

Ben assumed she meant later in the evening. He was impressed by the rooms and the furniture, asking, "How big is this place?"

"Fourteen hundred and thirty square feet. It's large

for an apartment, but it gives me room to have guests."

"You must have a great job at CIN Inc."

"Not really, I paid for it using my divorce settlement. My salary covers my condo fees and living expenses so if you're looking to latch onto a rich woman it's not me. I don't even receive alimony. I chose a cash settlement instead."

"No, I've other interests. I don't know you that well, but I enjoy dancing with you, and I am hoping to find other activities we would enjoy doing together," Ben said.

"Make yourself comfortable, I'm going to make coffee. Is decaf OK?"

"Yes, I prefer it."

Amy turned on the coffee maker, which had been set up earlier, took chocolate ice cream from her freezer, and two small bowls from her cupboard, which she half filled. She put the silverware, milk, sugar and ice cream on a tray which she brought into the living room, and served Ben who was sitting on the full couch, reading a skiing magazine from the coffee table.

"Thanks. Do you ski?" Ben asked.

"Yes, I belong to the Washington Ski Club. I go on one of their ski trips out West each year and their local ski trips when there's snow."

"I don't belong to the ski club, but I started skiing several years ago. That's an activity we could enjoy together, if it wasn't June."

"Maybe next winter." Amy said, thinking he already mentally has us in a long-term relationship. "Let me go get the coffee. Eat your ice cream before it melts."

She placed the tray on the coffee table and sat down on the couch touching him with her leg and arm.

He took the coffee, had one sip and placed it on the coffee table, turned to her, bent his face down and began to kiss her. She responded by opening her lips and throwing her arms around him, pulling him to her, crushing her breasts against his chest.

Several minutes of passion excited Ben, who could feel her leg pressing against his erection. He slowly moved his hand to her breasts and began to gently fondle them.

"I was wondering how long it would take you to do that. You couldn't keep your eyes off them since Friday."

"I didn't know you noticed."

"It was hard not to—don't stop."

Amy opened her blouse, loosened her bra, and moved his mouth to her nipple. Then she unzipped his pants and began to fondle his erection. He climaxed in a few minutes.

"I'm sorry I came so soon," Ben said.

Amy said, "Shush," holding his head to her breasts as she reached for a Kleenex and dried him. She moved his hand up her skirt, cooing in his ear, "It's my turn to come now."

He stimulated her with his hand and in a few minutes, she began to feel waves of pleasure. After she came, she thought, I am going to enjoy this business development assignment.

When Ben started to move, she said, "Stay still. I liked that."

"I came too soon."

"Don't worry. I'm satisfied. It takes practice to become perfect lovers. Come over for dinner this week and we'll get to know each other."

"Is Thursday OK?"

"Yes, show up at six-thirty. When you arrive give the desk your name and say you're going to visit me. They'll let you in." She kept hugging him, caressing his back, making Ben feel at home, relaxed, and wanted, not minding knowing he was losing control of their relationship.

Amy left work early to prepare for Thursday evening. Upon arriving home she set the table and prepared the food for cooking: cheese and crackers for appetizers; crab cakes, sweet potatoes, and asparagus for the entrée. She planned to serve mint chocolate chip ice cream for dessert. Since Ben did not drink, she prepared unsweetened ice tea.

Amy prepared her body as well as the dinner, showering and anointing it with lavender-scented perfume. She dressed in a low-cut red sweater, and a tight white skirt designed to render Ben powerless.

At 6:00 she retrieved a silent solid-state video recorder, enclosed in a jewelry box, she had purchased on the Internet. She checked to see if the battery had its full seven-hour charge and the lens was set up for low-light focus. She originally purchased the video recorder to review the fun she had in her youth when she was old. She aimed it at the bed and tested it to be sure it provided viewable video. Satisfied, she placed it on the dresser and turned it on. She put an audio recorder in a bookcase between the living room and the dining room.

After putting the cheese and crackers on the coffee table, she started baking the sweet potatoes, when Ben arrived. He gave her a kiss and flowers, saying, "Our wine substitute."

"Thanks. I'll put them in a vase."

"Can I help?" He followed her into the kitchen, like a lapdog, eager to please.

"No, the table is set, the food is prepared and I just have to cook it. Please pour us a glass of ice tea."

He handed a glass to Amy who was busy putting the asparagus into a steamer. She took the ice tea, saying, "Thanks, let's go sit on the couch."

Ben followed Amy, sat next to her, and obeyed when she said, "Try the cheese and crackers."

"I never knew I wasn't going to miss wine or whiskey years ago when I quit, but now I prefer water or ice tea."

"You should; it suits you better."

"Thanks. What's for dinner besides asparagus?"

"My favorites: crab cakes and sweet potatoes."

"I love crab cakes. I'm starving—when do we eat?"

"In fifteen minutes. The sweet potatoes are baking

and in ten minutes, I'll begin sautéing the crab cakes and steaming the asparagus."

"Has your firm considered bidding the DOE IT Consolidated Support opportunity?"

"Yes, I mentioned what you told me to my boss, without identifying you. He said, 'While it's great to hear DOE dislikes the incumbent, we have to understand why so we can prepare a winning bid. We have to offer them something to have them choose us over our competitors.'"

"I can tell you what we don't like about General Computing Support, or GCS. From the contracts office's standpoint, they're always late with status reports, work plans, and invoices. They're never correct when delivered. This gives us headaches in figuring out how much to pay them, how to budget for their contract in the future, and if their proposed planned work is legal. DOE technical managers try to use the Support Contract to cover any work they'd like done, even work not legally covered in the contract."

"Wow, you really sound pissed at GCS."

"Yes. But it's not just me, the technical staff's also upset. They tell me they have atrocious performance and they'll kill me if they win the re-compete. I think they mean it."

"I don't want you to die. Why don't you just cancel their contract?"

"We want to, but they have political connections."

"Our technical contract manager can't stand their program manager. He's late returning calls when there's a performance problem and acts as if it's their contract forever. They never meet their deadlines. GCS service support and help desk are terrible. We get constant complaints from DOE staff."

"Can't you change the contract to be performance based?"

"No, not the current contract, but the re-compete is performance based."

"I'm sure you'll find a better contractor next time."

"We're not so sure. They're very low cost and have political connections. I hope CIN Inc. decides to bid. I assumed you'd bid, since you attended the DOE IT Consolidated Support bidder's conference several months ago."

"We attend bidder's conferences for contracts we could potentially bid. They help us decide whether to bid. As I said earlier, I don't believe we've decided whether we're going to bid. A corporate committee makes the decision. I couldn't tell you even if I knew. It's time to cook, please bring in the cheese and crackers to the kitchen. Let's talk about something besides work."

Ben complied and tried to be charming, discussing his children, skiing, and other activities participated in by Washington singles while she cooked and when they ate dinner. She served coffee and ice cream on the coffee table in the living room. She noticed Ben rushing to finish his mint chocolate chip ice cream and said, "Didn't I feed you enough? There's more ice cream if you're still hungry."

"No, dinner was great and it filled me up. I just like ice cream, but I don't want any more, I have to watch my weight. I've heard girls don't kiss guys with fat asses."

"You're right." Amy reached over and kissed him.

They kissed, caressed, and fondled each other for five minutes until Amy said, "It's time to go to my bedroom."

She rose from the sofa took his hand and led him to the back of the apartment. Ben followed, staring at Amy's back and sensuous ass with anticipation.

Amy entered the bedroom, turned on the soft lights and gently pushed Ben onto the bed and started sensuously undressing. Her body mesmerized Ben. He starred at her, speechless, but kept his clothes on.

"Let me help you," Amy said.

Ben didn't talk as she removed his shirt, pants, and underpants. Amy began kissing and fondling him, encouraging him to do the same to her. This time he did not have to be led to her breasts. After several minutes, Amy moved Ben's head to her genitals. She said, "I love that, and I'll do anything to you or you can do anything to me when you do that."

"Please return the favor," he replied after she came.

She performed oral sex on him. After he ejaculated, she stimulated him again, and his erection returned. She maneuvered herself, and helped him enter her for a slow period of intercourse to end the evening.

"We've discovered another activity we do well together," Amy said.

"Yes, we have."

"We should do this again, soon."

"How about Saturday?" Ben said.

"I'm still in a beach house, so will have to meet during the week. I want to go to the Hollywood Ballroom next Wednesday. In October we can meet on weekends."

"Let's meet in Clyde's again."

After she closed the door, Amy knew she had him, nothing could stop her from winning the $2 million bonus.

Ben drove home sexually satiated. He stilled plan to see Laura during the summer on weekends and replace her with Amy in the fall.

Chapter 8 CIN Inc.'s Winning Processes

"I've information on the DOE IT opportunity," Amy told Pete in a phone conversation on Friday morning.

Pete asked Amy to meet him at noon for lunch in his office. While Pete had analyzed the opportunity for over six months, he waited for Amy's report on her first meetings with Ben, before requesting CIN Inc.'s executive management commit the funds required for a bid.

Amy, professionally dressed, without notes, entered Pete's office looking at the steak-and-cheese sub Pete had ordered and the chicken Caesar salad for her.

"Still know how to please a woman."

"I remembered you liked to graze."

"No calls," Pete told his administrative assistant.

"Do you want to eat or talk first or do both at the same time?" Pete asked.

"I'm not that hungry, I'll talk. You can eat. Don't ask me how I got this information."

"I understand."

"First, DOE hates General Computing Support, the incumbent, and are afraid they might win the next competition because of cost and political contacts."

"We can beat them on cost, but political contacts may be more difficult. Did he mention the names of the political contacts?"

"No, but I'll find out. Both the contracts and technical management offices have no use for the GCS program manager. He's arrogant and doesn't listen to their directives and he doesn't care when they complain. So we have to bid a program manager they trust and respect."

"We plan to bid Art Mitchell. Find out if your contact

knows him and if he's respected. If Art isn't loved, we'll have to find someone else soon." Pete took notes as Amy talked without identifying Ben as the source.

"I'll find out, but I hope you don't fire Art if they reject him."

"Since Art earns CIN Inc. revenue by charging his time to a contract, there's no way he'll be fired unless he rapes one of the government employees or steals from us." Pete said.

"I don't think he'll do that."

"I don't either."

"Ben has contractual bitches with GCS, saying their status reports, work plans, and invoices are always late and full of errors. He hates it because it makes work for him."

"That shouldn't be a problem for us since we're perfect in those areas on our DOE contracts and our potential references."

"GCS has performance problems. Their help desk and customer support are weak; they never meet their service-level agreements."

"Our low-end help desk and customer support at DOE are great. Let's have a regular luncheon meeting on Tuesday at noon to report any updates. The topics we discuss in these meetings should never leave this room." Pete said.

"I understand."

Since Pete worked on other projects, it took him several weeks to collect the material required for briefing CIN Inc. executive management, which he scheduled for June 25, 2009. The briefing stressed CIN Inc.'s capability to win the contract and a budget request to pursue the opportunity. The budget had three parts: pre-RFP issuance activities for $500,000, lobbying and marketing activities for $200,000, and formal proposal development activities for $1,250,000. The Executive Committee approved the $500,000 for developing the draft proposal, and $125,000 for lobbying and marketing activities. This satisfied Pete. He realized they had to win or the Executive Committee would hold him responsible for the loss.

That afternoon Pete appointed a senior capture team, staffed with business development and proposal writing specialists, including Amy as marketing lead. The other capture team members and their roles and responsibilities included:

- Pete, the capture manager, to lead the team to develop the winning strategy, and assemble the team of subcontractors to convince DOE that the CIN team would perform better than GCS
- Frank Nelson, an outside consultant as proposal manager to lead the development of the proposal in response to DOE's formal RFP
- CIN and subcontractor technical personnel to help develop the CIN offering to DOE
- Art Mitchell, to develop intelligence on DOE personnel involved in the proposal evaluation.

Pete e-mailed the capture team scheduling an opportunity kickoff meeting for Friday. He directed them to develop a formal proposal in response to the draft RFP, including a technical, management and cost proposal, staffing plan, and set of past performance references. Pete did not want to be surprised when DOE issued the formal RFP. He planned to have the draft proposal as complete and compliant with the requirements of the draft RFP as possible. If the final RFP was similar to the draft RFP, CIN Inc. could spend a month polishing the document. If there were significant differences in a specific area of the RFP, Pete could reallocate resources to these areas, knowing the other sections of the proposal were almost perfect.

Pete called George on a new untraceable cell phone, and asked him to meet for lunch on Friday, June 26, at a bench in front of the lion enclosure at the National Zoo. Both arrived at noon. Pete ate a steak-and-cheese sub, smothered with onions, while George started on a salad.

"Pete, I wish you'd improve your diet. I don't want to lose my best client."

"Don't worry; my parents are both alive and in their eighties. I have a small job for you. We're looking into bidding the DOE IT Consolidated Support Contract. General Computing Support is the incumbent, and we're told they're not performing well but have political connections." George was smart enough not to ask who provided the information.

"I want you to discover the political connections and what hold they have on DOE. I'll pay you your normal fee. I need the report in ten days."

"OK, I'll start after lunch."

"Did you and your wife ever take up dancing? You threatened to the last time we talked."

"Yes, we're starting tonight but not at the Hollywood Ballroom. I don't want Ben Kaiser to recognize me. We're going to learn the Argentine tango at the Colvin Run Community Hall in Great Falls, Virginia."

"That's a sexy dance for an old man."

"Emily won't be able to keep her hands off me for weeks."

They continued their conversation on non-DOE matters before leaving the zoo.

George went home and kissed his wife while she watched an instructional video on the fox-trot. "Don't get lost in work. Remember, we're going dancing tonight."

"I'm looking forward to it," George said as he entered his office. He loved having his wife regain her teenage enthusiasm for romance now that his children had left the house. He anticipated a love-filled evening after the dancing ended.

George opened the Internet and entered a search for

General Computing Support. He saved the company profile template in a non-GCS named file and began entering corporate information. He planned to locate what part of the company had political vulnerabilities. George read the executives' bios, reviewed their financial information, and entered the details into his database. He accessed Dun & Bradstreet and compared their financial report with the GCS financial statements and could find no problems, GCS did not have any historical or outstanding financial judgments.

George next wondered if there could be any connections between stockholders and politicians. Members of Congress had no legal restrictions on using inside information to purchase stock. He searched both Securities and Exchange Commission files and GCS information sources to find any members of Congress who owned GCS stock. Next, he accessed the EDGAR files, the Securities and Exchange Commission's Electronic Data Gathering, Analysis, and Retrieval System, which lists company officers, institutional and major stockholders, defined as those owning over 5 percent of the stock, as well as company filings to the Securities and Exchange Commission. After completing the search of the stockholders' data and recording the major individual stockholders in the GCS database, he found there were no congressional major stockholders. As he scanned the Securities and Exchange Commission filings, Emily knocked on the study door. "Dinner's ready."

"Be right there." George saved the new files, turned off the PC, and joined his wife.

George resumed working after an invigorating evening of dancing, marital sex, a sound sleep, and breakfast.

He reviewed the GCS Securities and Exchange Commission filings for the last four years and could not find data related to congressional ownership. He realized the easy and safe procedures for identifying stockholders were unsuccessful and began thinking of how to hack into the GCS corporate financial files.

George decided not to use the simple phishing e-mail approach he used on Ben Kaiser since he assumed GCS IT security would discover and block this attack. He decided to use Ben's phishing e-mail approach on the company executive officers' personal computers. It took until 3:00 p.m., with a break for lunch, to find the private e-mail addresses of the fourteen GCS officers. He used a sex ad for the phishing e-mail for the men and a free vacation ad for the women. George planned to use the vacation ad for the men, if the sex ad did not work. He sent the last phishing e-mail by 5:30 p.m., quit work, and wandered into the living room, searching for Emily to tell him what restaurant and movie she had chosen for the evening.

After an early church service and a home-cooked brunch and moderate servings of waffles, sausage, and scrambled eggs, George resumed work. He opened his e-mail and found three responses from the GCS officers, two operations vice presidents and the comptroller. George accessed the comptroller's computer and found the account and password database which he downloaded. He logged off the comptroller's PC and searched the downloaded database on his PC, finding the comptroller's user ID and password for accessing GCS financial files.

George's ability to open the comptroller's GCS account surprised him since most sophisticated IT systems use a hardware interface, with a login ID required for access. He found the stockholders' list within five minutes, downloaded it to his PC, and logged off from the GCS site. He accessed the comptroller's PC, and removed all traces of the electronic invasion, and planned to do the same to the other two executives as soon as they accessed his phishing e-mail.

The stockholders' list included 542 names. He matched the names with a directory of congressmen and found four: Ed Walinski (Iron City, Kentucky), Jim O'Neill (Utica, New York), Sam Johnson (Boise, Idaho), and Ernesto Gomez (San Antonio, Texas).

He next analyzed the company's operations, including their services and locations, entering this information into the GCS database. George discovered GCS had a facility in Iron City, Kentucky, a depressed coal mining area, remote from any DOE facility. This anomaly interested him. Why would GCS locate in a rural area of eastern Kentucky, unless they had bribed the congressman?

George searched the Internet for Iron City, Kentucky. He read a general description of the county, finding it one of the poorest in the state since the coal mines had closed in 1998, with 50 percent of the population leaving the county, and most of the remaining population surviving on public assistance. He found a page on the GCS facility identifying it as a help desk center, employing 454 individuals, making it the largest private employer in the county. A rational congressman would pressure DOE to award the contract to GCS to keep its largest employer.

George searched for information on Iron City's Congressman Ed Walinski. He saved it into his GCS database, including the margin of victory in the last two elections which did not exceed 2 percent in either election. He searched the GCS shareholder list and found Walinski owned eighty thousand shares, 4 percent of the outstanding stock, which did not have to be reported on EDGAR. George thought Representative Walinski had two killer reasons for exerting political pressure on DOE. George left his study to join Emily.

Amy saw Ben once or twice a week, usually on Monday and Thursday, since their intimate relationship began on June 7. They always spent the night at her condo because of the recording devices, even though Ben constantly invited her to have dinner at his house.

THE OPPORTUNITY

In the middle of July, as their evening ended, Amy, thinking he would be more amenable to giving her sensitive information in familiar surroundings, said, "Ben, I surrender. I want to see your place."

"Then I'll look forward to Thursday night, at seven."

Amy carried her new purse purchased on the Internet, which included wireless solid state audio and video recorders, to Ben's house arriving a few minutes before seven. She knocked on the front door and Ben greeted her overflowing with smiles. She handed him a box and kissed him on the cheek. Feeling his eagerness, she knew what Ben had been thinking since Monday.

"Hi, you live in a terrific area. You can walk to great restaurants on Connecticut Avenue."

"That's true but you'll enjoy the dinner here. What's in the box?"

"Open it."

"Cookies. They'll go great with ice cream for dessert."

"That's what I was hoping."

"Let me show you the house. It's a railroad house over eighty years old."

"What's a railroad house?"

"It's long and narrow, with the living area on the first floor, bedrooms on the second and a basement. You've already seen the front porch and you're standing in the living room."

He motioned Amy to follow him, past the living room into a section demarcated by two columns near the walls, "We'll eat dinner here in the dining room as you can see from the set table and sideboard."

Still walking with Amy following, Ben opened a door. "This is the kitchen. We're having lobster, corn on the cob, and salad. Everything is fresh. Like the best restaurants on Connecticut Avenue, nothing is cooked yet."

"I love lobster. I hope you have bibs. I'm wearing a new sweater."

"Of course I do."

"Good."

"I use the finished basement as my study and to watch TV. I've a pool table, if you want to play later. Follow me." He opened a door in the kitchen to a stairway, took her by the hand, and led her to his masculine basement.

"No, I don't play pool. This is your own private floor."

As they returned to the kitchen, Ben said, "Have some cheese and crackers and a glass of ice tea while I cook."

Amy, who was hungry, ate several, before she remembered to prepare one and give it to Ben.

"Thanks." He turned the stove burner on high for the lobster and prepared the salad while continuing to talk.

"Has CIN Inc. spent more time deciding on whether to bid the contract?"

"Yes, we're still discussing it, but we need more detailed information."

"I forgot to tell you GCS has a dismal record on their small-business-participation subcontracting. DOE is getting beat up by the Small Business Administration–SBA, because we're not meeting our small-business goals. I remind GCS of their deficiencies at every status meeting, and they promise to do better but ignore me. GCS management doesn't recognize or care that their SBA record counts as part of their proposal evaluation criteria for winning the next contract."

"Their loss. Our small business participation record is excellent, but I assume most serious competitors will satisfy your agency's SBA requirements."

"They'll have to, to win the contract."

"Does GCS use their political connections to overcome their contract performance and SBA problems?" Amy asked.

"Yes and they're congressional. GCS has employees

in several congressional districts that the congressmen want to protect. They threaten our appropriations when we tell them GCS is performing poorly. They don't want to hear it. All they care about is their votes."

"Isn't that illegal?"

"It might be, but DOE is not going to turn them into the FBI since Congress funds the agency."

"Scary, so if CIN Inc. has the best bid DOE's evaluation could be overruled by Congress?"

"Not directly but pressure could be put on the secretary of DOE to change the initial award. Welcome to big-time politics in Washington."

"I have a question I'd like to ask you, which you don't have to answer, but keep it confidential."

"OK."

"Selecting a qualified and personable program manager to bid is a critical part of developing a successful proposal. If the program manager is not liked by the evaluators, we'd lose the bid."

"That's true. Who are you thinking of bidding?"

"Art Mitchell, he joined CIN Inc. when he retired in January."

"Perfect, everyone loves Art. He's a great manager and the contracts office loves him, because his contractors submitted error-free status reports and invoices on time."

"Thanks. Please don't mention Art's name to anyone."

"I won't."

Ben continued cooking and served dinner within five minutes of the end of their business conversation. Amy smiled when Ben put a bib on her, thinking I've hit the trifecta: great bonus, good cooking, and a sex slave. She appreciated the non-business-related conversation, and concentrated on their past and Ben's children.

Ben kept talking as they ate the cookies, ice cream, and decaf coffee. Finally, in sweet exasperation, with a smile she said, "Isn't it time you show me the upstairs?"

"Yes."

"Let's clean up first. You don't want to walk into a dirty dining room and kitchen."

"You're right."

They walked upstairs ten minutes later. Ben proudly showed her the three bedrooms, the master bedroom last. Ben pointed at the bed and slowly walked into the room appearing nervous, in spite of their previous sexual meetings. Amy, in control of the situation, pulled him to the bed and began repeating their moves, passionately removing his and her clothes. Amy kept stimulating him and herself until he collapsed after three orgasms at 11:00. She did not bother to count hers. While Amy liked sex with Ben, thinking of her bonus stimulated her more than the sensuality of his body.

After they exhausted themselves, Amy did not offer, nor did Ben suggest she leave. Amy's goal was to complete Ben's sexual dependence on her in the morning.

When he woke up at 6:30, he gazed over at Amy, whose half-nude body rose and fell with her breath. He quietly left the bed went to the bathroom and relieved himself, noting that even though the voluptuous Amy slept a few feet away, he had no desire. He brushed his teeth and the soft sound of the flowing water woke Amy who got up and walked to the bathroom and shocked Ben with a passionate embrace.

"Good morning. That was fun. Why did we stop?" Amy said.

"Good morning. Exhaustion."

"Maybe, but that was last night. We're well rested now."

Amy rubbed her breast against his chest and said, "Ben, let's take a shower together."

He could not resist and felt his desire returning as he turned on the shower and retrieved two bath towels. The hot water and Amy's gentle hands aroused Ben who wondered at Amy's ability to revive him. She led him back to the bed and properly trained, he performed oral sex without her asking. Amy cemented Ben's addiction to her, transferring his general sex addiction to one person. Amy declined an invitation for breakfast, saying "I have to get to work by nine. I brought clothes for work."

After she left, Ben decided he did not need to see other women.

Amy met Pete for their regular luncheon meeting the next Tuesday.

"You didn't make a very convincing Santa at the Christmas in July charity beach party."

"I have the body for it and the wig perfected the image. I enjoy my role helping to get rich women to donate Christmas presents for the poor."

"Pete, Santa normally has children sit on his lap, not drunken, middle-aged women."

"They told me they enjoyed it."

"Those that volunteered did and they were so drunk they won't remember. It's the ones you grabbed and pulled to your lap that caused the problem."

"Is that why you, Joan, and Art dragged me from the party?"

"Yes. Art and I don't want to conduct meetings with you in jail."

"That would never have happened."

"You were very drunk and started abusing women you didn't know. One of them may have eventually screamed, called the police, and you would have been arrested."

"I don't remember much from the party."

"You kept drinking after we got back to the beach house and didn't go to bed until one thirty."

"I plan to reduce my drinking. Thanks for taking care of me."

"OK, you should. You could drink yourself into developing diabetes, or having a stroke or a heart attack."

Pete had Amy's chicken Caesar salad waiting while he munched on a meatball-and-cheese sub. Amy drank water while Pete had regular Coke.

"Pete, aren't you concerned about your health? Women don't like fat men."

"My health is fine. You might be different in your search for men. In Washington, women prefer men with money and power over a good body, and I've plenty of money and act as if I have power."

"I don't want you to die before I receive my bonus."

"Don't worry; your bonus is in a contract, and you have a copy."

"That's true. But winning depends on you developing a successful win strategy."

"With your help, I will. I promise I'll live past the award. What did you find out?"

"Plenty. The political problem is congressional. He didn't mention any names but said the incumbent GCS has facilities in congressional districts, and DOE fears the congressmen will pressure the Secretary of DOE to change a best-value award to us to a GCS win."

"I'll take it from here. Don't press him on that topic anymore. But tell me if he volunteers the names of the congressmen or congresswomen."

"He's pissed at GCS because they never meet their SBA small-business subcontracting goals. DOE is getting pressure from the SBA which means he is getting pressure since he's their contracting officer. He said he reminds them of their deficiencies at every monthly status meeting, and they ignore him."

"It will be easy for us to ghost them. We have an excellent record on small-business subcontracting."

"That's what I told him. But I held the best news until now. He and his colleagues love Art. It's a plus to bid him as the program manager."

"Excellent. I'm going to get Art more involved in the proposal process. Find out if they want to retain other

GCS or subcontractor managers. We should get them on our team before we submit the proposal. Ask about their security program. It's critical for DOE with their industry proprietary information and their nuclear programs."

"Will do."

They spent the rest of their lunch talking about the beach.

Pete stopped at a 7-Eleven he had never visited, on his way home, and purchased an untraceable cell phone. He followed his normal procedure, walking down a side street, and when alone, called George.

"George Steen."

"It's your friend. I found out the political connection is with Congress."

"Good, that's the organization I've been concentrating on. I'm glad it's not the Executive Branch; that's harder to investigate." George hung up.

George did not tell Pete he knew the congressmen involved preferring to wait unit the ten-day deadline meeting.

Pete called Art into his office on Wednesday morning. "Hi, Art. How is your DOE work going?

"Good, as far as I can see. We're on schedule and below cost on the contract."

"No problems?"

"None."

"Are you familiar with the DOE IT Consolidated Support Contract?"

"Of course. GCS, the incumbent, is hated throughout DOE. It's up for recompetition soon."

"We've heard GCS has problems. We're thinking of bidding it with you as the program manager. Since you were in a different organization there should be no conflict of interest."

"Thanks, that's a big program. What do you want me

to do with my current DOE contract?"

"Keep managing it and make sure you meet all your Service Level Agreements, schedules, and cost limits. If you don't, it could lower our proposal evaluation score.

This'll be a real training experience to supplement your reading of CIN Inc. procedures on how we develop a win strategy and write a proposal. I've hired Frank Nelson as the proposal manager. Amy Ericson is the marketing interface with DOE. I'm the capture manager. We've been holding weekly strategy meetings for a month. As the date for the RFP release becomes closer, we'll move to daily meetings. I want you to attend and provide inside knowledge of DOE operations to help develop our strategy. We hold the meetings at eight o'clock on Tuesday morning, in my office, so they shouldn't impact your meetings with your current DOE clients. Any questions?"

"No," Art replied.

After the meeting, Art called Joan.

"I've great news. I'll tell you the details when you come over for dinner. Pete has picked me to be the bid program manager on the DOE IT Consolidated Support bid. Amy has marketing."

"Great. What's for dinner?"

"Baked salmon in butter dill sauce, red Irish garlic potatoes, and a salad."

"I'll bring a bottle of Chardonnay. I'm looking forward to hearing the details."

"See you later."

Joan arrived at Art's condo carrying a bottle of chilled wine and a small overnight bag. She entered using her key.

"Hi, Art, it's me."

"Hi, I'm in the study, reviewing CIN Inc. proposal procedures."

She walked to him, caught him, grabbed him, and placed an openmouthed passionate kiss on his lips, and said, "Congratulations. I'm familiar with the opportunity. Tell me how you feel about being bid as the program manager."

"A little nervous. It's a big job compared to what I'm managing now. I've never worked on a large proposal and writing a proposal is more difficult than evaluating one, a task I performed at DOE."

"True. You'll be surprised at the work required to develop the technical, management, and cost volumes."

"Pete wants the key players to meet at eight o'clock every Tuesday morning and report the status of our capture management activities."

"I suggest we open the wine and eat dinner first, before you reread CIN Inc. proposal documentation."

Art served dinner which he had prepared and kept warm before Joan arrived.

Joan opened and poured the wine and said, "A toast to the DOE IT Consolidated Support program manager."

"To the proposed program manager."

"Art, don't be silly. You have to believe you're going to win the contract. If you're unsure of yourself, it will show at meetings at DOE and in the proposal."

"It'll take a while to get the winning confidence I'll need."

"Perhaps, but remember, Pete and Amy have been following this opportunity for years and they hired you, because they're confident you'll help win and be successful in managing the contract."

"You're right."

They finished dinner, without eating dessert, and retired to bed early. After making love they set the alarm for 6:00, so they could run together for an hour on the streets of Washington before beginning their work day.

After Tuesday's call from Pete, George decided to investigate the other three congressmen who held GCS stock. He accessed the GCS geographic office file and compared the locations to the three congressmen's districts. He discovered a perfect match for their districts and three GCS offices. He built a small spreadsheet from the GCS geographical office file for the four congressmen, with the first column identifying the congressman, the second column the location, the third column the name of the GCS office located in the Congressional district, the fourth column the GCS operations performed, and the fifth column the client's department. George had to revert to congressional data files to complete the sixth column, which identified congressmen's committee assignments. The four congressmen were their political party's ranking members on committees overseeing DOE operations. George became excited: one individual applying political pressure could be fraud; while four are a congressional conspiracy. He wrote up the findings and saved the material on a USB thumb drive.

Pete called George, as usual, on an untraceable cell phone.

"George Steen."

"It's your friend. Let's meet next Monday near the Jefferson Memorial on the Tidal Basin at noon?"

"OK." George hung up.

Pete wanted to explain the congressional situation to Amy on Tuesday and enlist her help in developing a solution.

Amy skipped the beach and went dancing with Ben on Friday evening at the Hollywood Ballroom, retiring to her apartment with Ben in the evening to enjoy each other. She invited him for dinner at her condo on Sunday, excluding dancing that evening.

Ben arrived with flowers, knocking on the door in anticipation of continuing his physical pleasure and emotional happiness.

"Ben, they're beautiful. I'll get a vase." She ushered him into the kitchen, taking the mixed bouquet of summer flowers and immersed them in water.

Ben, feeling rising sexual desire, smelled the baking squash and looked at the flounder on the counter, ready to be sautéed, thinking this is a perfect life.

After eating, Amy led Ben to the couch, sat next to him, stroked his arm, face, and chest, and said, "We have to talk."

"Go ahead. But I want to tell you the RFP will be released in six weeks."

"Great. You keep encouraging me to convince CIN Inc. to bid the DOE opportunity. Well thanks to your help our management has decided to bid. I told you, I'm in business development, but I haven't been completely honest. I'm the marketing lead for CIN Inc."

"I assumed that when I read your name on the bidder's conference attendance list."

"You're not mad."

"Of course not. I want a good firm to beat GCS, and you're kind enough to help. I'm doing it for DOE."

"Thanks for being so understanding." She kissed him passionately moving his hand to the exposed skin of her breasts, with her right hand, and using her left hand to fondle his genitals.

"Will you be able to keep helping us?"

Ben, who until now, had been providing information, which could be discovered by most firms with good market research, did not realize she was asking him for special favors related to the contract in return for hers.

"Yes, I'll help in any way I can."

Amy used her standard techniques to drive him to satisfy her, while convincing him he had found his last love.

After making love, Amy said, "Do you like our arrangement?"

"You mean, the dancing, dinner, and making love."

"Yes."

"I hope it continues."

"It will but we have to be careful. If CIN Inc.'s competitors see us together they might complain to DOE that our relationship unfairly favors CIN Inc."

"Well it doesn't matter. I don't choose the winner."

"We both know that, but we must be above suspicion or it could kill our careers."

"Are you saying we should stop seeing each other until the contract is awarded?"

"No. I'm enjoying myself too much to stop, but I'm suggesting we don't appear in public. I don't want to ruin my marketing career, and you don't want to lose your job at DOE. We're still a long way from retirement. You can come here or I can go to your house but we shouldn't be seen in public. We're seeing each other at least twice a week. I propose we continue. After CIN Inc. wins, I'll move to market another agency and we can date openly. Is that OK?"

"You're being very smart. I agree."

He had what he wanted and knew it would continue as long as he helped CIN Inc. win which he rationalized helped DOE.

George walked to the Jefferson Memorial, carrying a salad and a bottle of water. He found Pete eating a steak-and-cheese sub and drinking a regular Coke.

"Hi, Pete," he said, shaking Pete's hand and passing him the USB drive.

"How is it going?"

"Great. I found out a few interesting details related to our GCS congressional conspiracy. There are four congressmen involved. They receive political contributions from GCS. There are GCS branch offices in their districts and they hold significant amounts of GCS stock. I've documented the relationships. They have a vested interest in ensuring a GCS win."

"I'll read the details later."

"The report includes several of GCS's CPAS reports

on their poor past performance on the DOE IT contract and other contracts you might be able to use on the proposal. I included an analysis of the GCS win rate on contracts where they're the incumbent. It's bad, less than 50 percent."

"Thanks."

Pete planned to use Tim Carver, their political lobbyist, and Amy to neutralize GCS political backers.

The next Tuesday Amy entered Pete's office and said, "Ben told me the RFP is due out in six weeks, on Friday September 11, 2009."

"Great, the wait is over. We'll accelerate our proposal activities. How is Ben handling your relationship?"

"Very well. He agreed not to see me in public, so as not to alert our competitors."

"That's wise. I found out more on our congressional problem," Pete said. He summarized George's report.

"Is what they're doing legal?"

"Partially—members of Congress can buy stock with insider information. That's how many of them get rich. I'm not so sure influencing awards is legal."

"How are we going to convince them to back CIN Inc.?"

"There are two parts to my plan: enticement and fear. As our first enticement action, I'd recommend we contribute to their reelection campaign, so that CIN Inc. gets immediate name recognition when we call to schedule a meeting. Second, when we meet the Congressmen, we'll discuss our plan to bid the contract and to hire the GCS staff, ensuring employment to their voters. Third, if possible mention other potential opportunities for hiring the locals as CIN Inc. employees, enticing them into believing CIN Inc. could become a driver of prosperity for their districts.

"The fear factor has to be handled less blatantly. Convince them GCS is a loser and that they should switch their allegiance to CIN Inc."

"How?"

"I've reviewed CPAS reports on GCS's performance on several contracts. We'll summarize the reports in our meetings. GCS's recent win/loss rate on incumbent contracts is not good. They lost over 50 percent. We could subtly hint their stock might crash so the Congressmen might run from GCS before they lose their fortunes."

"When do we meet them and what will we say? It appears GCS has a hold on them." Amy asked.

"We'll meet with them soon. We'll show them CIN Inc. can help them more that GCS. I'll develop a strategy and a set of talking points, before I set up the meetings. Let's meet at nine o'clock on Friday morning to rehearse our presentation."

"See you then."

Pete greeted Tim Carver, a six-one trim, close-cropped gray-haired, early fifties, retired Marine colonel, and former congressional staffer on Thursday afternoon. "Hi, Tim, how's your golf game?"

"I still have a four handicap but manage to lose to congressional members and their staff unless they're my partner."

"Good, I want you to contribute money to four congressmen by writing a CIN check and not playing golf."

"Who?"

"Do you know Congressman Ed Walinski, of Iron City, Kentucky; Jim O'Neill from Utica, New York, Sam Johnson from Boise, Idaho, and Ernesto Gomez, representing, San Antonio, Texas?"

"Yes, they're always soliciting and accepting campaign contributions from lobbyists, not the most ethical public servants."

"You mean they can be bribed."

"We don't use those words. They can be influenced

to vote our way."

"Good. I want you to contribute ten thousand dollars to their Super PACS and twenty-five hundred dollars to their personal campaign funds in CIN Inc.'s name ASAP. Before you send the first donation, check what GCS has contributed, and match them or top them if legally possible."

"No problem. May I ask why?"

"Of course." Pete explained the congressmen's role in supporting GCS.

"I see. We want to dissuade them from backing GCS. Do you think they each can be bought for twelve thousand five hundred dollars?"

"No. You, Amy, and I will meet with them and convince them it's in their long-term interest to back us. I'll develop a presentation you and Amy can review and improve on tomorrow morning at nine o'clock. Make the contributions as soon as you can."

"I'll mail the checks tomorrow morning. I'll research our four congressmen, so I can contribute at the meeting."

Amy and Tim arrived for their Friday meeting. Pete greeted them enthusiastically, offered them coffee, and said, "I have a solution to the congressional situation but I want to get your input before we meet the fab four."

Pete pressed a button on his remote and flashed an outline of his strategy on a whiteboard:

- Money
- Employment
- Votes
- CIN skills

He looked at Amy and Tim. "Any questions?"

"Can you fill in the details?" Amy responded first.

"Yes." Pete said as he handed them the PowerPoint presentation. "Tim will send the fab four campaign contributions today so they'll recognize us when Tim calls. They love GCS because they made them rich. They'll realize CIN Inc. is an alternative if GCS fails. We'll tell them that if we win any contracts in their district where the losing contractor has employees, we'll hire them. Thus neutralizing GCS's hold on the Congressmen. Furthermore, we'll flatter them on how great their district treats government contractors, and that we will be moving existing operations to their congressional districts. They'll know they'll get reelected if they can bring another firm with new jobs to their voters. Amy, you'll do the presentation on CIN Inc. after the initial discussion. Just hypnotize them."

"Sounds perfect," Tim said.

"Tim, set up appointments at any time with the fab four. We'll clear our calendars to meet them," Pete said.

"I'll call on Tuesday after they receive their campaign contributions and e-mail you both as soon as I make an appointment."

Pete, Amy, and Tim stepped out of a cab three weeks later, on August 20, in front of the Rayburn House Office Building, for their thirty-minute meeting with Congressman Ed Walinski. They walked up to the entrance and presented their identification to the guard who called the congressman's office. A young tall blonde administrative assistant in her early twenties was dispatched to escort them to the office.

"I'm Kelly Ryan. You must be Amy and Pete. I already know Tim."

The trio followed her to the congressman's office. Pete appreciated her sensuality but reminded himself not to upset Walinski.

Kelly, led the trio through the receptionist's office and introduced them to the congressman, who asked, nodding at Tim, "What can I do for you?"

Pete responded, "We want to inform you that CIN Inc. is moving one of its IT help desk operations, from a Department of Education contract in Washington, DC, to

Iron City. The help desk requires a staff of two hundred which we will fill by hiring Iron City residents. We've rented office space and should start the move and hiring within thirty days. We are giving you the opportunity to announce the opening of our office in Iron City."

"That's good news. What are the details on the new office?" Congressman Walinski asked.

"Tim has developed material he'll review, and several draft announcement papers that you might find useful. We reviewed the economic potential of your district and plan to locate other offices here if our company's growth plans are realized," Pete answered.

Tim opened his briefcase, took out several documents and distributed them to the congressman and his staff. He spoke directly to the congressman.

"Ed, we've made this move, using a dummy corporation, so as not to alert our competitors, and as a way to keep our real estate costs low. The first document on the top of the package contains a map of our location, at the corner of Second Avenue and Main Street in downtown Iron City. We have signed a ten-year lease and tomorrow, after your announcement, we plan to move a skeleton CIN Inc. management team to Iron City and begin our recruitment process. CIN Inc. will place a company sign on the building a few days after the announcement. The next two sets of documents which we believe are suitable for a press release, should answer most of your questions. The short document summarizes the opening while the longer document provides a detailed overview. I'll e-mail you these documents in an electronic format so you can tailor them to your needs. I won't read them now in the interest of time, but my business card is stapled to them so you can call me to answer questions or provide more details. Tell me when the announcement will occur so we can proceed."

"Thanks, Tim. We'll try to edit your announcement this afternoon and Kelly will call you before it's released."

"Thanks," Tim replied.

"Amy will now summarize our long-term plans for CIN Inc.'s growth in Iron City," Pete said.

Amy, dressed in a subdued conservative business suit, handed out a fifty-page slide presentation. Seeing the congressman's facial reaction, she said, "Don't worry, Congressman Walinski, I don't plan to go over each page. I'll just summarize the presentation that includes detailed data which you and your staff can review at your leisure."

The Congressman smiled. Amy began by outlining the capabilities and growth potential of CIN Inc. She presented a table illustrating CIN Inc.'s performance criteria on its major contracts. She noted CIN Inc. has never had a stop work order issued on its contracts. She did not state that GCS has had several stop orders issued in the last few years. Pete selected CIN Inc.'s past contract performance criteria to raise questions about or ghost GCS performance history. She next switched to the CIN Inc.'s plans for Iron City, Kentucky, presenting a table of all the federal government contracts or subcontracts being performed in the congressman's district.

"Our business development organization will analyze each contract to decide if CIN Inc. has the qualifications to bid. CIN Inc. only bids when the current contractor had a poor performance record." She did not refer to the slides showing GCS's poor performance, growth and incumbent win rate, knowing the congressman's staff would alert him to the GCS data.

"CIN Inc. will always hire the incumbent's staff to keep employment levels unchanged in your district. CIN Inc. is planning to bid on the DOE IT Consolidated Support Contract held by General Computing Support. We believe we can deliver a better service for a lower price, and we want to make you aware of our efforts. Regardless, if we win or lose the opportunity, we will keep our new CIN Inc. office open so we can state in our proposal that CIN Inc. has a local Iron City office to support bidding other opportunities. Congressman Walinski, do you have any questions?" Amy said.

"No, but we might after we read the material. We'll call if we do."

"Congressman, thanks for your time. Please call us on any matter. We hope to work with you in the future in building our presence in Iron City," Pete said.

The trio descended the steps of Rayburn House Office Building, and when they reached the sidewalk, Pete said, "That went well. Tim, follow up to ensure we've neutralized GCS."

"I will."

"Three more to go. We'll be done by next week," Pete said.

Chapter 9 Writing the Proposal

Art arrived at the DOE IT Consolidated Support proposal strategy meeting in Pete's office at 7:55 a.m. on August 4, 2009, five minutes, before the actual meeting started.

"Pete, I'm very curious about implementing the proposal process I read about," Art said.

"You'll be shocked at how many resources we devote to winning a contract, including proposal development. It's the first opportunity for a company to impress a client of the quality of their work. The clients know the quality of the work will decline after the contract award since the government reimburses the bidders for writing proposals. We charge our proposal labor and materials to general and administrative expenses in our overhead."

"I didn't realize that. What stops contractors from buying the contract by spending exorbitant amounts?"

"Competition. If our general and administrative overhead is too high, our rates will be higher than our competition, and we'll lose on cost. The game is to submit a technically acceptable proposal and win on cost."

Amy walked into Pete's office, accompanied by a middle-aged man, with white hair and an arm extended in Art's direction, "Hi, I'm Frank Nelson."

"Frank's a consultant and our DOE IT proposal manager. He has run several of our major winning proposals," Amy said.

Pete handed Art, the CIN Inc. Proposal Procedures Manual, "You read this in your first month here, but now this will be your bible until we win the contract. Frank and Amy will take you to the war room and show you how we write proposals."

Art followed them toward the elevator. They descended one floor to the war room. Frank entered a combination into a cyber-lock. Art gasped, looking at a room full of tables, with writers at their PCs, and a wall posted with documents.

"You've never been in a war room?" Amy asked.

"No. What's happening? The RFP issue date is a month away."

"We're responding to the draft RFP," Frank answered.

"Won't the final RFP be different?"

"No, not much, and even it if is we've developed a great writing team, and the RFP sections that don't change will be in excellent shape."

"We don't leave anything to chance," Amy said. "The proposal outline, in storyboard format, is on the wall with draft sections and graphics underneath each section title. The wall is updated daily. Read the storyboards and draft updates every day after you're finished your regular job and make suggestions for improving each section. Write and sign your comments on sticky notes and place them on their relevant section, as others have done."

Over the next several hours Amy and Frank continued to explain the proposal process, reviewed the proposal outline, and story storyboards. Art met the writers who were CIN Inc. and subcontractors' staff.

"We don't expect you to absorb everything in one morning. Any questions?" Amy asked.

"I counted twelve people working on the proposal. Is that normal?"

"That's just what you see in the war room. Graphic artists, word processors, and reviewers working in other rooms are not here. When we work on the regular proposal, we'll have over forty individuals contributing."

"Lunch is here," a voice from the war room door announced. The workers left their PCs to eat.

"Do you feed them every day?" Art asked.

"Three meals a day, plus snacks. We don't want them to leave, lose their concentration, and take a few hours away from work to eat or drink," Amy replied.

Art walked around the war room, reading the draft proposal on the wall. In a few minutes, he noticed workers returning to their PCs, with sandwiches, sodas, and chips. He thought I am going to enjoy learning this process.

Amy entered Pete's office on Tuesday morning, August 11.

"Is Art surviving the proposal?" Pete asked.

"Yes, he's loves it—spending an extra two hours a day in the war room. He told me he enjoys learning."

"Any new information?"

"The proposal release date hasn't changed. DOE still wants to change prime contractors."

"Good. In addition to your marketing duties, I want you to run the proposal reviews. That way you can make sure the proposal includes our marketing themes. Include Art in the reviews."

"Thanks for the assignment. I know Art will contribute."

"He was a great hire. I'm glad the RFP won't be out until after Labor Day."

"So am I."

They spent the next fifteen minutes discussing their summer at the beach and the upcoming party at the Margarita House.

Amy wore a blue low-cut dress and an uplift bra. She consciously bent over as she opened the door to admit Ben on a Thursday evening. "Hi, hon. I've missed you."

Ben's eyes went to her exposed breasts. Ben felt her hand on the back of his head pressing his face against her soft breasts. She pulled him in and closed the door and kissed him on the forehead holding him fast to her, and said, "I missed you."

"You're horny."

"You're right. Follow me and don't resist." She removed his head from her breast took his hand and led him into her bedroom.

A half hour later, lying on her bed, she reached for her robe, and said, "It's time for dinner."

"Good, you just gave me an appetite. How long will it take to cook?"

"Five minutes, I just have to make the salad and microwave the lasagna which I made this afternoon."

"Amy, you're perfect."

"Do me a favor and pour the ice tea. It's sitting on the kitchen counter."

"OK.

They ate dinner, exchanged small talk, and Ben confirmed the proposed RFP release date had not changed. After dinner, Amy and Ben moved to a couch, and she started a new thread in their conversation.

"My boss called a meeting with the business development and operations staff working on DOE programs. He forbade us from contacting anyone in DOE whose job is related to the contract after the RFP is released. He stated he didn't want CIN Inc. to be disqualified for improper behavior. He further threatened if he found anyone engaging in illegal behavior, he'd fire them. I could be paranoid, but I swear he stared at me."

"Christ, he doesn't know of our relationship, does he?"

"No. If he found out, I'd be gone."

"I'm concerned your signing in at the condo desk every time you visit could complicate the proposal award, if the competitors find out. You should stop coming here."

"Are you dumping me?" Ben said.

"Hush." She cooed, "Don't worry." She reached for his penis, caressing it as she kissed his lips stimulating a new erection which she began massaging.

"I mean we should meet at your place, not mine, to protect our careers. I'm glad you understand. In a month my trips to the beach will end and I can see you on weekends."

"Good, I'll make you breakfast."

"I look forward to that."

"I brought us matching gifts." She handed Ben a small package wrapped in silver-colored paper.

"A cell phone!" Ben said.

"Yes, it's another precaution. I purchased them at a convenience store. It has one hundred dollars' worth of prepaid calls. Call me on the new phone number and I'll do the same. These phones aren't registered in our names so no one can detect our calls."

"Are you sure we need these?"

"Yes, if you want to keep meeting and keep your job."

"I guess it's necessary," Ben replied.

"Let's go to bed and celebrate our new arrangement."

Pete received a call from CIN Inc.'s contracts office at 4:20 p.m. on Friday, September 18.

"Hi, Pete. I just received an e-mail from DOE with the final RFP attached."

"Not bad for DOE, only a week late. Did you get a chance to compare it to the draft RFP?"

"No."

"I'll have Frank Nelson, develop a comparison document of the pre and final RFP. He should be done in an hour. I'll set up a formal proposal kickoff meeting for Monday."

"Good, I'll be ready."

"We'll work the weekend. I'll have meals delivered. I'll schedule a key proposal staff meeting at eight o'clock tomorrow morning in my conference room."

Pete called Frank Nelson and directed him to begin the formal proposal process, starting with developing the comparison document, and notifying the key proposal staff how to access it.

After finishing his call with Nelson, Pete opened his e-mail account and scheduled the Saturday morning meeting with the key proposal staff. He next scheduled the kickoff meeting in the proposal war room, for Monday, September 21, starting at 9:00 a.m. and invited the proposal staff, and the subcontractor contacts, notifying them the meeting would last until 5:00.

Pete called Amy, "Are you driving to the beach?"

"Yes, I'm with Art and Joan. We're on Kent Island. Are you coming?"

"No. I'm glad they're with you. It saves me a call to Art. Turn around; we just received the DOE RFP. We'll be working in Virginia all weekend."

They all heard the call since it was on Amy's Bluetooth cell phone speakers. Joan said, "I suppose you don't want to drive to the beach and drop me off before you return."

"I'd like to, but I don't have enough gas. Why don't we have a few drinks and dinner at Fisherman's Inn and return after rush hour. That way you can have a romantic Friday evening together," Amy said,"

"OK, it might be our last opportunity for love before the proposal is delivered," Joan said.

Three congressmen, the other members of the fab four, Jim O'Neill from Utica, New York, Sam Johnson from Boise, Idaho, and Ernesto Gomez, representing San Antonio, Texas, arrived at Ed Walinski's beach house at 5:00 p.m. September 19, on Tidewater Road in Henlopen Acres, Delaware. The cedar-shingled house, surrounded by large pine trees, had a beautiful view of the marshes north of Lewes. It was set back next to the Lewes-Rehoboth canal. Ed handed them their favorite drink as they talked with their wives while they waited for dinner.

As they ate dessert, Congressman Gomez after

finishing his flan said, "Martha, you're a great cook. Where did you get the steaks Ed grilled? They're better than any I've eaten at the DC-area restaurants."

"They're grass-fed local beef. We buy it from the C and J Farms Inc., on Woodland Ferry Road in Seaford, Delaware. I hope you liked the potatoes, broccoli, and salad. They're from our garden in Vienna."

The visiting congressmen assured her they now preferred grass over corn-fed beef and the vegetables were the best they had eaten all summer. Martha thought the wine must have been great to make them forget what they had eaten before this meal.

"It looks like we've finished dinner. If the women don't mind, the men will drink their brandy in the study and discuss a few critical legislative matters," Ed said.

None of the women minded since they had not seen each other in at least a month and had their own agenda.

Ed led the men out of the dining room through the living room to the mahogany-bookcase-lined study, filled with books he never had or planned to read, purchased from an interior decorator by the foot. He sat behind a large mahogany desk next to a credenza that he opened and retrieved a bottle of Courvoisier and four brandy snifters which he half-filled and distributed to the three congressmen.

They sipped twenty-one-year-old brandy and conspired to become wealthier using their positions to obtain insider information. But no one would ever see them having after-dinner drinks in Congressman Ed Walinski's study in Henlopen, and they never discussed these events in their congressional offices, fearing the offices could be bugged. Their conspiracy had worked for over ten years because they valued money over policy. To their voters they were happy representatives who appeared naïve during congressional debates.

"Tim and his boss at CIN Inc. briefed us on what

they plan to do in our districts. Does anyone think they had offered a bribe?" Congressman Walinski began the serious conversation.

"No," the three other congressmen said.

"Good. Now we have to decide what to do about CIN Inc. and at the same time protect our investment in Global Computer Services."

"I'm not so sure Global Computer Services has a future. I looked into its prospects after reading the CIN Inc. graphs on their growth problems and they don't look good. DOE has complained to my committee about poor performance on their DOE IT contract. I plan to sell my GCS stock and purchase CIN Inc. stock even if GCS wins the re-compete," Congressman Gomez said.

"My committee staff tells me the same thing as Ed's. I agree GCS's stock will crash. I'm selling mine. We should develop a coordinated schedule so we don't spook the market or alert the Securities and Exchange Commission even though we're not covered by insider trading restrictions," Congressman Jim O'Neill commented.

"We also need to develop a schedule for purchasing CIN Inc. stock," Congressman Sam Johnson said.

"We can trust CIN Inc. I looked into their growth prospects and they're excellent. They have a diversified client base, including the departments of Energy and Defense, and they receive excellent contract evaluations. They opened an office in my district, even before DOE released the RFP, as they promised," Sam Johnson said.

The other three congressmen stated CIN Inc. had done the same in their districts.

"Good. We're agreed on CIN Inc. as a long-term viable investment. Now what do we do about helping them win the contract?" Ed asked.

"If asked, we should say we heard DOE is unhappy with GCS and we want DOE to get the best contractor. I don't think we should attack GCS; if it gets back to them, they might react," Jim said.

"I agree, they might suspect we're doing what we're doing. We can bet DOE will ask us about GCS and our approach will take care of them, but how do we help CIN Inc. win? There'll be more bidders than GCS and CIN Inc.," Ernesto said.

"We'll have to let CIN Inc. win the contract without our help. If we endorse them, it could backfire at DOE and get them disqualified," Jim replied.

They agreed.

Frank Nelson prepared a sixty-slide presentation which he reviewed with Art over the weekend before the proposal kickoff meeting.

"Art, this document is supposed to summarize the work we'll be doing over the next forty-five days to write a winning proposal. Do you think it accomplishes that goal?" Frank asked.

"I'm at a loss for words. There's so much detail here. I recognize most of the slides from reading the CIN Inc. Proposal Procedures Manual but I don't know how we'll complete our assignments in forty-five days."

"Actually we only have twenty-five days to complete the Red Team review copy of the proposal that mimics the final proposal, with no mistakes or typos."

"Is that possible?"

"Of course."

"You're in for a lot of work, if you have to teach me proposal development and manage the proposal."

"Don't worry. I've done it before, and besides, I get paid by the hour."

Frank's presentation on Monday had its desired effect. He outlined the work to be performed and its schedule, motivating the writers from CIN Inc., the subcontractors, and consultants that they could win the contract. His presentation ended at noon. The group ate a catered lunch of salad and sandwiches in an adjoining room. In the afternoon each head of a proposal section explained their strategy and goals by reviewing the storyboards and documents on the wall. The group broke for cookies and brownies at 3:00 and resumed the presentations at 3:15. They ended at 4:30.

"Thanks, Frank and the section heads for excellent presentations. Show the proposal schedule slide. Team members, this schedule is your friend and lover; you do not want to cheat on the due dates or we might lose our relationship," Pete said. He summarized the major due dates of the schedule and provided additional verbal incentives for sticking to it.

"This room is open twenty-four hours a day and seven days a week. The security desk has everyone's contact information, including a copy of your photo ID, so you can enter the building at any time and stay and work as long as you want. There are sofas in the lounge so you can crash for a few hours when you're exhausted. The kitchen is always full of food and nonalcoholic drinks so you don't have to break from writing when you get hungry or thirsty. There are no weekends during the proposal," Pete said.

He addressed Jim Larson, the lead writer of the transition plan section. "Jim, you've started customizing our company's transition plan to the requirements of the RFP. Brief Amy, Art, Frank, and me on your progress at ten o'clock on Wednesday morning in my office. Art, access our knowledge base and read the transition plan template before Jim's presentation."

The meeting ended at 5:00. Most of the participants did not leave, but talked with those from other companies.

After the presentation Amy asked Art, "What do you think of our proposal manager?"

"He's dynamic, a great planner, and has promised to teach me the proposal procedures. I feel sorry for him having to train me as well as manage the proposal."

"Don't worry about him. He knows he won't get much sleep for the next six weeks, but he earns more than both of us combined as a consultant."

"You're kidding."

"No. You'll see when the proposal's finished. He earns every cent."

"I hope so."

Pete joined them saying, "He's great and did exactly what I wanted. He'll form a team out of a diverse group of people from different firms, set expectations with his proposal schedule, and stress the importance of meeting deadlines. Make sure both of you attend his standup meetings each morning at eight o'clock. Art, you'll learn how to run the proposal for winning the re-compete of the contract."

"How many doughnuts did you eat this morning?" Amy asked Art after the kickoff meeting.

"I don't remember."

"I saw you eat three," Amy said looking at his stomach.

"Really, why are you counting?"

"Joan asked me to watch you. She told me she doesn't want you to gain weight and crush her at night."

"She didn't say that."

"Yes, she did. She said you're not running because of the extra work. Proposal eating without exercising is the perfect formula for turning you into a balloon."

"I don't have time to run in the afternoon since I stay at the office until seven o'clock reviewing the day's proposal work."

"Run at lunch. It will help you cut down on proposal food. There are showers in the building."

"I'll try tomorrow."

Art's admiration for CIN Inc. grew as he read the transition plan template. The plan included detailed instructions on all aspects for taking over a contract: scheduled meetings with the client and with the incumbent contractor, hiring staff, learning client incumbent contractor procedures, accounting and billing, opening regional offices, preparing status reports, et cetera. Art spent several hours reviewing the detailed Microsoft project schedule for implementing 430 transition tasks.

Pete opened the transition plan meeting stating, "We have plenty of coffee, but no doughnuts. I want everyone to stay awake. The integration of the transition plan with the technical and cost proposals is critical. DOE reviewers would question our capability if there were inconsistencies. When we win, it will be Art's blueprint to manage the first six months of the contract. The presentation should last at least two hours. To stop a mutiny we'll serve sandwiches at noon."

Jim Larson began his presentation stating, "Please interrupt me at any time if you have questions or don't understand what I'm saying."

Art listened in awe as Jim, in his PowerPoint presentation, translated the template into actions he would have to manage. He took extensive notes, stating where he thought the transition plan could be improved; including those areas he believed should be revised since they insulted DOE. Jim accepted his comments without arguing, changing the PowerPoint presentation to accommodate his recommendations. Art feared he did not have enough contract management experience to begin a CIN Inc. takeover of the contract before the presentation. As Jim spoke, Art realized he had an easy-to-follow blueprint for success.

The meeting lasted more than two hours, but as Pete promised, he served sandwiches at noon. After Jim finished the presentation, Frank, the proposal manager, spoke, "Jim, present the status of the transition plan at our daily standup meetings. Review the proposal wall hangings and in your daily presentations to identify any inconsistencies between the transition plan and the draft proposal. We'll work with the writers to resolve them."

Art called Joan after the meeting. "Hi, Joan, I have to apologize for working too much on the proposal and neglecting you. Can you come over to dinner tonight?"

"Sure. Is six-thirty OK?"

"Yes. Please bring your running clothes."

"OK. But you stopped running."

"I'm feeling better about the proposal and winning the contract. I realize I can't change my whole life for it."

"Good, you can tell me tonight why you feel better."

Joan arrived and let herself into the condo. She found Art in the kitchen preparing a healthy Caesar salad topped with lump crabmeat.

"Hi, that looks good. Are you eating healthy again?"

"Yes, Amy said I was getting fat so I've gone back to my healthy lifestyle."

"So that's why we're running tomorrow."

"Yes."

"Tell me what has made you confident of winning?"

"It's not just winning. I now believe I can be effective in managing the program after we win. I felt lost when Pete asked me to be the DOE IT program manager. Your and Pete's insistence that I learn CIN Inc.'s capture and proposal management procedures help remove the uncertainty I had of winning. I started believing we could win from attending the weekly and now daily status meetings. I realized I didn't have to write the complete proposal. Jim Larson presented our first draft of the proposal transition plan today. It convinced me CIN Inc. could successfully transition from the incumbent. Both Pete and Jim Larson accepted my recommendations for modifying the plan. I then realized I was in control and they looked to me for guidance in improving the proposal. From now on I'll be more aggressive."

"Good. I told you that's why they hired you."

"You did, but I just realized it today."

THE OPPORTUNITY

After dinner they went to bed early, made love, awoke at six and had a five-mile morning run. Joan had to run a slow pace so as not to outdistance out-of-shape Art.

A week later, at the end of the daily standup, Amy asked Art, "How do you think the proposal is going? Do you think the group will be ready for the Pink Team review of their design and integrated themes?"

"Great. We'll be ready for the Pink Team."

"We'll know by Friday. You should enjoy your first formal proposal review."

The Pink Team review started at 8:30 a.m. on Friday, ten days after DOE released the RFP. Amy began the meeting explaining the review process and described the comment sheet she distributed to the twelve Pink Team review members. The simple form impressed Art. It directed the reviewer to record their evaluation of whether the text reviewed was compliant with the RFP, to identify weak sections, and to offer improvement suggestions.

Art filled out his forms as he read each draft document. He judged the proposal to be in great shape and turned in his forms at noon. He dared not eat the high-calorie unlimited lasagna and salad, with Amy watching, but went running on the sidewalks of Tysons Corner. After a forty-five minute run, he returned and showered in time to attend the Pink Team evaluation summary presented by Amy.

"I want to thank all the writers and reviewers for their work on the Pink Team review. The findings show that we have made significant progress since the kickoff meeting, but we still have a long way to go before we have a winning proposal. We'll distribute the comments to each section leader who will be responsible for addressing each one by the Red Team review in two weeks, either by accepting them or providing a reason for their rejection."

Art looked around at the serious faces of the writers and wondered what he missed. Art listened as Amy's presentation described each problem and suggested solution. Art realized he had a lot to learn about reviewing a draft proposal.

At Monday's proposal standup meeting, Amy told Art, "I keep missing you at lunch. You look thinner than two weeks ago."

"I'm running."

"I know. Joan told me she is not worried about being crushed anymore."

"I hope she isn't tired. The running makes me more virile."

"She won't complain about that. How did you like the Pink Team review?"

"I felt sorry for the writers whose sections received a poor evaluation. They worked as hard as the others."

"Don't worry; they're used to it. They never expected to have a perfect Pink Team document in two weeks. If you think they worked hard last week, wait till you see them over the next two weeks. The Red Team document has to be as perfect as possible. The goal of the Red Team is to create a well-written, edited proposal with final graphics that could be delivered to DOE if they changed the proposal due date to the Red Team completion date. It has to be of high enough quality to win the contract."

"Is that possible in two weeks?"

"Yes, just wait."

Art watched in amazement as the Pink Team document metamorphosed into a finished document of the quality Art had evaluated while at DOE.

Amy led the Red Team review with the same review procedures and reviewers used on the Pink Team. She started with the same opening statement she used for the Pink Team saying they had more work to do before they had a winning proposal. She noted and Art agreed, "Our proposal is compliant, the engineering solution great, and the themes spread adequately through the document. Now we have to improve our writing, eliminate typos and grammatical errors, and upgrade the graphics to beat our competition."

Art watched with fascination as the Red Team review slide presentation demonstrated again that his review missed many problems. He had to train himself to read for grammar, typos, and style, something he did not have to do at DOE since they had a publications department to review and edit documents before their release.

Friday afternoon after the Red Team debriefing, Pete invited Amy, Art, and Tim for a drink in his office. When they arrived, he handed Amy a glass of Merlot, Art a bottle of Dogfish Head Indian Pale Ale, Tim a glass of Chardonnay, and made a vodka Martini for himself. He raised his glass and said, "To a successful Red Team. Art, what do you think of our proposal processes?"

"Complex and thorough. Does every firm bidding use these procedures?"

"If they want to win they do. There will be some companies who will try to win on cost, but their proposals will be so poor they won't make the technical cut."

"We're almost finished. The next two weeks will be different from the first four. Over half the proposal writers will leave. We'll use the senior writers and the proposal section heads to implement the Red Team Review recommendations. You, Amy, and Tim will continue to concentrate on your areas of expertise. Art, I want you to start getting involved with the cost proposal and in developing the basis of estimates, or BOE, for each RFP requirement. Frank will teach you our BOE procedures. You have to examine each labor loading we bid and justify it in the BOE forms. Tim, make sure we don't write anything that'll piss off the fab four. Amy, keep reviewing the document to make sure our marketing themes are included in the prop."

Art spoke first. "When will Frank be available to

teach me CIN Inc.'s BOE procedures?"

"He's expecting you in his office at ten tomorrow."

They talked for another hour, accepting Pete's offer of another drink, while they waited for the late Friday afternoon traffic to dissipate.

The preparation of the final proposal went as Pete and Frank planned, completed three days before its due date. Art wondered what they would do for three days. He did not have to wait long for Frank to appoint him along with the other senior members of the proposal team as part of the book-check review team. They sat in a room with all the volumes of the technical and business proposals, except the cost proposal, in front of them. Frank called a page number and each reviewer turned to that page and examined it for printing errors, ink smudges, or problems with the paper. When a reviewer identified a problem he or she removed the offending page and inserted a perfect replacement page.

"Is this review important?" Art asked Amy after an hour into this process.

"Yes, all the time we spent collecting data, developing our team, and writing the proposal would be wasted if our proposal contained imperfect pages. It would show the client we don't care about the quality of our proposals and the work we deliver to them. Yes, it's important!"

The next day Frank and a few support staff started loading boxes with the proposal and associated CDs for delivery to DOE.

"Why are there twice as many proposal documents boxed as required for delivery?" Art asked Frank.

"Suppose we only have one set and the van driving to DOE malfunctions and there's a traffic jam. The proposal might not be delivered before its due."

"Now I see. We'd lose. The other volumes are a backup plan."

"Yes, with a different route planned. If the secondary van is not called telling the driver the delivery was successful by a specific time, the backup van leaves CIN Inc. to deliver the proposal."

"Smart thinking."

"But not paranoid. I worked for a firm over ten years ago who had contracts supporting the US submarine fleet. They had several recent hires and decided to train them in proposal preparation since they had not received their security clearances and couldn't be assigned to a contract. They bid an RFP they had no hope of winning. They heard the client loved the incumbent. So they went through developing, boxing, and delivering the proposal from Washington to Connecticut. We rode the train through New York to Mystic River as did our competition, but we had a backup plan of a car delivery. Unfortunately for them the employee on the train died of a heart attack before he reached his destination and they had no backup plan. The Navy disqualified the incumbent for a late delivery and my firm won the contract and two re-competes," Frank said.

"Christ, we don't want that to happen here."

"No, we don't. Every firm has multiple stories of the dangers of not having a backup proposal package ready for delivery."

CIN Inc. delivered the proposal at DOE Headquarters at 1000 Independence Avenue, SW, Washington, DC 20585, three hours before it was due on Friday, November 13.

Chapter 10 The Evaluation Process

The Monday morning after the proposal delivery, Art walked into Pete's office. "Pete, I felt strange this weekend. I had nothing to do. No pages to read, to write, and no proposal to check. What do I do next?"

"Relax and take a few days off to clear your mind. In a few months we'll be back answering DOE questions. Art, have you ever been part of a proposal evaluation?"

"Yes."

"What happens at DOE?"

"The same as in other agencies. DOE management assigns evaluators to grade sections of the proposal related to their technical specialties. They're expected to work full time evaluating the proposals. There is a two-stage evaluation process. Most of the evaluators have full-time jobs which still have to be performed, even if they're assigned backup staff to work in their absence. First, the evaluations look for any reason to disqualify a proposal as being technically unacceptable to shortcut the evaluation process, including: the proposal isn't neat, or graphics are not well presented, or it is full of typos and grammatical errors. CIN Inc. was so anal during the Red Team process, we'll pass that test. Failing to answer all the requirements of the RFP is the easiest way to disqualify a proposal. Other poor proposal attributes including factual errors, invalid engineering concepts, poor contract references, weak bid personnel, et cetera, are used by the evaluators to mark a proposal as technically unacceptable.

The second phase is more positive. The evaluators are looking for the contractor they will have to live with for the next five years. This phase is more detailed. Any questions the evaluators have about the proposal are documented and included in the best and final offer DOE will send to the technically qualified."

"How long does DOE take to evaluate a major proposal?"

"A few weeks to complete the technical evaluation. It may take a few months to have the evaluation documented, reviewed by the DOE contracts office, and approved by the DOE contracting officer, before they can formally disqualify the technically unqualified bids. We might not receive a best and final offer for three to six months."

"That's what I thought. Make sure your performance at DOE excels over the next six months so they'll want to hire us for the next five years."

As Amy promised, she visited Ben at his home to keep her intelligence line open. She always took the subway so her car could not be observed parked near his home. Amy didn't learn anything new during the proposal preparation process since Ben did not have access to CIN Inc.'s competitors' proposals. However, after DOE began evaluating the proposals, Ben volunteered invaluable information including the names of the nine other firms submitting bids.

Two months after the proposal's submission, on a Tuesday morning, January 19, 2010, Ben called Amy on his untraceable cell phone. "Amy, can you come over tonight? It's very important."

"When?"

"For dinner at seven."

"See you then."

Amy walked from the subway station wondering what Ben would tell her. She knocked on the door which Ben opened with a mischievous smile on his face. He pulled her in, hugged her, and said, "Congratulations."

"For what?"

"CIN Inc. has passed the first cut. Of the ten bidders, the evaluation team rapidly rejected five, there are four left besides CIN Inc. DOE will send CIN Inc. a request for a best and final offer."

"Great." She kissed him passionately, thinking, I will have to thank him after dinner.

"Unfortunately, the incumbent GCS also made the first cut. While CIN Inc.'s proposal had the highest technical score, it had a higher proposed cost than GCS's."

"Do you know how much higher?"

"Six percent. What do I get for the information?"

"Anything you want after dinner. I'm starved."

During dinner Ben provided information on the weaknesses and strengths in CIN Inc. and the other companies' technical proposals.

The next day she walked into Pete's office. "Pete, I'm going to Starbucks. Would you like to join me?"

Pete, surprised by her invitation, but convinced by her Mona Lisa smile, said, "Sure."

As they left and started walking across the parking lot with no one closer than fifty feet, Amy ended their idle conversation by saying, "I received evaluation status and cost information last night."

"I assume it's about DOE."

"Yes. I hope you have a good memory since I don't want to write anything that could haunt us later."

"Go ahead."

She relayed the information Ben had provided, paying particular attention to the cost differentials and CIN Inc.'s technical deficiencies.

When she finished, Pete said, "Thanks. I guess we'll start writing our best and final offer now before DOE requests it, although we won't call it a best and final drill. You're on your way to winning your bonus."

Pete opened the next Monday's DOE IT opportunity

meeting, attended by Amy, Art, and Frank Nelson by saying, "It's been two months since we submitted the proposal. During our last two weeks of writing, we were too close to critically evaluate our assumptions and approach. This weekend I took the proposal home and read it at my leisure. I've discovered several weaknesses that should be examined. We should revise those sections to improve our proposal." Using a remote, Pete displayed a bullet list on a whiteboard:

- Too many management labor hours compared to worker hours
- Help desk assumptions on productivity are too conservative, resulting in higher labor hours bid
- Skill levels of the maintenance software developers are too high, adding to cost.

"In preparation, for the best and final, I'd like Art and the bid technical section managers to look at ways to cut our proposed cost, either through bidding fewer staff or implementing more productive procedures and software. Art, take the lead and find the technical experts to examine and improve the current proposal. I don't want this effort to become a major event that will alert our competition. Work out of your offices and not at a client's location. At this stage, until DOE requests us to submit a best and final proposal, we won't amass forces in the war room.

"Have your draft responses delivered to me within two weeks. Frank will supply you with all the word processing, graphics, and editorial support you require. I want the revised sections to be in shape to be submitted as part of the best and final proposal."

"Do you want us to review the proposal to find other problems?" Art asked

"Yes. But don't delay in addressing the problems I mentioned."

"I became bored after the proposal submission. Now I feel my adrenalin rushing again," Art said.

"Good, but don't sacrifice your current DOE work."

"I won't."

Pete continued to feed the DOE IT capture team additional areas of weaknesses, which Ben had confided to Amy, until Art's team completed their rewriting to his satisfaction. Art and his staff also discovered other areas where the proposal could be improved. By the end of the rewriting effort, Art reduced their bid cost by 10 percent.

Amy's weekly meeting proved satisfying for both her and Ben. She continued to receive information on the weakness of the other contractors, which she used to develop text to insert in the best and final proposal that would ghost their weak approach.

Pete received a call from the CIN Inc. contracts office at 4:20 p.m. on Friday, April 16, 2010. "Hi, Pete, I just received an e-mail from DOE with the best and final offer attached."

"When is it due?"

"In a month, on Friday, May 14, 2010."

"How many questions?"

"Thirty-two."

"That doesn't sound like too many to answer in a month. I'll call Frank Nelson to start the process, and schedule a kickoff meeting for Monday morning."

Art waited in the war room with nine others, far fewer attending than at the first kickoff meeting. He observed the relaxed tone of the participants compared to the earlier meetings. No subcontractors attended.

Pete began, "DOE asked us thirty-two best and final questions. We anticipated twenty-six of the questions and are in good shape. The response is due in four weeks and with our previous work I expect we'll write a winning proposal. Art and I will develop an approach to answering the questions we did not anticipate. Frank will present assignments and a schedule for completing the response."

Amy left the meeting after Frank's presentation, without talking to Pete, knowing what she had to do next. She walked into the parking lot and called Ben on her untraceable cell phone.

"I was expecting your call. How about coming over for dinner at seven?"

"See you then."

Ben opened the door with a smile as Amy rushed in and embraced him, placing her hand where Ben would not mistake her intentions. She pushed him up the stairs into his bedroom and paid him in advance for the answers to the missing questions.

CIN Inc.'s processes for completing the best and final went well; convincing Art he made the correct move by becoming a government contractor.

CIN Inc. delivered the best and final proposal to DOE headquarters five hours before it was due.

Chapter 11 Contract Award

Pete received a call at 4:15 p.m. on Friday, July 23, 2010, "Hi, I'm Ben Kaiser, DOE contracts office calling to congratulate you and CIN Inc. DOE has decided to award the DOE IT Consolidated Support Contract to your firm."

"Thank you, Mr. Kaiser, our firm and staff will do everything to ensure DOE made the correct decision."

"DOE would like to meet on Tuesday or Wednesday with your management team and our contract managers to discuss the transition from GCS to your company. I'll contact you on Monday to schedule the meeting."

"The CIN Inc. management team looks forward to meeting the DOE team."

"Do you have any questions?"

"No, I assume we'll develop questions before the meeting."

"OK, until Monday. Have a nice weekend."

"Amy, I guess you overheard the conversation. You're a rich woman."

"You're a richer man."

Amy, burst into Art's office, yelling, "Congratulations. We visit your new client next week."

"What new client?"

"Art, CIN Inc. won your new DOE contract."

"I enjoyed the proposal. Now I have to work for a living."

"Don't worry; they're your former colleagues."

"That's why I'm worried."

Art liked to bring organic gifts to the office to celebrate

significant events. He harvested twelve yellow spring and zucchini squash the next Monday morning before work, and brought them to the management win party planning meeting held at noon. He placed them on Pete's conference table with a note, "Please take at least one. They are healthy and organic."

"Where did you get these, Whole Foods or Giant?" Jim asked.

"Neither—from Joan's garden."

"I brought something more refreshing than the vegetables and sandwiches on the table," Pete replied.

He reached into his credenza and took out four glasses and two bottles of chilled champagne, opened the first bottle, poured it, and distributed the glasses.

"Is it organic, like the squash?" Amy asked.

"I don't know."

The alcohol expanded their original party planning goals. Pete decided to throw a CIN Inc. win party in two weeks his staff would never forget.

Pete, Amy, Art, and Jim Larson met at 2:00 that afternoon in Pete's office to plan the DOE kickoff meeting that Ben scheduled for 10:00 a.m. on Wednesday, July 28.

Pete addressed the group. "I've prepared a presentation for our meeting which I've e-mailed to you. Art will conduct the presentation. Read the PowerPoint slides and prepare for the meeting. You'll deliver the slides with your name in the footnote. We'll meet at ten tomorrow morning here to run through the presentation. Take a few minutes to read it this afternoon, and forward any suggested corrections by four o'clock today. I'll send back the revisions tonight."

Pete drove Amy, Art, and Jim to the West Falls Church Metro at eight thirty and they took the subway to the Smithsonian station, across from DOE Headquarters. They arrived thirty minutes early and strolled across the street to the DOE entrance. After signing in, Ben's administrative assistant escorted them to the DOE contracts office conference room.

When they arrived, she said, "You're ten minutes early. Please take a seat. Can I get anyone something to drink?"

Everyone declined. She continued, "I understand you have a presentation. Here is the PC you'll use. Give me the USB drive and I'll set it up."

Pete thanked her and tested the video system. When he finished, Ben's administrative assistant left the room.

At 10:00 a.m. the DOE contingent entered the room, including Ben; Roger Meeks, the Contracting Officer's Technical Representative (contract technical manager); Mark White, the Information Technology area contract manager; Martha Lincoln, the DOE facility manager; and Mary Pincer, the DOE contract security officer.

Ben opened the meeting by saying, "We'd like to congratulate CIN Inc. for their excellent proposal. Let's start by everyone at the table introducing themselves and discussing their role in the contract."

Ben looked at everyone at the table as he spoke to stress his authority and power on the contract, barely glancing at Amy. After the introductions, Ben stated, "The DOE staff at the table will discuss how they'll work with CIN Inc. and its subcontractors to ensure a smooth transition and operation of the contract. Mary will begin and discuss how we expect the CIN Inc. team staff to apply for and receive their DOE contractor identification badges so they'll have access to our facility."

The DOE staff did a capable job delivering their requirements for working with the CIN Inc. team. When they finished, Ben spoke, "This concludes the DOE part of the meeting. I understand CIN Inc. has a presentation of their plans for the transition and the contract long-term management. We look forward to hearing your approach."

Art walked to the podium, "I'm glad to be returning

THE OPPORTUNITY

to DOE to manage the DOE IT Consolidated Support Contract. I've spent most of my professional career at DOE, and I'm familiar with its policies and procedures as well as knowing every DOE staff member at this meeting. Thus, I expect our transition and long-term operation of the contract to satisfy DOE's requirements. Please call me for any concerns related to the contract. Indeed, interrupt any of the speakers during this presentation if you require clarification of what they're saying."

Art presented his plans to manage the contract. He introduced Jim Larson, who summarized the transition plan. Amy followed Jim and outlined CIN Inc. internal quality assurance program to discover potential problems so they could be corrected before they affected contract performance. She said, "If it's OK with DOE, we plan to meet with the CO quarterly to present our QA report."

"We look forward to receiving your report," Ben said.

Pete followed Amy, and assured DOE to call him if the CIN Inc. managers didn't perform to DOE's standards. He handed his business card to each of the DOE staff to emphasize his sincerity. He ended his discussion by thanking DOE for its faith in CIN Inc. and promised to deliver contract excellent performance. Art finished by summarizing the presentation.

Art used the transition plan to manage the contract during its first six months of operation. His transition role included meeting with DOE managers, determining their needs and problems, and asking for suggestions on improving CIN Inc.'s performance. He left the details of implementing the transition plan, including hiring incumbent staff, opening regional offices, et cetera, to Jim Larson. Art felt like a symphony orchestra conductor who successfully implemented the transition plan score with the parts played by competent musicians. Art, Amy, and Pete did not hear of any negative comments during the first six months of the contract.

Pete threw the win party, not because he wanted to congratulate every worker on the proposal, which he did, but because he liked parties and the company paid for it. He called the Argentine Steak House in Tysons Corner, located a half a block from CIN Inc.'s office to reserve the restaurant for Monday evening, August 9. The restaurant had a great salad bar with cold seafood and exotic cheeses he loved that showed on his waist. He knew the company's employees would appreciate the waiters circulating between tables carrying skewers of steak, fish, lamb, and chicken they expertly sliced to the waiting diners. The unending servings of wine and beer should improve the morale of the staff as long as they followed his advice and took a cab home.

"This is my first win party here. Are they always this elaborate?" Tim asked Pete, an hour into the party.

"Not always. It depends on the value of the contract win. Since the DOE contract is valued at over one billion over five years my boss told me not to spare any expense."

"It seems you obeyed your boss."

"I did, and tonight I'll eat and drink too much knowing it's not good for me, but I'll do it."

Pete made a welcoming speech in a strong voice, thanking the CIN Inc. staff and subcontractors who participated in the proposal. After the speech, he circulated, thanking the subcontractor managers attending the party while he could still walk without a wobble. Everyone sat at their tables as Pete announced the waiters were ready to serve the food. He led the group in going to the salad bar where he filled his plate with garden salad, shrimp salad, and chilled salmon. The waiters began serving the skewers of meat and fish after half the guests had returned from the salad bar.

After dinner the crowd congregated in the open in front of the tables. Pete, leaning on a building column, teetered from his vodka martini and fourth glass of wine.

He looked at Amy in a way no boss should be caught looking at an employee. Art noticed Amy saw Pete staring. With his straitlaced morals, Art tried to engage Pete in a conversation so he would redirect his eyes, saying, "Pete, what's your next opportunity?"

"Unfortunately, not Amy."

"I meant, business opportunity."

"It's your girlfriend, Joan's Health and Human Services Consolidated Grant Management opportunity. You might be seeing less of her, which will give you more time to manage the DOE contract. Where is Joan?"

"She'll be here in thirty minutes. She told me her boss gave her an assignment she has to finish before the party."

"Good. I didn't think it would take that long."

"You never do."

Art walked over to Amy.

"I tried to get Pete to stop staring at you," Art said.

"I'm a woman in my thirties and don't care since he's complimenting me. I might just go up to him and ask for a raise. When's Joan coming? She missed dinner," Amy said.

"She hates going to all-you-can-eat parties; she'll be here soon. She thinks it's crazy to run to keep her figure and then ruin it in one orgy of food and alcohol. When Pete asked where she was, I said she was working on an assignment he gave her."

"Good response. You've learned to play to his ego. You've come a long way from DOE."

After her conversation with Art, Amy decided to play with Pete in retribution for his stare.

"Pete, what's your favorite here?"

"I like the lamb chops and the shrimp salad. It's hard to get baby barbecued lamb in most restaurants."

"I didn't know your favorite was food. From your beach behavior, I assumed it would be the wine, or the vodka martini, or one of the Latin waitresses serving you."

"All of the above."

"That's what I thought. I noticed your eyes devouring

them—and not taking the time to savor them."

"You can make fun of me now, but remember my strategy and your marketing helped CIN Inc.'s stock price go from twenty dollars and fifty-five cents the day before the announcement to over twenty-five dollars now. We're both going to be rich in a few years. Make sure you stay at CIN Inc. so you can collect your entire bonus."

"I plan to."

Joan arrived at the party after dinner and walked over to Art, kissed him on the cheek, and said, "I'm going to get a glass of wine."

"I'm sorry you had to work and missed most of the party," Pete said to her at the bar.

"Anything for CIN Inc."

She ordered a Chardonnay, raised the glass and toasted, "To CIN Inc. and its DOE IT Consolidated Support win, and to Art. May he successfully manage the contract and still have time to see me in the next six months."

"I'm sure Art will do OK. They love him at DOE. You won't miss seeing him because of his work, since you'll be very busy with the HHS Consolidated Grant Management or CGM opportunity capture."

"I'm sure we'll find time for ourselves."

She walked back to Art and whispered in his ear, "Did you tell Pete I missed dinner because I was working?"

"Yes, he wouldn't understand if you missed a dinner, because you feared eating too much. That behavior is incomprehensible to him."

"He told me between your managing the DOE IT contract and my work on the HHS opportunity that we might not be seeing much of each other."

"I guess he doesn't know we spend almost every night together."

"No one does, including Amy. Let's keep it that way."

Two days after the win party, Amy dressed in a thin, low-cut light-blue blouse and shorts, rang Ben's house bell. She wondered if their relationship would continue now that CIN Inc. had won the contract. She knew it had to end, but hoped not before she found another virile sex partner.

Ben opened the door with a smile, embraced Amy, and pulled her inside the foyer. "How was the win party?"

"Great. I skipped work yesterday, because I had too much to eat and drink."

"We're having a light dinner tonight, Caesar salad with grilled chicken. I figured you'd not be in the mood for a heavy meal. I've a bottle of champagne on ice for you to celebrate our win."

"Thanks, but I go light on alcohol tonight."

"You'll have to drink one glass of champagne. You can take the bottle home."

"Not on the subway."

"True. I'll save it for your next visit."

"Good."

"A toast to the CIN Inc. win hoping their performance on the contract justifies the award and to us on our satisfying relationship." Ben raised his glass of ice tea to tap Amy's champagne glass.

After she sipped the champagne, Amy saw him looking at her cleavage and said, "Let's sit on the sofa."

As he sat down, she pushed his head to her breasts, unbuttoning her blouse, and said, "Let's continue our joint satisfaction before dinner."

He did not object and began his normal foreplay. They moved into his bedroom.

They broke for dinner and spent an hour eating and recovering from their lovemaking. As they finished eating, Amy said, "Pete told me he is going to assign me to another opportunity in a few weeks."

"Does that mean we'll stop seeing each other?"

"No. We'll have more time to stay in bed since we

won't have to talk about DOE."

"That sounds good. How often can we get together?"

"We still have to be careful to avoid being exposed and losing our jobs. I'll still be going to the beach on weekends until the end of September, so once a week is prudent. We should continue to use our secure cell phones."

"I hoped we could spend more time together."

"We will, just not now. It's early. Let's continue our mutual satisfaction activities."

The fab four congressmen took advantage of a warm October weekend in Washington, three months after the award, to drive to Ed Walinski's home in Henlopen with their wives on a Friday afternoon. They planned to play golf on Saturday at Kings Creek Country Golf Club in Rehoboth, have an evening cookout with their grass-fed beef steaks, and retire to the study to sip brandy and discuss the DOE IT contract.

They walked into the study, tired from the golf and overeating, and waited for Ed to pour the twenty-one-year-old Courvoisier.

Ed spoke first. "Let's raise our glasses in a toast to CIN Inc.'s excellent performance."

They obediently and joyfully raised their glasses, smiling as they sipped the strong brandy.

"My contacts at DOE tell me CIN Inc. is ahead of schedule in transitioning the contract and are meeting or exceeding their performance goals. Has anyone heard differently?" Ed continued.

"No," they answered.

"While I'm happy for DOE to receive improved service, I'm ecstatic over the performance of CIN Inc. stock up 25 percent since the contract award two months ago. If this keeps up over the next five years, we'll have justified dumping GCS as well as being closer to a comfortable retirement," Congressman Jim O'Neill said.

THE OPPORTUNITY

"To a rich retirement," Jim toasted as they simultaneously raised their glasses. They repeated his words as they sipped the brandy.

"My constituents told my office they're being treated excellently by CIN Inc., which, except for a few problem employees, has hired the incumbent's staff. They've been given career counseling by the CIN Inc.'s Human Resources representatives who are encouraging capable employees to sign up for training so they can be promoted to higher-salaried technical jobs. They promise to bring more work to Boise if the employees are trained to perform the work. If they're successful and our districts become prosperous, we may never lose an election and never get to enjoy our rich retirement," Congressman Sam Johnson contributed.

"Are you praising or criticizing CIN Inc.? I don't want to work forever," Ed commented.

"It's praise. I don't want to be retired involuntarily by losing an election," Ernesto Gomez stated. "CIN Inc. is doing in San Antonio what they are doing in Boise. They're fulfilling the promises made at our initial meetings. Their actions are not entirely altruistic. They get to bid cheap labor which helps them win new contracts."

"They're doing the same thing in Utica. I recommend we take no actions, refrain from talking to DOE, and let CIN Inc. give jobs to our constituents and make ourselves rich," Jim O'Neill said.

"I'd propose a toast to that sentiment. Your glasses are empty," Ed said.

They picked up their glasses with their wobbly arms and extended them to Ed who filled them from the bottle conveniently at his side.

"I assume you have received campaign contributions for the next elections," Ed continued.

"Yes," they said.

"To our marriage with CIN Inc. May it develop and prosper," Ed said.

After Amy and Pete read DOE's six-month IT contract performance evaluation on Friday, February 25, 2011 they congregated in Art's office at noon and congratulated him as the program manager. Pete, as expected, brought two bottles of champagne to celebrate.

After an appropriate toast to Art, Pete began talking. "Do you know what this evaluation means to CIN Inc.?" He continued before anyone could answer. "We'll grow from a middle-size company into a large corporation so that in five years, using the DOE contract as a reference on other bids, our wins will soar and our revenue will reach the multibillion-dollar range."

Everyone looked at him not responding. They knew that since he drank champagne for lunch he didn't want to stop speaking.

"I'm going to exercise my stock options ASAP and buy additional stock on the open market. It should go up by 200 percent in the next five years. You should follow my lead, but don't do it until our press release is issued. Then we won't be prosecuted for insider trading."

"Pete, perhaps you should wait until the second and the third performance evaluations before you invest all your money," Art said.

"No, you get a few chances in life to get rich. With you managing the contract, Amy marketing DOE, and me providing executive leadership our performance scores can't fall," Pete countered.

"I'm not sure you're correct. Something could happen in DOE or Congress that could affect our performance and the stock could crash. Amy, you're too young, but Pete should remember the dot-com stock bubble of twelve years ago," Art said.

"Forget him, Amy, and do as I say if you want to get rich quick," Pete replied.

Chapter 12 The New Opportunity

Amy, still euphoric from the DOE contract award after seven months, sauntered into Pete's office at 11:00 a.m., Tuesday, March 8, 2011, and with a smile said, "Is there anything more for me to do on the DOE IT contract now that the transition's over?"

"Yes, you have to conduct the quarterly QA meeting to make sure Art's managing the contract properly."

"Of course. But that's not a full-time job."

"Correct. I've a new marketing assignment for you. It isn't as large as the DOE contract; however, your bonus, should we decide to bid and win, won't be inconsequential. The opportunity is in a new agency for you, Social Security. It's their IT support contract, scheduled for a rebid in the late summer of 2112. The current contract is held by Binghamton Information Technical Associates Inc. I'd like you to develop a capture plan PowerPoint presentation of the opportunity, including an analysis of whether we can win. Complete the preliminary analysis of our chances in two weeks and the full capture plan in two months."

"You're a slave driver. I planned to enjoy the rest of the winter skiing."

"No time for that. If the Social Security opportunity doesn't work out, I'll give you another one. Be unbiased, and give me a true evaluation. You don't want to waste your time for two years and not earn a bonus. We have other opportunities, if Social Security is a no-bid."

Amy left Pete's office, smiling at the thought of a new campaign and stopped at the vending alcove, removed two yogurt containers and a bottle of water from the refrigerator and walked thirty feet to her office.

She signed on to her PC and accessed the CIN Inc. process repository and downloaded the template for CIN Inc.'s capture plan. This was Amy's first experience in developing a complete capture plan. Pete had developed the plan for the DOE IT opportunity, and Amy planned to use it as a template for completing her new assignment. Amy welcomed the new responsibility and knew Pete expected a first-class draft of the plan in two weeks.

Eight years earlier when Amy learned the CIN Inc. capture process, she considered the process too elementary to be a highly skilled activity. Seven years ago, when Amy was new to business development, she asked Pete, "Why do marketing/capture managers receive high salaries for executing a simple process?"

"Because a company's profits are so large from winning a major contract, and it takes a special personality to implement all the capture plan template's requirements. Most marketers don't have the patience to do the mundane research. They believe they can't lose and misinterpret the competition's information they collect. Others don't know how to build teams and they make other errors, which, as an ex-teacher you won't make."

"Thanks for the lecture. I promise not to fail."

Amy opened her strawberry yogurt container and started reading, remembering Pete's counsel. Between sips of water and consuming both yogurts she filled in as many blanks as she could from memory. She accessed the FedBiz, INPUT, and Social Security reference databases to search for missing information related to the contract and completed the first task as scheduled by the end of Tuesday. She identified CIN Inc.'s weaknesses and identified ten potential subcontractors she would court over the next six months to join the team finishing by Thursday afternoon. On Friday she reviewed her material and edited the capture plan presentation.

THE OPPORTUNITY

Amy planned to identify key Social Security personnel connected to the contract on Monday that she should include in the marketing section of the capture plan.

Amy spent the weekend enjoying tennis, dancing, and erotically planning to find a new sex partner from Social Security. She arrived at her office on Monday morning reviewed her e-mails and found nothing critical. She accessed the Social Security website to identify officials connected to the contract. Finding ten, she entered them into the call plan section of the presentation. Amy eliminated four women as potential partners. She accessed individual search databases to find out more about the six remaining individuals, discovering three were married, two divorced, and one had never married. The unmarried males' ages were acceptable for an erotic marketing partner.

While Amy knew of the incumbent company, Binghamton Information Technical Associates Inc., she had no detailed knowledge of their performance. She planned to use her personality to obtain unpublished information on their reputation.

On March 15 Amy walked into Pete's office for their regular 11:00 a.m. Tuesday meeting.

"How is the capture plan coming?" Pete asked.

"Fine, I've completed the slides on the opportunity, our strengths and weakness, and a list of potential subcontractors to make a winning team. I'm now working on the slides for the key Social Security contract staff including those I'll add to my client call plan. I've begun to evaluate Binghamton Information Technical Associates Inc.'s capabilities, but I want the Social Security staff to tell me how they performed when I call them. A good draft will be completed by next Tuesday. But, I could use help in finding out details of three Social Security contract-related staff: Jim Brogan, the contracting officer; Steve Gardner, the technical lead; and John Wilson, the security officer."

Pete smiled when he realized they were all men thinking Amy wanted to replicate her DOE winning ways. "How soon do you want the information?"

"Next Tuesday. I want to make the first go/no go decision ASAP, so I can move on if the opportunity isn't a match for us."

"I'll try, but I still want to review the first draft of your capture plan next week."

Pete left the office for lunch, walked to his car and retrieved an untraceable cell phone and called George.

"George here."

"It's your friend. Can we meet at five o'clock today at Lock Ten at the C&O canal?" Both men hung up their phones.

Pete arrived and noticed George sitting at a bench. George rose when he saw Pete and they both began walking east on the canal.

"You look a little pale. You must be spending all your weekends indoors working," George said.

"I am. But I'm drinking and eating too much. I've gained five pounds since Christmas."

"I noticed but didn't want to mention it."

"Thanks. I want you to perform a high-level background check on three Social Security employees by next Monday."

He handed George a piece of paper containing the names.

"We can meet at Lock Seven for lunch."

"See you then."

George drove the short distance from Lock Ten to his Chevy Chase home. As he entered he shouted, "Hi, Emily. I'm home."

"I hope you're not too hungry. I'm thirty minutes

late. Dinner should be ready by seven."

He kissed his wife who handed him a beer, as she talked.

"Seven's fine. I'll be in my office."

He started three versions of his investigative report template on his PC. He had accessed his normal sources and made significant progress, when his wife called.

"Dinner's ready."

He could not repress his disappointment as he glanced at grilled chicken, without barbeque sauce, sautéed zucchini, and a salad.

"George, don't look so pained, I'm keeping you alive, rather than killing you with cholesterol."

"I've lost five pounds since Christmas. If I keep losing weight, I'll die of starvation by Memorial Day."

"I'll let you eat steak tomorrow, but I'm not going to grill it; you'll have to."

"Thanks."

After dinner, George returned to his study and resumed his search. He found Jim Brogan, the contracting officer, age forty-three, divorced for five years, two children, no arrest record, liked skiing and tennis, graduated with a business degree from the University of Maryland at College Park, and a law degree from George Washington, earned while enrolled part time. Brogan had spent his entire career at Social Security. He owned a two-bedroom condo in Columbia, an SVU, and a thirty-foot sailboat which he kept on the Magothy River in Maryland.

George assumed Brogan, on the surface a typical middle-aged hardworking Washington professional, would elicit little interest from CIN Inc. However, he realized no one is perfect and after he finished the preliminary analysis of the other two, he planned to return to Mr. Brogan.

George next examined John Wilson, the security officer, age thirty-six, single, never married, nonathletic, worked at Social Security for five years, had no arrest record, graduated with an IT degree from George Mason, and shared a condo in Wheaton, Maryland with Sam Newman, as a joint owner and an active member of the *Log Cabin Republicans*. George found he was openly gay and campaigned for legalizing gay marriage. While George had nothing against gay marriage, he knew Pete had no interest, since Amy could not develop a marketing relationship with Mr. Wilson.

George felt tired and decided to join his wife, who was watching TV, rather than continue working.

George woke refreshed, reflecting he always slept better when he made love to his wife the previous evening. He went to the kitchen poured himself a cup of coffee his wife had prepared the night before using their programmable coffee maker and carried it to the office. George searched for personal information for Steve Gardner, the technical manager. He discovered that George was forty-one, divorced twice, no children, skied and sailed, had a DWI arrest seven years ago, with a six-month suspension of his license, held a computer science degree from the University of Maryland, and was working on an MBA part-time at Maryland. He had been at Social Security for six years previously employed at various companies, working on and managing federal contracts. Gardner lived alone, in a two-bedroom condo, in Laurel, Maryland. George considered Gardner an ideal candidate for Amy's marketing charms and decided to complete Gardner's investigation before moving to Brogan.

George accessed Gardner's Facebook account and analyzed his friends, dividing them into several categories by sex, age, professional, and nonprofessional. Gardner held a membership in the *Columbia Ski Club*. While he had professional friends, most were nonprofessional women, ranging in age from twenty-two to fifty-five. He noted Gardner's similarities to Ben and decided to hack into his e-mail, using the e-mail address provided by Facebook.

George sent Gardner an untraceable phishing e-mail,

related to skiing to implant a Trojan horse to his hard disk. He returned to analyzing Brogan's background since he knew it could take several minutes, to hours, to days for Steve to open the phishing e-mail. George found Brogan had far fewer nonprofessional friends than Gardner. He had four female, non-familial entries, around his age. Brogan was a member of the DC-based *The Tennis Group* and Annapolis-based *Singles on Sailboats*. He sent Brogan a phishing e-mail related to sailing. George decided to wait to receive notification that either had opened their phishing e-mails before continuing further and joined his wife for breakfast.

"Would you like to go for a healthy walk on the C&O canal before lunch?" George asked.

"Yes. What's got into you?"

"I'm enjoying you too much to leave your life early."

She thought I'll make love to him again tonight since he's connecting sex with good habits. She wondered what her children would think of their erotic behavior.

George's phone rang in the late afternoon, announcing Jim Brogan had opened his phishing e-mail. George, sitting on the sun porch with his wife and reading a short baseball novel, *Calico Joe*, by John Grisham, excused himself and went to his office. He examined Brogan's keystrokes as he responded to his e-mails. Since the software recorded the keystrokes, George accessed Brogan's browser history, confirming his belief that the husband of the sexy Emily was the only male in DC who did not access porn. Brogan's porn history was not as extensive as Ben's.

George observed heavy use of www.match.com, which was normal for a single adult. His match.com profile described him as five-ten and thin. His pictures showed a good-looking man with a full head of black hair. George downloaded the profile and read several of his match.com e-mails, from women, winking or writing, inviting him to contact them.

He noticed two women sent a large proportion of the non-match.com e-mails, which, after reading, George concluded Brogan had two steady girlfriends, one of whom played tennis and slept with him on a regular basis, while the other shared his dinners and bed.

George read the *Singles on Sailboats* e-mail. Brogan spent every other weekend sailing with the group, but never with either of the two girlfriends. George credited Brogan intelligence for not mixing his women with his sailing.

He felt Brogan must have extreme physical stamina to service at least two women and a disciplined mind not to be confused over whichever woman he was with. Brogan's promiscuity, led George to believe he would succumb to Amy's marketing skills. He decided to stress this opportunity with Pete. George decided not to place a tracking device on Brogan's car because of the short period of the investigation. He could always place the device later if Pete showed an interest in Brogan.

George returned to the living room and Emily said, "George, please start the grill now. Remember, you are barbequing steak tonight."

He smiled, having forgotten his wife had planned a sinful meal for dinner and said, "Yes, dear." He walked to the backyard and started the charcoal fire. While waiting for the fire to catch, he asked his wife, "What else are we having?"

"Baked sweet potato and salad."

While he would have rather had a white potato, smothered in butter, sour cream, chives, and bacon bits, he surrendered to his wife health care practices. He settled for the healthier sweet potato and butter since the alternative could have been broccoli.

George received the an e-mail notice from Steve Gardner after dinner, while he and his wife watched the seven o'clock news. George rose from his seat. "Something's come up. I've got to go to my office."

THE OPPORTUNITY

"Don't spend all evening there. I want to go to bed early so you can give me a full body massage. My muscles are sore from gardening."

"I'll be an hour or two." His wife's expanded sexual drive impressed him. He knew asking for a massage implied sex and was glad he took the thirty-six-hour active-time-span, Cialis, the previous evening. He noticed she, as well as he, had lost weight with their healthy diet, and assumed the weight loss increased her libido.

George logged on to his PC, telling himself not to skip any steps in the investigation, since Emily would wait for him as long as he did not take over two hours. He accessed Steve Gardner's Internet history, finding significant differences from Brogan's. Even though both accessed porn, Gardner's had a more intense habit. He specialized in viewing large-breasted women in sex videos. George believed Amy would drive Gardner crazy. While Steve Gardner accessed www.match.com, he visited the www.adultfriendfinder.com dating site on a regular basis. George downloaded Gardner's match.com profile, which stated he was five-nine and overweight. His picture showed a good looking man with wavy blond hair and blue eyes.

He accessed the adultfriendfinder website. George He admitted their pictures and text stimulated him and he was glad he had been asked to massage his wife that night. He accessed Gardner's e-mail and realized Gardner was kinkier than Ben. He thought Amy would be successful working with Gardner. George catalogued a list of bars, restaurants, and other locations Gardner frequented. He filled out his report entries for Gardner, turned off his PC, and greeted his wife within the two-hour deadline.

"George you finished early. Let's go to the hot tub before you start my massage."

George approached Pete sitting on a bench at Lock 7 on Monday.

"George, I almost didn't recognize you. Are you losing weight?"

"Yes, five pounds since Christmas. Emily has me on a diet, plus we dance at Colvin Run. I'm more healthy and virile than I've been in years. You ought to try a healthy lifestyle."

"Everyone seems to be concerned about my health," Pete said as he unwrapped his oil-drenched Reuben.

"That's better than being told you look good, when you don't," George said as he began eating his chicken Caesar salad.

"Thanks for that positive reinforcement."

"No problem. I don't want to lose a good client."

"That's the second time in a week someone said the same thing to me. I wish someone would give me advice on my health because they like me, not because they'll lose income."

"If we phrased it that way, you wouldn't believe us or listen. But you understand our economic motives."

George patted Pete on the chest as he was talking and slipped Pete the encrypted, self-data-erasing thumb drive in his left upper jacket packet.

"Maybe you're right. I'll try to reform. Thanks for the advice."

George summarized his detailed findings and said, "I recommend forgetting Wilson."

"I agree."

Pete shook hands with George. They walked away in opposite directions.

Amy spent the two weeks after Pete assigned her the Social Security account entering information into the CIN Inc. bid capture plan template. As with any analysis, she prepared herself for discovering CIN Inc. did not have a chance at winning the re-compete. As she worked on the report, she became confident they could win. She discovered that the incumbent contractor, Binghamton

Information Technical Associates Inc., was not well liked, their subcontractors were unhappy, and her marketing contacts outside of CIN Inc. told her Social Security was searching for a new support contractor.

Amy delivered the completed report to Pete on schedule in his office at their regular Tuesday meeting.

"Here's the draft capture plan. So, Pete, what happened this weekend?"

"Nothing—I thought you'd be proud of me, following your advice. I had dinner with Art and Joan on Saturday evening at L'Auberge Chez Francois in Great Falls, and I didn't have one drink."

"Or tell one joke. Art said you were boring and didn't embarrass them."

"So you want me to start drinking again?"

"No, but one weekend does not make a new life."

"True. Here's something that may get you to quit your sarcasm and treat me with respect." Pete said.

She opened up the envelope, looked at its contents and screamed, "Pete, my god. I didn't know I'd get my bonus so soon."

"It's not your bonus; it's for helping me save my life. Don't you think it's worth four hundred thousand?"

"At least. Thanks."

"Don't spend it right away."

"I never spend my bonus. I'm saving them for an early retirement."

"Good. I should have followed your example; I'd be retired now. Two of the three Social Security staff you asked me to investigate have potential for you to market: Steve Gardner and Jim Brogan. Visit the third, John Wilson, to gain intelligence and to sell CIN Inc., but you'll never develop a close relationship with him. He is in a gay relationship and not the least bit interested in women."

"OK. How are the other two?"

"Market both, but choose one as your primary target. Both love women and are divorced. Jim Brogan is similar to you, very athletic, including skiing and tennis, while Steve Gardner is closer to DOE's Ben, addicted to alcohol and large-breasted women."

"Sounds, like an adventure."

"Brogan should be easy to meet since he's a member of *Singles on Sailboats* and *The Tennis Group*. Gardner is a member of the *Columbia Ski Club*."

"I'll guess I get active in the ski club and the tennis group. At least we have until summer of next year before the RFP is released."

"Good," Pete replied, providing her with more details of Brogan's and Gardner's behavior, before they adjourned.

The draft capture plan convinced Pete to ask for corporate funds to support the effort. Pete pitched the capture plan presentation to his bosses, asking for a commitment of $300,000, part of which included Amy's salary. His bosses approved his request.

Amy, regardless of what she had told Pete had made her decision before the meeting ended. She preferred to prey on weak, sex-obsessed men rather than strong men like Brogan. Gardner's sex obsession excited her, especially since she felt sexually deprived being restricted to weekly liaisons with Ben.

She reviewed Steve Gardner's habits and decided to try to meet him at the next *Columbia Ski Club* meeting on Monday, April 11, 2011, as reported on the ski club's website, at the Columbia Doubletree Hotel from 7:30 p.m. to 9:00 p.m. A happy hour in Morgan's Bar in the hotel preceded the meeting starting at 6:00 p.m.

Armed with a picture of Steve Gardner, Amy arrived at a respectable 6:30. She glanced around the bar and smiled as she identified Steve leaning on the crowded bar sipping a Samuel Adams Pale Ale. Not hesitating, she walked toward him and moved into the small open space next to him. She waved at the bartender, who asked,

"What will you have?"

"A glass of Chardonnay."

"Do you want to start a check?" he asked.

"Yes," she said, handing the bartender her credit card.

Amy turned to Steve knowing he stared at her body during the wine transaction. "Hi, I'm Amy. This is my first time to a ski club meeting. What happens at the meeting?"

"I'm Steve. If you're not a member working on one of the committees, the meetings can be boring. They discuss club plans, schedules, and budgets. The happy hours preceding the meeting are a lot more fun. Do you ski much?"

"No, I'm not even a good skier. I'm single and heard ski clubs are great for meeting men and for improving your skiing."

Amy noticed Steve's not-so-subtle reaction of breaking out into a broad smile when she announced her availability. They continued talking until the meeting started, both exchanged personal information to inform the other of their desirability as a partner. Amy noticed Steve could not keep his eyes off her breasts. She continuously changed positions to arouse him.

"Amy, I enjoyed talking to you. Please give me your phone number? I'm afraid you'll be bored by the meeting and leave early and I won't have a way to reach you," Steve said.

"Of course. I enjoyed meeting you. But I'll stay for the beginning of the meeting."

Amy handed Steve a personal card with nonbusiness contact information. She didn't want Steve to know where she worked until they became friendlier. Amy wondered how long Steve would wait to call. Remembering his background and seeing him in person, she knew he was more than a replacement for Ben. At least with him, she could share a glass of wine.

Steve could not believe his luck Monday evening and

constantly fantasized about Amy, struggling mentally about when to call her. He knew calling too early would make him appear too interested while waiting too long would make Amy think she was a second or third choice. Steve settled on Wednesday evening and had difficulties concentrating at work waiting to call. He did not worry about being rejected by Amy, assuming he had read her signals correctly.

Amy's cell phone rang at 8:00 p.m., the phone screen displaying a number she did not recognize.

"Hi, Amy. It's Steve Gardner. We met at the *Columbia Ski Club's* meeting on Monday. Do you remember me?"

"How could I forget your blond hair and blue eyes?"

"I'm speechless. You left the meeting early. I guess you found it boring, as I suggested."

"No, I wasn't bored, but I had to prepare for an early morning meeting. I'm glad you called. I enjoyed talking to you."

"I'd like to take you out to dinner on Friday evening and continue our conversation."

"I'd like to go. You have my address on my card. When do you want to pick me up?"

"At seven. Is Clyde's near you OK?"

"Yes, I love Clyde's. Park on the street near my condo. Just announce yourself at the desk, and they'll let you come up. We can walk to the restaurant from my place."

Amy prepared well for Friday evening. She left work early at two and purchased a six-pack of Samuel Adams Pale Ale. At home she prepared for the evening by cleaning her home and changing the sheets on her bed. She showered and washed her hair. At six-thirty she sprinkled modest amounts of lavender perfume on her neck and shoulders and dressed in a comfortable low-cut white blouse and red skirt designed to enflame Steve's desire. She planned on wearing a modest red sweater to tone down her attire while walking to and eating in the restaurant.

Steve, not wanting to be late left Laurel at six. He arrived twenty minutes early and parked on Park Avenue a half block from the Elizabeth Condo's entrance. He waited in his car for ten minutes before walking to the Elizabeth. The marbled foyer impressed Steve, as he announced himself at the receptionist desk. "Hi, I'm Steve Gardner, here to see Amy Ericson."

"She's expecting you. Take the elevator on the right. She's at nine hundred."

Amy waited twenty seconds to answer the door after she heard the ring. "Hi, come in."

"Hi, this is a great neighborhood."

"Yes, I love it here. Do we have to leave right away or can we have a drink while I show you my condo?"

"We can stay. I wasn't able to get a reservation until eight."

"Great. I can give you a Sam Adams Pale Ale or a glass of wine."

"Sam Adams. You remembered from Monday night."

"Yes, I did." Amy walked into the kitchen, handed him the bottle, and poured herself a glass of Chardonnay. "Follow me."

Steve accepted the beer and walked behind her, gazing at her backside.

"This is the dining room with the L-shaped living room in front of us. The two bedrooms are in the back."

Steve followed her, mesmerized by her sensual walk.

"The first door on the left is a full bath while the door on my right is a bedroom which I've configured as a study. The master bedroom is ahead and includes a full-size bathroom."

Steve knew Amy had designed this room as he looked at the king-size bed and matching dresser resting on a cream-colored soft rug with a view of the Bethesda suburbs from the corner windows. The visual scene plus the feminine aroma of the room further enticed Steve into Amy's trap.

They returned to the living room, sat on a sofa and continued sipping their drinks.

"This place is beautiful. How large is it?" Steve asked.

"Thanks, I picked out the furniture and drapes, myself. At fourteen-hundred and thirty square feet, it's as large as many single-family homes. I wanted a large apartment, so I could spread out and entertain."

"Do you throw a lot of large parties here? It certainly has the space."

"No, just small dinner parties for my friends."

"It's twenty to eight. We should get going."

"OK, let me get my sweater."

They enjoyed a leisurely walk on the warm April evening through Friendship Heights, with Amy describing her favorite stores and restaurants. They crossed Wisconsin Avenue to Chevy Chase Center and entered Clyde's. After being seated, Amy ordered a Chardonnay, while Steve continued with Sam Adams.

"This is a great choice. I love Clyde's. The food is great and it's close to home," Amy said.

"I like it too. Do you know what you'll have?"

"No."

"Me too."

"I'll have the single crab cake," Amy said, after reading the menu.

"I'm leaning to the salmon salad."

"Sounds healthy."

"It might be, but it tastes great. So, Amy, after seeing your condo and the neighborhood where you live, since you haven't discussed your job I wonder if you are unemployed and wealthy."

"No, not quite, I work and I purchased the condo with my divorce settlement. When I was married I taught elementary school, but after my divorce, I decided I couldn't live the way I did when married. I listened to a girlfriend who advised me to change my career and get into government contracting. I joined Computer Information Networks Inc. eight years ago as a business development specialist. It pays significantly more than a teacher's position. What do you do?" She planned not to tell him he was her next marketing target.

"I have a degree in computer science from Maryland. I've had several great jobs where I expanded my technical knowledge. I joined the Social Security Agency six years ago where I manage their IT support contract."

"That must be interesting."

"It is, but I realize to move to the next income level, I have to expand my education, so I'm enrolled in a part-time MBA program at Maryland."

"Very impressive."

Amy and Steve continued exchanging personal information throughout the rest of the meal. Both ordered decaf coffee after finishing eating hoping to prolong the dinner. When the check came Steve started to reach for it, but Amy said, "I insist we split the check." Amy would charge her dinner to CIN Inc. as a marketing expense.

They continued their conversation on the walk home. When they reached her apartment, Steve wondered if he should kiss her good night when she opened the door and said, "Would you like to come in? It's early and I still have five Sam Adams left."

Steve, realizing she had postponed his decision to kiss her, said, "Sure."

"Sit down on the couch, I'll get the drinks."

She hung up her sweater in the hall closet before she entered the kitchen and noticed Steve's intensity staring at her breasts. Amy knew he's lost. She carried the drinks into the living room and bent over to hand Steve his ale.

"I'm enjoying tonight," she said.

"So am I."

"You're very quiet compared to Monday night and

dinner. What's the matter? Are you shy or nervous?"

"Neither."

"Right. This might help," she said as she ran her right hand through his hair and used her left hand to pull his face to her lips.

Steve woke up first at seven-thirty, smiling, thinking he might be dreaming spending the night with a woman with the most voluptuous body he had ever seen. Gazing at her for several minutes he became aroused, and after she woke up said, "Hi. I really enjoyed last night."

"So did I. Do you have any plans for the morning?"

"No."

"Good. Why don't we shower together and enjoy each other some more before I make breakfast."

Steve left at two in the afternoon, wondering if Amy shared his sexual obsessions. He decided to cancel his subscription to adultfriendfinder.com.

Chapter 13 Amy Leaves DOE

In April 2011 after the delivery of her third QA report and
continuously seeing Steve two to three times a week, Amy
resented having to fit Ben into her schedule. She did not
need him for sex or for sustaining the contract after its
high performance evaluation. While it might be cruel, she
knew it would be safer to end the relationship. On
Thursday, April 28 when she had no plans to meet Steve,
she called Ben on their untraceable cell phones. "Hi, it's
Amy."

"Hi, this is a surprise. What's up?"

"You're not driving, are you?"

"No, I'm home. Why?"

"This isn't easy for me since we have been seeing
each other for so long."

Ben remained quiet.

"Ben, I like you. We had great sex, but I don't have
an emotional attachment to you, and women need
emotional attachments."

Ben continued his silence.

"I've met someone else who is providing what I
missed in our relationship."

Ben shocked, couldn't react.

"So I have decided it best if we break it off without
meeting again."

Ben did not answer, but felt nauseous never expecting
Amy to say their relationship had ended, since he planned
to marry her.

"Ben, you must have known this was coming. Our
meetings are now purely physical and not very frequent."

He found the courage to speak and said, "No, I had

no idea. We were perfect together."

"No, Ben, we weren't."

"I can't talk now." Ben did not want to have Amy hear him crying.

"OK, I wish you luck in finding what I've found."

Ben hung up the phone, thinking he had as the tears flowed..

Amy thought that wasn't so bad. Now I have to tell Pete I want to leave DOE, since I'm not seeing Ben.

On Friday morning, Amy called Pete. "Hi, can I have a half hour of your time today?"

"Sure, noon in my office? I'll order lunch," Pete said.

"OK. I'd like a shrimp salad and water."

As Amy entered his office she noticed her salad and a Ruben on the conference table. "Thanks. It looks good."

"Mine looks good, yours looks healthy. Your phone call and formal request for a meeting surprised me. What do you want to talk about?"

Pete proceeded to chomp on one end of the sandwich, causing Russian dressing to drip down his chin, missing his shirt, and land on his napkin.

"A few things you said at the champagne lunch in Art's office two months ago." Amy didn't touch her salad.

"Perhaps I was too aggressive in advising you to invest everything in CIN Inc. I'll understand if you diversify."

"Pete, that's not it. I want to thank you for the bonus and the compliments on how I helped with the win and in earning a high contract evaluation score."

"You deserved the bonus and the praise."

"Thanks, but you said with Art as the program manager, you as the executive, and me marketing DOE, the contract could not fail."

"Yes, I did."

"Well that contradicts what you told me when you assigned me the Social Security opportunity and still wanted me to continue working on the QA meetings. You didn't say to continue marketing DOE."

"I realize QA is not marketing, but I meant marketing new task orders."

"Pete, my skills are in marketing new opportunities not in task orders. Everyone in DOE loves Art. They tell me when I interview them for the QA work. He is constantly bringing in and training his staff in how to develop new task orders. You don't need me. I'm asking you to remove me from the DOE contract. Please find a QA expert to prepare the reports."

"I agree with your arguments, but I'm concerned your leaving will affect our evaluation scores. How will Ben view your leaving?"

"I told him months ago I'd be leaving."

"That doesn't answer my question."

"Our evaluation scores will be lower if I stay on the contract, than if I leave."

"Why?"

"You're a man of the world. Figure it out."

Recognizing Amy's seriousness, Pete correctly assumed Amy had dumped Ben.

"OK, I'll talk to Art to prepare him for the change and find a QA replacement."

Amy relaxed, felt the tension leave her body and hungrily dug into the salad.

"What progress are you making on developing the complete capture plan for the Social Security opportunity?" Pete changed the subject when he realized he had satisfied Amy's goal for the meeting.

"Great progress; it's a better opportunity for CIN Inc. than the DOE opportunity was at the same stage of the capture process. I'll have the plan completed on schedule as always."

"As I expect."

Now relaxed, they spent several minutes eating without talking. Finally Pete who hated silence, said, "I assume you miss the beach house as much as I do. Do you have any activities planned before May 1?"

"Yes, I'm joining the Columbia Ski Club."

Pete broke into a full smile, showing a partially chewed Ruben, thinking Amy is now back in her favorite element. "I hope the Social Security opportunity is as successful as the DOE effort."

Ben had called Amy on her regular cell phone multiple times since her last phone call, but she declined to answer after seeing his name on the cell phone screen. After a month she decided she had to talk to him to reinforce their earlier conversation. She answered the ringing cell phone on Thursday, June 9.

"Hi, Ben. How are you?"

"Thanks for answering. I'm better than when I last talked to you."

"That's good. What are you doing?"

"Working and still missing you. I want to meet you one more time."

"Ben, I don't want to continue maligning you, but you have to realize it's over between us. Stop calling me."

"I'm trying, but one more meeting should give me closure."

Amy wary of a private meeting, having seen Ben display physical aggression at the beach, replied, "Why don't we meet at the Smithsonian Mall on a bench in front of the East Wing Art Gallery?"

"When?"

"Next Friday at noon."

"Should I bring you lunch?"

"No, I'll bring my own."

Amy walked toward the bench, and as expected she saw Ben sitting looking around waiting for her.

He spied her twenty feet away stood up and said, "Hi, Amy. You look good."

"You look good too."

Amy sat down and unwrapped her roast beef on rye sandwich, while Ben took the lid off his chef salad.

"What do you want to talk about?" Amy said.

"You and I."

"Ben, there's no you and I."

"There will be; just hear me out."

"Ben, what's the point?"

"I'm hung up on the idea of us, and can't get you out of my mind," Ben said, almost crying.

"You should have known we were just having fun, talking about our contract, eating dinner, and making love. I never led you on," Amy said with a straight face.

"I can't help it. I still want to be with you and if you don't, I'll ruin your career."

"How will you do that?"

"By telling our bosses how you won the contract."

"Ben, don't make me laugh. I never asked you for any information on the bid; you volunteered everything."

"That's not true. Besides, I'm sure other people have seen us together. I had to sign in every time I went to your condo."

"You can't prove a thing you just said, but I can. I made video and audio recordings of our meetings in my condo and your house."

Ben, shocked, did not reply.

"I wouldn't talk to anyone. Remember, videos are forever, especially if I put them on the Internet where they'll be seen by millions."

Ben, still silent, felt like he had worms in his stomach, eating his flesh and approaching his heart.

"You wouldn't expose yourself," Ben said after being quiet for a minute.

"Why not? I have enough to live on and retire. You on your government salary couldn't survive without work, and you'd be disbarred if you accused me. I wonder how your daughters would react to seeing you making love and performing graft at the same time. Give me your private cell phone."

"Why should I?"

"So you won't harass me and so you can't give it to someone else. Ben, hand it over."

He complied.

Ben, knowing he could not argue with Amy, despondently stood up and walked away with suicide on his mind. Ben spent the rest of the afternoon wandering around the parks near the Smithsonian Mall that were overflowing with colorful spring flowers. He did not return to work, realizing he had to talk to someone or he might really kill himself. At 5:00, looking over a sluggish Potomac River, he opened his cell phone and dialed Laura, his old girlfriend.

At her condo, Amy took both cell phones, removed their SIM cards and cut them into small pieces. She went for a walk in the evening and deposited the cell phones and the dismembered SIM cards in separate storm sewers.

Chapter 14 The Newspaper Investigation

"I never should have left you," Ben said, as he sat down to dinner with Laura on Saturday, June 11, 2011.

"Once we said it would last forever, but Amy's body blinded you from seeing our future," Laura replied.

"Yes, I fell for her body, without learning about her personality. She wanted to trap me and learn about the DOE IT Consolidated Support Contract. She never told me she loved me."

"Too bad men never learn the value of a good stable long-term relationship. You hurt me for months when you dumped me. You're suffering now and I'm not sorry."

"It hurts, but not as much as before. Now I'm mad and want to get even."

"What happened?" Laura asked, wanting to hear of Ben suffering.

"There wasn't a big fight. After CIN Inc. won the contract, she was always busy so we saw less and less of each other. I called her on it, and she ended our relationship. She said she was seeing someone else."

"Your behavior is very common. A federal contracting officer bribed by sex."

"I didn't plan to be bribed by sex. We went dancing on our first date and she seduced me that evening."

"Ben, Amy really played you. She must have had a long-term plan to control you." Laura thought I am sure she did since I did, but Amy won because she was new and had a better body.

"Yes, I guess she did. That's why I never should have

left you. I want to see you again."

"Ben, you don't want to start a relationship with me, another marketing female. Men just try to prove the woman is wrong in the relationship by dating her clone. Find another woman. While there's a difference between Amy and me, it's not as large as you think. Find someone outside the federal government contracting world."

"Are you sure? We had great times earlier."

"It's over. I've moved on, and so should you. Find someone with the same interests and not just sex."

"That hard to do since the only people I meet are in the federal government."

"It's not that hard. Join a tennis, golf, or skiing group—and there's always the Internet."

"Laura, it's not that easy for me. I'm not a ladies' man."

Laura refrained from laughing, "You'll have to change. You used to be a drunk and now you've stopped drinking. Change your behavior toward women. You always let them control the relationship. Be a man and take charge next time."

"Did you control us?"

"Of course. You don't realize how malleable you are. How and why do you want to hurt Amy?" Laura asked, not wanting to discuss their relationship further.

"Because she took advantage of me—she used me."

"Take control of your next relationship and it won't happen again."

"Amy is only interested in money. She told me she doesn't want to live the way she did when she was married, economically dependent on her husband. That she went into marketing because a grade-school teacher can switch careers and get rich on bonuses in marketing."

"Amy's dream is no different than those of other women who trained to be teachers, nurses, and social workers. After a divorce, women realize their previous occupations won't keep them in their married lifestyle. I'm one of those women. Ben, learn more about women before your next relationship."

"I assumed by helping her earn her bonus, she'd appreciate me. I was dumb."

"How did you help her?" Laura asked.

"I suggested technical and cost strategies to help CIN Inc. win."

"You mean the contract held by the team my firm worked on that we bid and lost!"

"Yes."

Laura, knowing his weakness and loneliness, could help her firm protest the CIN Inc. win and regain the contract. Pressing her advantage, "Can you be more specific on what you told her?"

Ben, still hoping they could revive their relationship, complied. For the next hour, he provided Laura with enough information to convince the DOE inspector general to issue a stop work order. During their conversation Laura realized while Ben kicked his addiction to alcohol, he would never shake his sexual cravings.

"Ben, another reason we can't get back together again is that I found someone, I'm happy and I don't play around," Laura said.

Ben did not expect Laura's reaction. When he left her years ago for Amy, she said she wanted to continue the relationship. He expected her to welcome him and express sympathy for his treatment by Amy, but now felt worse than at his last meeting with Amy. He tried to control his emotions and resist the drive for alcohol's soothing effects, still remembering drinking's false promise of making everything better, but always drove him into depression.

Throughout the night, Ben wondered what he should do. He realized his life with Amy had ended and would never restart with Laura. He decided to do nothing.

After Laura left Ben, she thought that bastard! After we

met I became his occasional lover like Amy to help get my company revenue and he has the nerve to confide in me and want to get back together again.

She let her emotions boil, deliberating how to exact revenge without divulging her earlier relationship with Ben and without implicating herself. Laura went to her car and turned on her silent solid-state recording device and listened to their conversation as she drove home.

Laura wondered how she could use the information without losing her credibility marketing DOE or making her liable for criminal prosecution for her profitable affair with Ben.

After returning home, finishing her second Cosmo, she decided to anonymously expose Ben and pay him back for giving the contract to Amy. She reasoned nobody knows better than her newspaper reporter friend, Ralph Summers, how to turn a rumor into a well-believed event. Knowing that alcohol can lead to unplanned dialogue on the phone, she decided to call him in the morning.

When Ralph answered the phone Sunday morning, he recognized Laura's voice. "Hi, Ralph. We haven't spoken in a long time."

"True, what's up?"

"I have a great news story for you."

"Can you summarize it for me?"

"Not on a cell phone. It's extremely sensitive. Let's meet for a drink so we can talk in private. Are you available Monday afternoon?"

"Yes, why don't we meet at the Front Page at three?"

"Fine, you could win a Pulitzer Prize for this story if you write it with drama and excitement."

"In the past I've been expected to win one, but I never have."

They met in the attractive, well-appointed newspaper reporters' hangout on New Hampshire Avenue, where six reporters, who had just met their deadlines, sipped wine or guzzled beer.

Laura, seeing the group of reporters eager for the next headline, said to Ralph before he could order a drink, "It's crowded in here with people who would do anything to steal your story. Let's go to DuPont Circle and talk."

"OK, but you're going to buy me a drink when we finish talking."

They strolled to the Circle. Ralph, and his artistic eye, took in the half-filled chess tables and the elegant fountain.

Laura pointed to a deserted bench. They both sat down.

"Let's begin," Ralph said.

"My firm held a subcontract to GCS on the one-billion-dollar DOE IT Consolidated Support Contract that DOE re-competed last year. The GCS team lost and DOE awarded the new contract to CIN Inc."

Laura stopped talking as she noticed one of the reporters, carrying a Dixie cup of whiskey amble by attempting to listen to their conversation.

"Hi, Jim. Didn't you get enough to drink in the bar?" Ralph addressed the intruder.

"Yes, but I decided to take a stroll on this warm day to see the flowers. What are you two talking about?"

"A personal matter. We used to date several years ago and we're catching up on old times," Laura answered.

"Lucky Ralph," Jim said as he walked away.

"He noticed us leave the bar and didn't believe my story," Laura said.

"Yes, we'll have to be very careful, an investigative reporter talking to a government contractor on an extremely sensitive matter. Besides I don't want to share the fame. I assume the contract award wasn't legitimate."

"Smart guess," Laura answered.

"Not so smart. I could tell from your hard smile when we met in the bar, you're pissed at something."

"Very observant."

"I'm an investigative reporter. I must be observant. What happened?"

"I received a call from an old friend, Ben Kaiser, the DOE Contracting Officer, who told me the whole story."

Ralph, seeing the contempt expressed on her face as she mentioned Ben's name figured this could be complicated.

"The CIN Inc., marketing specialist seduced Ben, and he provided her information that helped win the contract," Laura continued.

"Are you sure it was confidential information?"

"Yes, he provided me with very specific details. Ben told Amy about GCS's weakness in their operations, so CIN Inc. could write their proposal making our team look bad. He told her what the evaluators specifically looked for in the proposal, material not presented to the bidders. Ben gave Amy a list of the evaluators and the scoring procedures so CIN Inc. could tailor their proposal. DOE found half of the bidders unacceptable. They sent CIN Inc., GCS and three other firms a RFP for a best and final request. Ben told her of the details of GCS price proposal, enabling them to undercut my team's bid."

"Those are pretty damming charges. Do you have any proof besides your word against his?"

"It wouldn't be fair to you for me to come with this accusation if I didn't." She reached over, stroking his face, moved her hand down his arm and reached for his hand, slowly depositing a USB drive in his palm. She removed her hand when she felt him grip the drive and continued talking. "The proof is his own voice."

"Thanks."

"Use the information only if you don't name me as the source."

"I agree."

Laura felt relieved after she left Ralph and hoped their meeting didn't ruin her career.

Ralph returned to his office inserted the drive into his PC, placed earphones on his head and began to listen to Ben

THE OPPORTUNITY

confess. He noticed Laura's voice had been disguised in the recording and wondered if it would affect the validity of Ben's confession. The recording would be easier to use if Laura's voice had not been modified, but he realized she had to protect herself.

Ralph wondered if Ben had mental problems as he spouted a continuous confession in a high-pitched voice. Halfway through the file Ralph realized while he might not win a Pulitzer Prize he had a great story of sex and government corruption.

As he continued to listen, Ralph philosophically knew the press, while having the capacity to bring goodness and damage others would hurt Ben, Amy, and her company. The most likely to survive was Amy, but Ben was doomed. Ralph had started taking notes at the beginning of Ben's ramblings and wrote a rudimentary outline for the story.

Ralph realized Ben's anger over Amy's treatment caused him to irrationally answer Laura's incriminating questions. The sound of his own heart beating with excitement was the only sound Ralph could hear over Ben's voice as whined his life away. He continued structuring the outline. Ben's narrative gave him a perfect timeline of the corruption for phase two of the story, but missed how the liaison of Ben and Amy started. He had to include their relationship in the first phase of the story. As always he had a simple plan. Find out who Ben knew using LinkedIn, Facebook, and the DOE phone directory, and interview the most promising candidates.

Ben's facts Ralph discovered in the social networks chronicled the normal college and career development of a typical government bureaucrat. Not exciting but necessary for the newspaper. He next planned to call Ben's ex-wife, knowing that her response could range from a no comment to a deluge of vindictiveness. After the ex-Mrs. Kaiser picked up, he said, "Hi, I'm Ralph Summers from the Washington Reporter. Is this Linda Kaiser?"

"No, it's Linda Fairmont. I couldn't wait to get my

maiden name back and remove my identity from that loser."

"We're writing a series on midlevel government officials, describing their typical life and how they help the government function. I want to discuss your ex-husband."

"Ha, the simple truth is that he's an alcoholic, womanizing bum, and I'm sure his work ethic doesn't help the government. I don't care what anyone else says; he's a disgrace to humanity."

"Please tell me details that we could use in the article."

"How much time do you have?"

"All day."

"I'd like to start with his drinking. When we were dating, he used to appear sober when he picked me up. I believed a speech defect caused his slurred speech, but after we were married I found out three beers or martinis at lunch caused it. I don't know what he did at work, but I'm sure he participated in as many alcohol lunches as possible. He used to brag that his clients picked up the tab at fancy restaurants."

"How often did he do this? I read that Carter outlawed the three-martini lunch."

"No, Carter just eliminated alcohol from the list of available business tax deductions."

"Did he say if he gave anything in return for his free lunches?"

"Yes, he said he signed task orders they gave him at the end of the lunch.'"

Ralph knew his ex-wife's words may decide Ben's fate.

"Linda, it sounds like Ben engaged in petty corruption."

"I couldn't tell how petty it was. Some of the task orders cost over a hundred thousand dollars."

"Your marriage ended twelve years ago. Do you know if he still behaves this way?"

"My daughters said he stopped drinking. I assumed that wasn't out of a moral reform in his character, but his arrest for DWI."

"When did that occur?"

"Eight years ago."

Linda continued providing damming statements on Ben's behavior for the next thirty minutes, including his liaisons with women contractors, which she discovered during their divorce.

Ralph asked his last question. "Ms. Fairmont, can I quote you in the newspaper on what you have told me?"

"Please do."

After ending his conversation with Linda, Ralph wrote a tentative title for the series, "Federal Official Allegedly Preys on Female Contractors, Exchanging Sex for Contract Awards."

Ralph now felt with Linda Fairmont's answers and Laura's recording the Washington Reporter's editorial board had to approve the series before publication. They would not approve a story that could lead to a liability lawsuit. He decided to extend his research to strengthen the series, before asking for the board's approval, by interviewing an executive at GCS, who worked on the DOE IT contract.

Ralph left his office, purchased an untraceable cell phone, and called Laura.

"Laura Clark."

"Hi, it's Ralph. Can I meet you at the same bench in DuPont Circle where we talked yesterday? You name the time."

"Four o'clock"

"See you then." Ralph hung up.

He arrived a few minutes early, but saw Laura, reading a magazine, sitting where they talked. He sat next to her., "I want to thank you for the information yesterday. To protect your identity I called on an untraceable cell phone. I suggest you buy one. Call me when you have it."

He shook her hand transferring his untraceable cell phone number.

"Thanks for protecting me. I will."

"I have been doing background checks for the story and found Ben might have been exploiting contracting women throughout his career. Was Ben married when GCS held the DOE IT contract?"

"No, he divorced several years before the award."

"Who was the incumbent contractor before GCS?"

"Dynamic Information Systems. Why?"

"I talked to his ex-wife, Linda. She told me he has been trading sex and other favors for contract or task order awards for years. I have to validate her story to show Ben's behavior is compulsive. I'd want to talk to someone from Dynamic Information Systems, preferably a female who worked with Ben."

Laura tore off a small corner piece of a page of the magazine, took out a pen and wrote a name and phone number on the paper, handing it to Ralph by patting his chest and slipping it into a jacket pocket. "She's a friend of mine. Please don't tell her I'm your source."

"Thanks. I won't. Can you provide me with someone at GCS I should talk to?"

"I don't think he had any sexual liaison with GCS's staff, since most of their managers were male, but he sure liked to go to lunch and play golf at GCS's expense." She tore off another piece of paper, wrote a name and gave it to Ben.

"Thanks."

"This guy hated Ben's guts, but had to be nice to him since he was GCS's contract manager."

As Ralph walked back to his office he retrieved Laura's slips of paper and put them in his wallet.

He examined the names and numbers as he sat at his

desk and decided it was too late to call. The next day he first contacted Sandy Reynolds from Dynamic Information Systems at 10:00 a.m.

"I'm Ralph Summers from the Washington Reporter. We're doing a series on midlevel government officials, describing their typical life, and how they make the government work. I understand you might have worked with Ben Kaiser."

"Yes, I did, when I worked for Dynamic Information Systems years ago as a marketing representative before I was married. Why do you want to write about Ben?"

"We want to profile several excellent public servants and balance the article by discussing some who aren't so excellent."

"Well Ben fits in the latter category."

"Why?"

"Ben was a sleaze always expecting us to take him to a three-martini lunch before signing a task order. He never even hid his behavior. When I saw him after work, he was always drunk, hitting on female contractors and not just from our firm. Unfortunately, some of the women thought their compliance necessary to have him approve task orders and they succumbed to his requests. I didn't cooperate with him. I told him I'd tell his wife if he didn't stop bothering me. He laughed. So I called her. She was furious and filed for divorce."

"Was Ben aware you called his wife?"

"Yes, his wife told him after the divorce."

"Did he exact any retribution for your call?"

"None that I can prove. However, my old firm lost the re-compete two years after the divorce. I left Dynamic Information after the incident, to get married, but I assume he still held a grudge against my old firm."

"You may not be able to prove your contention, but we're compiling information on Ben that makes it highly probable. Can I use your name in the article?"

"Yes. If you quote me, state that Ben was an anomaly,

the only one I've met in over fifteen happy and rewarding years working with federal government officials."

"That's a deal."

They continued talking for another fifteen minutes. She provided substantiation for some of the earlier material Ralph had collected.

Ralph called the next contact, Jack Harrison, at eleven. "I'm Ralph Summers from the Washington Reporter. We're doing a series on midlevel government officials, describing their typical life and how they make the government work. I understand you know Ben Kaiser."

"Yes, I do. Why do a story on him? He's a snake."

"We want to profile several excellent public servants and balance the article by discussing several who aren't so excellent."

"Ben fits the not-so-excellent category. I used to manage the DOE IT Consolidated Support Contract for Global Computer Services and he was DOE's contracting officer, basically my boss at DOE. All he cared about was getting our status reports in on time and keeping on budget. When we told the DOE technical manager they had problems with their infrastructure that affected the IT user response times, the technical manager went to Ben and asked for more money and a task order to correct the problem. Ben always said no. Since response times suffered, we received poor evaluations.

In the first year of the contract we invited the DOE managers to a charity golf event. Ben accepted. Most DOE managers paid their own way, to avoid a conflict of interest. Ben allowed GCS to pay his bills. He called me two days later, saying he had found extra money to fund the response-time task order. He suggested we meet for lunch at the Market Inn to talk over the task order and to hand me the signed task order if we agreed on its content. GCS picked up the tab and I received a signed document. The lunch taught me how Ben conducts business."

"Why didn't you complain?"

"How could I? My job depended upon growing the contract and Ben showed me how. If I complained, I doubt he'd be fired, but I'd never receive another task order or win the re-compete."

"You lost the re-compete. Do you know why?"

"Six months before DOE released the RFP we found that CIN Inc. was making a move. They had hired a well-liked program manager, Art Mitchell, from DOE. When we first won the contract, Ben suggested we set up regional offices in poor areas of the country to hire low-income workers. We discovered CIN Inc. was opening regional offices in these areas and transferring non-DOE work to establish a presence for the re-compete bid."

"Why did Ben mandate offices in rural areas?"

"I guess you're ignorant of how Congress operates. The four congressmen representing these regions are members of congressional committees that control DOE's budget."

Ralph wrote in his notes, political corruption could be better than sex and favors.

"So Ben helps the congressmen and they reward DOE."

"Correct. CIN Inc. would lose the contract unless they had pacified the four congressmen."

"Can a congressman veto a contract award?"

"Not legally. But if a congressman indicates he doesn't want a company, most evaluators recognize awarding that company the contract may impact their agency's budget."

"Check and I bet you'll find CIN Inc. contributed to their congressional campaigns before they won the contract."

"Isn't that a bribe? Isn't that illegal?"

"No, all companies do it. GCS contributed to their political campaigns."

"How did you lose the contract?"

"We don't know. Both companies were technically qualified, but they bid a lower price than GCS. We couldn't figure how they could bid so low."

"Read my article and you might find out why."

"I will. I'm curious, since GCS fired me when we lost—a normal procedure for losing managers."

"I'm sorry to hear that. Can I use your name in the article?"

"Yes, GCS and DOE can't discipline me; I'm retired. I never looked for another job after GCS fired me. I'm beginning to think your story is more centered on corrupt, not good public employees."

"Read the article, and you be the judge."

"I enjoyed talking to you. If you have any more questions please call me. I always carry my cell, and I'll answer, even if I'm on the golf course."

"Thanks. I enjoyed the conversation. You've been very helpful. Call if you want to add anything."

"I will. Your number is on my cell."

Ralph felt great after hearing Jack Harrison's answers, his agreement to be quoted, and to continue his cooperation. Ralph thought, Ben must have hurt and pissed off the world. He probably didn't realize the impact of his behavior. I'll have no misgivings destroying him.

Ralph felt elated as he realized he had the foundation of a great story, which, while a Washington story, should catch the attention of the national news networks. He decided to pitch the series to his boss, the paper's editor, John Mason. At noon on Wednesday, June 15, he completed the paper's special request article template and called Mason, who set up an appointment for 4:00 p.m.

Ralph walked into Mason's office, who briskly said, "What do you have?"

"My proposal is documented in Washington Reporter format," Ralph said as he handed him the proposal.

"The document's only to cover our ass. Describe

your article."

Ralph began with Laura's call, not mentioning her name, and summarized the events of the last several days. He gave Mason an outline of the proposed three-part series.

Before he could begin presenting it, Mason speed read it and burst out, "Christ, Ralph that the best potential story I've heard in six months. The outline's great. In the first article, you summarize the corruption charge with high-level details to whet the reader's appetite. Make sure you describe the importance and size of the contract, CIN Inc., as well as identifying those who you interviewed. It's good you state corruption is a rare occurrence in federal contracting, but when discovered it should be exposed to deter others in the future. The second part continues to lure in the readers, summarizing Ben's history and behavior in previous contracts and describing the contracting process and how an immoral contracting officer can corrupt it. The last section is great, presenting the proof. Are you sure you can't release the name of your informant?"

"Yes, they said if I released their name they'd deny it and say they never talked to me."

"OK. Your article will start a DOE investigation which you can cover.

Mason opened his credenza, pulled out two glasses, a bottle of single malt scotch, poured several shots into each glass, and said, "This deserves a good drink. Sorry, no ice. Continue."

Mason sat on the edge of his chair gripping the outline, listening to Ralph bring life to the sparse words on the paper. Mason let him talk except in a few sections where he offered advice, which Ralph realized improved the outline and accepted without argument.

"When can you get me a finished article?"

"In two days, if I'm assigned a research assistant to help me investigate the congressional angle."

Mason picked up the phone and dialed. "Joe, Mason here. Come to my office immediately."

"Good kid, very smart, twenty-two, recent journalism graduate from Maryland. He's a son of one of my golfing buddies. He has done routine work well in the last four months. It's time to see if he can help on a major story with an impossible schedule both of us workaholics will give him."

Joe knocked on the door. Mason shouted, "Enter."

"Joe, I'm sure you know Ralph."

"Only by reputation. I never met him," Joe Graham answered in awe.

"Well, you have now."

"Good to meet you." Ralph reached over and shook his hand.

"Tell him what to do," Mason blurted.

Ralph summarized the article, ending his discussion with, "I need help finding information on the relationship of the four congressmen to Ben Kaiser, to the DOE IT Consolidated Support Contract, and CIN Inc."

"I look forward to the work. I had a political science minor."

"Joe, this is a great opportunity. Ralph used his expertise as a research assistant to rise to his status as a nationally syndicated columnist. You'll treat this work as top secret, no matter how much you want to tell your girlfriend or father. No information can leak or those identified in the article may start a preemptive defense against our charges," Mason said.

"I understand the need for security."

"Good. If I learn you're the source of a leak you'll be fired, the paper will never give you a reference, and I'll break your dad's new putter. I won't kill you. If I tell your dad you're responsible for the putter, he'll kill you himself."

"That's true. I'll be quiet."

Mason changed the topic. "What's great about

Washington?" He did not wait for a response, but continued, "Metro's subway stops at my office and a block from my home. Do either of you drive home or do you take the Metro?"

They both replied Metro. "Good." Mason poured them a good drink of scotch and raised his glass "To the greatest potential story of the year."

Ralph arrived at work at 7:30 a.m. on Thursday and began transcribing his notes into the outline of the story. Joe showed up at 8:00 a.m. and said, "I've developed a plan to find information on the congressmen. Want me to tell you my plan?"

"The summarized version."

"I'll use the Federal Election Commission's website to find out if CIN Inc. has been contributing to the congressmen. The CIN Inc.'s website should tell us if they have offices in the four congressional districts. I'll follow this up by accessing local websites of each of the four districts to discover more information related to CIN Inc."

"I'd do the same for GCS. You might find morally questionable information about CIN Inc. that is commonly accepted business practice and GCS will provide a baseline. Complete the election campaign contribution section first, summarizing the details in a table, and write a few paragraphs I can use in the second part of the article by eleven," Ralph said.

"Will do."

John Mason sent both Ralph and Joe an e-mail, asking them to be in his office at noon for a status report.

"Ralph, what do you have for me?"

Ralph handed Mason a table of the detailed outline and the status of each section which Mason scanned. "Looks good for a beginning, but I notice over half the section's status is not started. Will you be able to complete the article by COB tomorrow night or do you need more resources?"

"We'll meet the deadline. Resources are not a problem. We'll work all night if needed."

Joe glanced at Ralph wondering if he was serious.

"Correct answer. I recommend adding a few paragraphs summarizing earlier contract corruption scandals for the first part of the article to put the DOE contract problem in perspective."

"Will do. Joe finished his first assignment early so he could tackle that next."

"Great. Let's meet again at five o'clock for an update."

They left Mason's office and Ralph said, "Do you want to get lunch?"

"I brought a brown bag today. I figured I'd work through lunch. Were you serious about having to work all night? My girlfriend invited me to dinner at her house at seven o'clock."

"Occasionally we work through the night, but we're in good shape on this one provided you can finish the table and write a few paragraphs describing previous corruption cases by two."

"That should be no problem."

"Good. Do you own a laptop?"

"Yes."

"Bring it to your girlfriend's tonight in case Mason thinks up other ways to improve the article. It's good training for your girl to show her how top-flight reporters work."

"I thought I was a research assistant, not a top-flight reporter."

"Tell her it will help you become one. If you work at her home tonight, do it in private."

At the five o'clock meeting, Ralph handed Mason an updated status sheet.

"Great, Ralph; it's less than 20 percent empty. I see

Joe completed the section on the earlier corruption cases. Are you guys going to stay here and work tonight?"

Ralph answered for both of them. "No."

"Good." He turned toward his credenza, took out his bottle of scotch, and poured three stiff drinks.

After he handed the drinks to his writers he toasted, "To the greatest story of the year. When can I start reviewing what you have?"

"Right now," Ralph answered.

"Good. I'll start after we finish our drinks. I'll e-mail you my suggested changes by seven. We'll meet here again at noon. I'd want to give it to the copy editor by two o'clock tomorrow. Is that possible?"

"Of course." Ralph planned to incorporate Mason's comments in the evening at home.

The next morning Ralph and Joe met at 7:00 to review the current version of the article and scheduled assignments.

"I've finished rough drafts of the missing sections, and I've prepared a list of missing information for you to find. Tackle them in order of priority on the list, and send me an item as soon as you complete it. Complete it by eleven," Ralph said.

"OK." Joe looked at the twenty-two items, and assured himself he could complete the tasks by the deadline.

At noon Ralph and Joe walked into Mason's office, with Ralph saying, "We're ready for the copy editor."

"Great. Is it OK if I read it before I give it to her?" Mason responded.

"Sure."

"Go to lunch and return at one."

At their meeting, Mason said, "I made a few changes. Read them, and if you accept them send it to copy editing. I'm planning to put the article on the front page of the Sunday edition and follow up with the next two sections on

Tuesday and Thursday. We'll revise the last two sections based on the reaction to Sunday's article."

At Ralph's desk they read the revised article, accepting his corrections, and sent it to the copy editor. Joe objected to some of Mason's phrasing, but Ralph advised, "It a good practice not to insult your boss. That's what you do when you reject his suggestions. If the writing is feeble, I'd tell him, but I'm smart enough to know he's the paper's editor and may be a better writer than I am."

Joe listened carefully and decided to follow Ralph's advice.

Chapter 15 Impact of the Article on CIN Inc.

Pete and Amy enjoyed the beach house the weekend of June 19, 2011, while Joan and Art hiked on Old Rag Mountain in Virginia. After breakfast, Pete picked up the Washington Reporter at Fifer Orchards Market on Route 1. Halfway down, on the right-hand side of the page, he noticed an article titled, "Contract Corruption Alleged at DOE." He scanned the article as he walked back to the beach house and broke into a cold sweat as he read his, Amy's, and their flagship DOE contract names.

Pete called his boss, Jim Shafer.

"It's Pete. I'm sorry to call on a Sunday morning."

"I planned to call you having just read the Washington Reporter article."

"Let's meet Monday morning to discuss our response strategy."

"Be in my office at ten. Paul Saunders, our lawyer will attend the meeting to ensure whatever we decide to do is legal." Pete didn't like the sternness in Saunders voice.

When he returned to the beach house, Amy was on the porch reading a book and drinking coffee.

"Amy, I've more interesting reading." He handed her the paper and pointed to the article.

Amy read the article. It shocked her. The words tangled in her mouth as she tried to understand its content and implications. Her first reaction—her professional life had ended. The article portrayed her as one of Ben's lovers who allegedly traded contract information for sex. She felt better realizing there were others, noting the article did not mention his previous girlfriend, Laura. After finishing the article she looked at Pete.

"You're right. It's an interesting story. I wonder what's in the next two articles," Amy said.

"We have to analyze today's article and develop a damage control strategy. Our competitors will scream to the DOE inspector general's office to have the contract cancelled, but I'm not ready to let that happen."

"I agree. Unless they can prove the accusations, they can't cancel the contract. I swear I never asked Ben for any information related to the contract during the proposal."

"Good. Let's hope you don't have to testify to that in court. It appears Ben has a history of dating his contractor's staff. Not illegal. Even if there's no proof of corruption, Ben's career at DOE is over."

"I never cared about his future especially when I met him at the beach and you slugged him. Our future on the DOE contract concerns me."

"That's cold but realistic. I have to meet with my boss and our corporate lawyer at ten tomorrow to develop a response," Pete said.

"If anyone, including DOE, calls for a comment, say no comment, but that CIN Inc. is developing a response. I'm going to call the rest of the staff and tell them the same thing. We'll meet in my office to develop a joint strategy to nullify the article at eleven."

Pete had left the beach early, dictating ideas into his portable recorder as he drove. When he arrived home he transcribed his notes into a set of PowerPoint slides:

- Deny any knowledge of Ben Kaiser's behavior and relationship with his contractors
- State that Amy denied asking Ben Kaiser for confidential contract information during the proposal
- Cite hard work and efforts including resources spent on the proposal, opening regional offices, and CIN Inc.'s promise to hire incumbent staff

- Reference excellent contract evaluation scores, showing DOE had made the correct decision in awarding the contract to CIN Inc.
- Promise CIN Inc. will work with DOE to investigate the causes of the allegations in the article
- Wish to continue the mutually beneficial relationship between DOE and CIN Inc.

Pete entered Jim Shafer's executive vice president's office on Monday morning. Paul Saunders, an attorney from CIN Inc.'s external law firm, sat next to Jim the conference table.

"Pete, what does this article mean?" Jim asked.

"I've talked with Amy and she swears she never asked Ben Kaiser, the DOE CO, for any confidential contractual information."

"I hope she's telling the truth. Our competitors will call to have the contract cancelled and re-competed. Develop a strategy to discredit the article by two o'clock and return here. If we lose the contract, you'll lose your job."

"I understand. I've already started. I'll meet with my staff at eleven and we'll have the strategy by two."

"Instruct your staff not to talk to anyone. If DOE calls your staff, refer the caller to me," Paul, the lawyer, said as he handed Pete his business card.

"I told my staff not to talk to anyone yesterday."

At his get-well staff meeting Pete attached his PC to a projector and started talking after Amy, Art, and Tim, the congressional liaison, arrived.

"You've read the Reporter article. We're here to develop a strategy for nullifying its impact on the DOE contract and to CIN Inc. I talked to Amy. She swears she never asked for confidential bid information from Ben."

"Art, do you know the impact on your operations?"

"I received a call from Roger Meeks, our technical

contract manager, who asked if I had read the article. When I said yes, he said, 'While the article includes damming information against CIN Inc. and DOE's contracting officer Ben Kaiser, everyone is innocent until proven guilty.' I thanked him for understanding, and he replied, 'You're doing such a great job. We don't want the article to affect your performance so continue working as if it was never published. If DOE investigates the charges in the article, I'll recommend DOE restrict it to DOE and CIN Inc.'s management so as not to impact our working relationship'" Art replied.

"Did you tell him to call our lawyer, and repeat what he said?

"I will."

"I didn't expect that reaction," Pete said. "Meeks may think we're guilty, but wants to protect his operation and stop us from resigning as their contractor. He doesn't understand the contracting business. Regardless of his motives, that's good news. At this point there'll be no stop work orders. The article included a brief reference to the fab four congressmen, stating more details will follow in Tuesday's article. Tim, how will the congressmen react?" Pete asked.

"Slowly. They'll deny knowledge of Ben Kaiser's behavior and say they'll wait and cooperate with an investigation. They'll issue no-comment statements until after the publication of the complete series," Tim replied.

"So it's not as bad in the short term as we might have expected. My boss, Jim Shafer, has asked me to prepare a strategy for nullifying the article. I have a six-slide presentation. Art, develop a seventh slide summarizing your conversation with Meeks," Pete continued.

Pete delivered the draft presentation, making changes to the electronic file suggested by his staff. When he finished he said, "Art, I saw you scribbling notes while I talked. Can I assume they are the DOE-Meeks slide, and if they are, please dictate them to me?"

"You're correct. Are you ready?"

"Go ahead."

After Pete finished the final editing of the presentation, he handed them his draft of the CIN Inc. press release, which he read out loud asking them for their comments. He printed out the final version and said, "Review it one more time. This has to go to my boss."

Pete entered Jim Shafer's office at 2:00 p.m.

"What do you have for us?" Shafer asked.

"A PowerPoint presentation my DOE contract management staff and I prepared. When I read the article on Sunday I was devastated. However, since talking to Amy and my staff I'm more upbeat and have a plan to nullify the impact of the article."

"Good to hear. Give me the thumb drive," Shafer replied.

After Shafer inserted the thumb drive into his PC, Pete delivered the presentation. He won over his skeptical audience as they nodded in agreement, especially when Pete presented the DOE technical contract manager Roger Meeks slide and Paul Saunders, the lawyer, verified his call from Meeks.

"At least our revenue stream won't stop immediately. Meeks appears afraid we'll abandon the contract," Shafer said at the end of the presentation.

"We agree. We've prepared a draft press release for your review," Pete replied.

They read the document, with Shafer nodding approval, while Paul Saunders penciled in suggested edits.

"Excellent. It sets the right tone, denying any knowledge of Kaiser's general behavior and stating we never asked for private bidding information, as well as offering to work with DOE if they investigate the allegations in the article. Paul, what did you think?" Shafer said.

"I agree with your evaluation, but I have a few

suggested changes both from a grammatical and legal standpoint."

Paul handed his marked-up copy to Shafer who reviewed and approved it, and returned the revised text to Pete, saying, "Make these changes, e-mail them to me and I'll send out a press release. Hopefully there will be no surprises in the next two articles."

The CIN Inc.'s executive vice president's office issued the following press release to the news wire services, the local radio and TV stations, and regional newspapers, including the Washington Reporter.

CIN Inc. applauds the efforts of the Washington Reporter to investigate corruption in the federal government. Many of their stories have identified and stopped illegal activities. However, we believe the allegations in their current expose of potential corruption in the Department of Energy's (DOE) contracts office related to CIN Inc. are incorrect. Neither CIN Inc. nor its employee, Amy Ericson, has ever requested DOE confidential bidding information from Ben Kaiser on the IT Consolidated Support Contract. We were not aware of Mr. Kaiser's alleged previous behavior on other contracts.

CIN Inc., as one of the thousands of honest federal government contracting companies, pledges to cooperate with all DOE investigations of the allegations in the Reporter article and will continue to deliver superior service to DOE on the IT Consolidated Support Contract and other contracts.

Mason e-mailed Ralph the CIN Inc. press release at five thirty with a note stating, "It's very general and doesn't have to be answered in Tuesday's article. In the interest of fairness we'll include it at the end of the article."

THE OPPORTUNITY

Steve Gardner, loved his new sexual and personal relationship with Amy. He felt empty when he did not see her, even though they met three times a week. Steve wondered if he had met his future wife. He had finally found someone with a sex drive as insatiable as his. His feelings changed instantaneously when he read the Ralph Summers's article on Sunday. While he had planned to spend Monday night at Amy's condo, his anticipation and desire faded as he understood the implications of the article. Amy used sex to compromise a DOE employee for confidential information. She traded sex for money. Was he her next target?

Gardner loved her sensuality, but feared their relationship may damage his career at Social Security. He debated with himself on how to talk to Amy, without ending the relationship, and realized to protect himself he must call Amy by noon.

"Hi, Steve. I'm looking forward to seeing you tonight."

"That's why I called."

"Aren't you coming?"

"Amy, I read the article in the Washington Reporter. The accusations against you concern me. We should wait until your situation is resolved before we get together."

"The statements in the paper are lies. I never asked the DOE contracting officer for confidential information."

"I believe you, but I still want to postpone getting together."

"There's nothing I can do or say to change your mind?"

"No."

"Thanks for calling. I hope to see you again."

"Me too. Bye, Amy."

Pete and Amy talked the next Saturday morning, on a walk between Dewey and Rehoboth, after a June thunderstorm.

They usually enjoyed the mile of warm scented beach, permeated with the smell of decaying sea life. However, this time they ignored the environment only thinking of the three Reporter's articles.

"Do you think Ben would destroy his career to get back at you?"

"I don't know. He's irrational and very hung up on me. My threat to place our videos on the Internet, where his daughters could watch them, seemed to quiet him. But he must have talked to someone else who went to the reporter."

"You took videos!" Pete said, shocked and surprised.

"Yes, to protect myself and CIN Inc."

"What kind of videos?" Pete asked, still incredulous, but slightly aroused.

"Everything, our conversations, our meals at my house, and our pillow talk," Amy replied.

"As your boss, I should review them to make sure CIN Inc. is not libeled."

"Pete, what earthly good could come of that? I know what you want to look for and there's no chance of that."

"Even if I can't view them, I can imagine."

"Grow up; there's more to see on the beach on a Saturday afternoon, than in the videos. The audio recordings are more important than the videos."

"What do you mean?"

"Ben volunteers the information we used to help win the contract in the audio. I didn't ask him for anything."

"I don't want to watch the videos and I'm glad you didn't tell me they exist. CIN Inc. cannot be accused of bribery if we're unaware of the videos and conversations."

"Exactly!"

"The recordings could send you to jail if the FBI obtains a search warrant and finds them, even if you didn't ask for the information from Ben, since your relationship helped win the contract. I recommend you get rid of them."

THE OPPORTUNITY

"Let me think about that. It's the only proof I have that I didn't entrap Ben."

"Don't think too hard. You'll never know when the police will obtain a warrant. There'll be no time to destroy them."

Amy left the beach early Saturday afternoon, driving home unsure whether she should destroy the memory cards containing the audios and videos or hide them. She thought Pete's motivation was self-serving. He wanted them destroyed so he could not be implicated in directing her relationship with Ben. She believed the audios and videos would save her if legally charged, but she realized her marketing career would be over if they were released.

She decided to hide the memory cards where a search warrant could not reach them. After arriving home she went to her bedroom dresser, retrieved the recorders and full memory cards earlier removed from the recorders. She removed the memory cards still in the recorders and placed the cards in two layered waterproof ziplock bags. She took the bags, the recorders, and a garden spade, and drove to the C&O canal parking lot at Carderock off the Clara Barton Parkway. She walked over the small bridge spanning the canal to the tow path, thankful she saw few walkers and runners. She turned down a path toward the Potomac River. Halfway toward the river she turned into the woods and found a large oak tree she knew she would never forget. She used the garden spade to dig a hole four inches wide and a foot deep in the soft moist soil. She placed the layered ziplock bags at the bottom of the hole, covering it with dirt, old leaves and a six inch circular rock.

At the river's edge she tossed the recorders and the garden spade into the river out of the reach of a search warrant. She thought I'll retrieve the cards when I'm old and gray, so I can see how my breasts looked when they were firm.

Chapter 16 DOE's Investigation

The DOE inspector general opened the meeting at 10:00 a.m. on Monday, June 20.

"I've asked you to come to my office, in response to a call from the secretary of DOE. He asked me if I'd read the DOE story in the Sunday edition of the Washington Reporter. He said it puts us in a very bad light, and expects me to develop a strategy for responding to the article, including, and if needed, to initiate a special investigation of Ben Kaiser. I'd like each of you to present a summary of your thoughts on the article."

Four additional DOE staff attended the meeting: Ben's boss, Harvey Dwyer; Roger Meeks, the contract technical manager; Audrey Tompkins, from the inspector general's office; and Bob Rothman, the DOE press secretary.

"Harvey, you can go first, since you're his boss."

Harvey, knowing that the article reflected on his management ability, chewed his fingernails, thinking of a response to save his job.

"The article includes criminal allegations without providing proof. We should develop a plan to react to the potential outrage by the CIN Inc's' competitors, if and when the Reporter provides the proof. However, since no contractors have accused Ben of unethical behavior, we should presume he is innocent until offered proof. I called Ben to discuss the article and his administrative assistant said he was home sick."

"I bet he's sick—afraid to face our questioning. Harvey, your suggestions are a very conservative wait-and-see response. My boss wants us to be more active in finding out the truth and not wait to read it in the Washington Reporter. Sunday's article promised to provide proof of the accusations this week," the inspector general responded.

"Roger, your thoughts?"

"My immediate concern was continuation of CIN Inc.'s excellent performance on the contract. Most of us know Art Mitchell, the CIN Inc. contract manager. He would not condone the behavior alleged in the article, and I feared he would quit as the contract manager. If he and others leave, the performance of the contract may deteriorate. Since the contract supports most departments of DOE, CIN Inc.'s departure may impact DOE's mission.

"I called Art this morning and assured him Ben was innocent until proven guilty and that he's not responsible for Ben's behavior. I praised his work and asked him to continue, and I told him if DOE has an investigation he would not be included."

The inspector general said, "Good initiative, I hadn't considered the impact of the article on CIN Inc.'s productivity. I've invited Audrey to lead an internal investigation. Harvey and Roger, give Audrey everything she wants. I appointed her so we could have an independent review of Ben Kaiser's behavior. Harvey, while I respect your ability to discover what happened, the internal politics in your office won't distract her. Audrey, tell us your impression of the article, and how we can help you."

"If the article is true, it appears Ben works just as hard in the evening as he does during the day. I'll assume it's true, since I don't think the Washington Reporter would publish an accusatory article without proof. They don't want to be sued and lose credibility with the public. I'll look for evidence related to each point in the story. If I find contradictory evidence, Ben will be absolved of that accusation; if not, we'll ask the Department of Justice if his actions are criminal, and if he should be prosecuted."

Harvey, listening to Audrey, chafed at being a participator rather than the lead investigator. He looked directly at her as she addressed him.

"Harvey, I'll need a complete history of the contracts Ben has managed, including the details of the award, and data on why the competitors lost. Send me the original information as you compile it and don't wait until you have a complete set of documents. I'll start the investigation, but won't get to the critical parts until I can review the Reporter's promised proof in Tuesday's and Thursday's editions."

The inspector general addressed, Bob Rothman. "Bob the secretary wants you to write a press release to answer the Reporter's charges."

"I wrote my first draft yesterday afternoon after I read the article. I've been modifying it to include the information we discussed today."

"Good. We can read and edit together."

They commented on the draft press release line by line. Bob entered their agreed upon comments into his laptop. When he finished, he said to the inspector general, "I'll e-mail you a copy."

"Send one to the secretary asking for his approval. When he releases it, put it in on our website. We'll meet in my office on Friday at three o'clock and discuss any new developments. Audrey will report her progress."

Audrey Tompkins, a straitlaced woman in her forties, dressed in formal business suits at work. She had the reputation of being a strong but just woman in DOE. She had experience as a criminal prosecutor in Indiana, and moved to Washington, DC, when her husband accepted a position at the Department of the Interior. At DOE she conducted investigations of employee fraud, sexual discrimination, and contractor irregularities.

Audrey parused the first article and identified sixteen

specific charges of corruption at DOE and in Ben's past. She planned to organize her report around these charges. Next, she started compiling and reading information on the case so she could ask meaningful questions. She called the individuals named in Sunday's article, explained her role in DOE's response to the article, and asked if she could meet them at DOE or a location of their choosing Wednesday, Thursday or Friday morning. They agreed. She planned to interview Ben last, after she had completed the original interviews and developed specific questions to either prove his guilt or absolve him.

Tuesday's article provided additional information on Ben's career, and potential crimes, and proof of the earlier accusations. Audrey added ten accusations to the original sixteen charges of corruption. The article identified those who accused Ben of these crimes; she called them and scheduled interviews. Audrey developed more questions to ask during the interviews.

Thursday's article provided more proof of specific instances where Ben had committed felonies, exchanging sex for information. The article stated the original information came from an anonymous source, but that it had been verified by those identified in the articles. Audrey knew if the original sources was credible, their testimony would put Ben in prison.

Audrey worked fourteen-hour days to complete her report by Friday afternoon. She received more detailed answers in her interviews, than provided to the reporter of the article. She concluded DOE should ask the Department of Justice to take over the investigation and indict Ben, even without interviewing him.

Audrey brought five copies of the preliminary report to the DOE inspector general's meeting. She noticed that in addition to those attending the Monday meeting, Alice Fay, the DOE personnel director sat at the table.

The inspector general started the meeting.

"Thanks for coming. It has been a very interesting week, with two more articles published, which paint a dismal picture of Ben and reflect on DOE's contracts office."

Harvey Dwyer felt nauseous when the meeting started. The feeling increased when the inspector general paused and looked at him.

Harvey reported Ben did not show up for work on Tuesday, but e-mailed saying he was taking personal leave for the next week. Harvey contacted Alice and the inspector general for advice. Harvey said, "The three of us met on Wednesday morning and took the following actions Alice will describe."

"Good afternoon," Alice said. "They are designed to protect DOE and to remove Ben from contractual relations with CIN Inc. and other contractors. Harvey e-mailed Ben, granting his request for personal leave, but requested he answer questions from a representative from the DOE's inspector general's office. We had planned to have Audrey ask the questions. Ben replied that the lies in the Reporter articles concerned him, and that he had hired a lawyer to protect his rights, who advised him not to answer any questions until after publication of the third article and to answer questions only in the lawyer's presence. We respect his legal rights, but we concluded from the last e-mail that he's as guilty as Nixon. We took the following action to help resolve the problem, recognizing his lawyer would never let Ben answer meaningful questions.

"We drafted a letter encouraging Ben to resign, guaranteeing his pension if he left DOE and wasn't convicted of any criminal charges. A courier delivered the letter to his residence yesterday. He received it at three thirty. He hasn't responded to our offer."

"Thanks, Alice. Roger, report on the impact of the articles on CIN Inc. performance."

"CIN Inc. is continuing to deliver at the highest

levels, even though DOE could cancel the contract if Ben is found guilty. There has been no impact on DOE's operations."

"Good. Audrey will deliver her preliminary report."

She handed the report to the other attendees and began.

"The report is organized into three major sections. First, background information of the CIN Inc. bid and contract is presented. Second, Ben's alleged history at DOE and other organizations is summarized, as reported in the article and information I obtained from external interviews, Harvey, and the personnel office. The last part of the report includes twenty-six allegations included in the articles, my findings as to the truth of the allegations, and summarizes the interviews I conducted with the individuals mentioned in the articles. He's guilty of at least twenty of the allegations. Without interviewing Ben, I cannot make a judgment on the others. From Alice's discussion, I assume his lawyer will never let Ben answer any of my questions. I propose we call the Department of Justice, turn over my findings, and ask them to continue the investigation. If the evidence warrants, they should issue Ben a criminal indictment."

"Thanks, Audrey, for writing an excellent draft report, which everyone can read this weekend. I agree with her recommendation and both of us will meet with representatives of the FBI this afternoon at four. Since we're going to transfer the investigation to the FBI, we won't meet again; however, be ready and open if an FBI agent questions you about the corruption charges or your relationship with Ben. Thanks for your help."

Chapter 17 Articles' Impact on Ben

Ben read the article while eating breakfast. He refused to answer his phone, which rang constantly all day. He was in a stupor Sunday. At night, Ben cried after reading the article for the sixth time, wondering who provided the reporter with the information used to damn him. After noticing the omission of Laura's name, he knew the answer. He wondered why she had been so vindictive after he spilled his heart out to her over a week ago. Since it was 11:00 p.m., he realized it was too late to call her.

Ben felt just as bad on Monday when he decided not to go to work. He e-mailed a short note to his administrative assistant, citing illness as his excuse, which he understood would fool no one.

Laura fished the cell phone from her purse at 8:00 a.m., and seeing Ben's name as the caller, pressed the "do not answer" button. She had no desire to be confronted by Ben.

While depressed and worried, Ben had a law degree, specializing in contract law, and understood he was unqualified to defend himself. He called an old friend Alex Shapiro, a criminal defense attorney, a fellow student at law school.

"Alex Shapiro. Can I help you?"

"Alex, Ben Kaiser. The Washington Reporter printed an article that included me in yesterday's paper. I'm calling you for legal advice."

"Good move. I read the article. Can you come by my office this morning?"

"Yes. What time?"

"Eleven. Criminal defense attorneys have a more

difficult time collecting their fees than liability attorneys. We always ask for retainer fees up front before we take a case, since we never know if the defendant will jump bail, get killed, commit suicide, et cetera. So I'm asking you for a retainer. I'm sure you understand. Please bring a check for ten thousand."

"OK. It will take more than a few hours to get a check that large. Could we meet tomorrow?"

"Is one in the afternoon OK?"

"I'll see you then."

"My first legal advice is not to talk to anyone mentioned in the article or anyone from DOE or the FBI. When you talk, I want to be present."

"Of course. See you tomorrow."

Ben followed his lawyer's advice and kept silent on Monday and Tuesday morning. He went to his bank on Monday afternoon and transferred money from his savings to his checking account.

"Good afternoon, Ben. I never thought I'd see you under these circumstances," Alex Shapiro said as his administrative assistant led Ben into his office.

"I didn't either." Ben handed Alex an envelope containing the check.

"Ben, while the two newspaper articles accused you of illegal activities, they have not presented proof except for general quotations from those involved. The authorities have not charged you with a crime, so we can't develop a defense strategy. I don't want to discuss the newspaper articles and I don't want you to comment on your guilt until the authorities charge you. What I plan to do today is describe what will happen if you are charged. Is that OK?"

"Yes."

Ben spent the rest of Tuesday and Wednesday in his home, followed his lawyer's advice, and didn't answer his phone.

Ben had trouble sleeping, woke up early and nervously awaited the Thursday installment of the Reporter's corruption articles. He heard the paper land on his walk and took it into the house, paralyzed by fear of what it might report. After five minutes he opened the folded paper and found the final installment on page one. He read, and started shaking and crying as he realized the major portion of the article repeated verbatim the confession he had given Laura and verified by others.

Ben stayed home in his stupor, fighting the urge to return to drinking to end his pain. At three on Thursday a car pulled up in front of his house, and a middle-aged man walked to the door and rang the bell.

Ben opened the door, and the man asked, "Are you Ben Kaiser?"

"Yes."

The man reached into his coat and handed Ben an envelope. "Here is a message from the Department of Energy. Have a good day."

Stunned, Ben closed the door and opened the envelope, dreading its contents. DOE offered to accept his resignation, and preserve his pension, with the option remaining open to prosecute him. He read that if he did not resign, the Department of Justice may indict and prosecute him, and if convicted, send him to prison and cancel his pension. His resolve to stay sober crumbled.

He retrieved and guzzled the rest of the now vinegar tasting champagne he had purchased to celebrate the DOE IT Consolidated Support Contract award with Amy eleven months earlier. The initial impact of alcohol destroyed years of sobriety.

He left the house, walked a few blocks, and purchased a fifth of vodka. He drank it with orange juice until he passed out on his living room couch with the DOE letter on the coffee table staring at him.

THE OPPORTUNITY

Ben woke up early Friday morning; his head hurting and experiencing an overwhelming thirst, which he quenched with the remaining orange juice. He cried when he realized he had broken eight years of abstinence. Still not sober, he blamed Laura for the fall, not himself. He wanted to find out why she had confided in the reporter. He had thought, as old lovers, she would sympathize with his plight. Laura and Amy were just like his ex-wife; they used him no matter how well he behaved toward them.

Ben staggered off the couch and noticed his unrecognizable image shaking in the mirror. He had not shaved since Sunday and he wore two-day-old, dirty, wrinkled clothes. He smelled his body odor and remembered he last showered on Monday. Feeling he could not confront Laura the way he looked, he went into the bathroom. His shaking hand cut his face three times while shaving. He washed his wounds, placed bandages over the wounds, turned on a hot shower, and let himself soak for a few minutes before he washed the grime of the last week off his body. The facial cuts reopened in the shower as he dried himself. After rebandaging the cuts, he dressed in clean clothes, walked into the kitchen, had more orange juice, made coffee, and ate two waffles.

After finishing his breakfast without getting sick, he filled a thermos bottle with coffee and drove to 5410 Connecticut Avenue in Chevy Chase, DC, arriving at 7:45. He assumed she had not left for work and would not buzz him into her apartment. He sat in his car on Legation Avenue where he could see her car in the parking lot next to the building. Ben sipped his coffee, and stared at the entrance to her apartment. At 9:15 he saw her leave the entrance and walk toward her car. He jumped from his car and ran to intercept her. She clicked her keys to open the door just as he arrived at her car.

"Laura."

"What are you doing here?"

"Why did you tell that reporter about our

conversation? I thought we had a special relationship."

"Are you kidding? What world do you live in? You drop me for that fat slut, gave my prime contract to her firm, and almost caused my firm to go bankrupt. I recorded our conversation and gave the reporter a USB drive copy. You're disgusting. I read other women said you always trade contract funds for sex."

"You don't understand," Ben said, shocked at her rebuke. He started to walk toward her.

"Don't come any closer," Laura shouted.

Not stopping, Laura reached into her coat pocket and aimed the pepper spray directly into his eyes. Ben screamed, feeling the unbearable pain. His eyes instantly closed, blinding him, and his nose started running in reaction. He stood where she sprayed him. She smiled looking at him suffer, entered her car and drove away. He dared not move, afraid of walking into moving traffic. After ten minutes, the pain faded, and he moved his arm to find a car to lean on. After twenty minutes more he could open his eyes, and he saw his parked car. Still coughing, he dabbed his runny nose with his handkerchief and stumbled to his car to drive home. He stopped at a liquor store, succumbing to the irresistible drive to take the only medicine he knew to stop the pain.

Ben poured his first drink of the day at ten. Two women who hated him had recordings implicating him in serious felonies. Amy, who he loved, had told him she never wanted to see him again. DOE wanted him to resign, and if he did, he still might be prosecuted and sent to prison. As he continued drinking, he began to visualize ending the pain and hopelessness by going to sleep forever. He went to his bathroom and retrieved two containers of OxyContin prescribed for severe pain after dental surgery over the last four years. Ben's fear of addiction had been so great that previously he took only two pills from each bottle, willing to suffer the pain rather than return to chemical dependence. He walked back into the living room and put the containers next to his letter from DOE.

Ben remembered the time his parents put down his childhood dog. While Ben felt great pain, the dog experienced nothing forever.

Ben had played a high-stakes game with Amy and had lost. He wanted to be like his dog, ending his pain. He emptied both containers into his right hand and threw some of pills into his mouth swallowing them with orange juice and vodka. It took him three tries to complete ingesting the drugs. He last thought of his daughters, realizing he could not stop what he started.

After meeting with DOE Friday afternoon, FBI Special Agent Jennifer Tompkins returned to her office with the background information Audrey used to prepare her report. She knew the time criticality of the investigation, since Ben Kaiser, an intelligent, financially stable individual, could flee from his home, go overseas, or change his identity and disappear in the US. She requested and received permission from her boss, Jack MacDonald, to work over the weekend and read Audrey's material. She went home at 9:00, when she was too tried to continue working.

Jennifer returned to her office on Saturday, continued the research, and became incensed at Ben's callous treatment of women and disregard for his contracting officer's responsibilities to protect DOE from financial abuse. She prepared a search warrant for Ben's home, hoping to find additional evidence before Ben destroyed it.

At noon, she called her boss. "Jack, I'm sorry to bother you at home, but I've drafted a search warrant for Ben Kaiser's home. I want to e-mail it to you."

"Go ahead. Hold on while I read it.

"The search warrant's perfect. Bring it to Judge Clayton, DC Court, who's on call. Call me when it's signed."

Jennifer called Judge Clayton at his home. "Hi, this is FBI Special Agent Jennifer Tompkins. I'd like to speak to Judge Clayton."

"He's playing golf at Congressional Country Club. He'll be home at two. Is it anything critical that you need to see him right away?" his wife, Molly, asked.

"No. I have a search warrant I would like him to sign." Jennifer assumed critical meant a national security matter or a serial killer.

"I'll call him to make sure he doesn't change his plans and is home at two."

"Thanks very much." Jennifer e-mailed Jack to say she had an appointment at two to have Judge Clayton sign the warrant.

She called Jack as she drove from Clayton's home. "Jack, it's Jennifer, I have the signed warrant."

"Good, go to our office, make a couple of copies and leave one on my desk for the files. I'll meet you at the office at four and we'll drive to Kaiser's home."

Jennifer and Jack, plus two other agents wearing FBI jackets arrived at Ben's house at five. Jack directed the other two agents to guard any exits they found at the back of the house, while he and Jennifer approached the front door with the warrant. Before knocking Jennifer glanced through a front window and noticed Ben motionless on the couch.

She showed Jack, who said, "He looks passed out." He radioed Ben's condition to the other agents.

"Knock on the door. If he doesn't wake up, we'll enter forcibly," Jack said.

When Ben did not move, Jack picked the lock, and they went into the house.

"Ben Kaiser, we're FBI agents with a warrant to search your home," Jack announced.

Ben still remained motionless. Jennifer walked over and checked his pulse.

"He's dead."

"Open the back door and let the others in, while I call the DC police. Don't touch anything in this room, while you search the other rooms. The vodka and empty containers of OxyContin on the coffee table make it look like a suicide," Jack said.

The FBI found nothing incriminating in their search. They seized his cell phone and laptop. The DC police arrived and took the body away for an autopsy. In the evening the DC police issued a press release stating that Ben Kaiser, found dead by the FBI at his home, had apparently committed suicide.

Chapter 18 Congressional Reaction

The Washington Reporter articles shocked and dismayed the fab four congressmen. However, as veteran politicians, they didn't panic. They realized the articles didn't incriminate them, but included their names for shock value. They arranged to meet for a Sunday golfing outing, without their wives, at Congressman Ed Walinski's vacation home at Henlopen on Saturday, June 25, to discuss their strategy.

They arrived in separate cars around seven in the evening. Ed had purchased four subs.

"You all look hungry. The subs are your favorites from Casapulla South."

He placed them on the table, and went to the refrigerator to retrieve their favorite drinks and condiments.

"While we're eating, I'm going to discuss our response, if any, to the Washington Reporter articles," Ed said.

Jim O'Neill from Utica, New York, reached for the steak-and-cheese sub, and started talking.

"We should investigate all contingencies, including our relationship with Ben Kaiser. The articles may be positive publicity for us. My hometown paper published an editorial on the article, praising me for bringing CIN Inc.'s long-term work to our depressed district. They stated the article does not charge my actions were illegal, but that I was caught up in an unrelated scandal on the DOE IT Consolidated Support Contract."

Sam Johnson from Boise, Idaho, chomping on his Italian sub replied, "My local paper wrote a similar article."

Ernesto Gomez, representing, San Antonio, Texas, chewing his meatball and provolone sub, continued, "My paper too. There's nothing like free publicity."

Ed responded to the happy chorus, "Mine too. Remember these papers are loyal to us and should be expected to support us unless we're directly accused of corruption. I'm worried what the FBI, an unbiased agency, will say about us. If they accuse us of a crime, supported by evidence, I doubt if our newspapers will be as positive as they are now."

These sobering words dampened the group's enthusiasm. Ed continued, "I've prepared a series of questions. Their answers will tell us if we have problems."

"Go ahead," Ernesto said.

"At our meeting here on September 19, 2009, we agreed we should not either publicly or privately support CIN Inc.'s bid for the DOE IT contract. Did anyone violate our agreement?"

"No," they all stated.

"Good. That eliminates any charge the FBI could make that we directly supported CIN Inc. in a quid pro quo relationship, where CIN Inc. would bring jobs to our districts in exchange for us pressuring DOE to award them the contract.

"Second, has anyone met with or had a direct communication with Ben Kaiser, not related to DOE business in our offices or outside of a congressional hearing?"

"No," they again answered.

"Good. I assume we're telling the truth, since the FBI has ways to discover when people meet or communicate. If we didn't privately contact Kaiser, that means we couldn't have directly coerced him into awarding CIN Inc. the contract.

"Third, CIN Inc. has contributed the legal corporate maximum to our campaigns. Has anyone received backdoor contributions besides their legal contribution?"

"No," they all shouted.

"Good. The FBI cannot alert the Federal Election Commission and charge us for directly supporting CIN Inc. in exchange for money.

"Finally, has anyone had private or physical contact with Amy Ericson? While we love our wives, we met her at CIN Inc.'s introductory presentations. She's sexy and curvaceous. She appeared very friendly at my meeting."

"No!"

"Gentleman, don't be insulted. The article charged she traded sex for the contract with Ben Kaiser. Why wouldn't she do it with us if she had the opportunity and thought she'd be successful? That's my last question. We don't have to worry or respond to the articles. Does anyone want to say anything else?"

Before they could answer, Ed's cell phone rang. Looking at the screen, he said, "I have to answer. It's one of my staff."

"Sorry to bother you, Congressman, but I read over the news wire that the FBI discovered Ben Kaiser dead at his home. He apparently committed suicide by overdosing on prescription drugs and alcohol."

"Thanks. You did right to call me. Follow the Kaiser story and call me tomorrow with updates."

Ed smiled and said, "I have the pleasure to announce that the FBI found the dead body of Ben Kaiser at his home. They believe he committed suicide."

The other congressmen smiled.

"While Ben's death will help protect us, we should be concerned, since we found the FBI is now involved. There's nothing more to discuss here. Let's finish our dinner and have a few drinks."

Chapter 19 The Washington Reporter's Final Article

Mason called Ralph Summers at 8:30 a.m. on Sunday. "Ralph, we just received a notice that Ben Kaiser committed suicide. The FBI found him yesterday afternoon. We need to include an article in Monday's paper to follow up the original three."

"I'm at the office writing it."

"Great. Call me when you're ready for me to read a draft."

Ralph had arrived at the office ten minutes before the call and had typed in a draft outline for the article: report Ben's suicide, summarize the previous three articles, speculate on the causes of Ben's suicide, and discuss the future of the investigation. He felt he would have no problem writing the first two sections, but decided to call Amy Ericson, Laura, and the others he interviewed to determine what caused Ben to commit suicide.

Amy picked up her cell phone at three.

"Hi, Ralph Summers of the Washington Reporter. We mentioned your name in our paper last week. Can I ask you a few questions and give you a chance to respond to the statements in the articles?"

"I want to respond. Go ahead."

"Did you know Ben Kaiser is dead?"

"Christ, no, I didn't. How did he die?"

"The police think he committed suicide. Do you want to comment on his death?"

"I'm sorry for Ben. However, I've no comment." Amy realized she could not be charged or convicted of corruption with Ben dead. Before it had been a case of he said—she said, and she had the embarrassing videos to prove her innocence, now she could keep them private for her old age.

"Any comments on the allegations in the article?"

"Yes, I don't know your source, but they're complete fabrications. I never asked Ben for confidential bidding information related to the DOE IT bid."

"Would you repeat that claim in court?"

"Yes. Your paper is a more stringent court than the states. You drive people to death."

"Thank you for your time."

Ralph next called Laura on his untraceable cell phone. When she answered, he said, "It's Ralph. Did you hear Ben killed himself yesterday?"

"Yes, I've been listening to WTOP."

"Do you have any comment on what caused him to do it?"

"Yes, your articles."

Ralph could not understand why the woman who started the story blamed him and not herself for his death. "I just talked to Amy Ericson, who denied any exchange of sex for information."

"What did you expect?"

"Unless you identify yourself as the source of Ben's confession, the FBI will have to drop the case."

"Ralph, Ben's suicide is punishment enough. I don't want my name released and ruin my career. Ben has paid for his behavior. I'm in no mood to try to ruin both my and Amy's life."

"Are you sure?"

"Yes."

"OK, thanks for bringing me the original story. We'll have to have a drink when it's over."

"Mister, I don't know what you're talking about; I didn't bring you anything, but I'd enjoy the drink."

Ralph returned to writing. There was nothing to add to his original speculation about Ben's death. He included Amy's denial of the article's earlier charges in Monday's draft. After receiving and reading the draft, Mason made a few editorial changes, e-mailed it back to Ralph, and called.

"Ralph, Mason. Could you talk to your anonymous source and get the person to identify him or herself? If you don't, the FBI may end the investigation."

"Mason, I tried. It's no use. They don't care if it ends. They think Ben's suicide is penalty enough."

"They're probably right. Send the draft to a copy editor and I'll tell the night editor to make sure it's on page one. It was a great two weeks; too bad it had to end, but you'll find another great story."

Chapter 20 CIN Inc. Staff Reaction

Amy called Pete, who was driving home from the beach Sunday afternoon. He pressed the Bluetooth cell phone button on the steering wheel. "Pete, I just found out Ben committed suicide."

"Are you kidding?"

"No, the FBI found his body yesterday. He took a prescription drug overdose."

"Let me find a place to pull over, it's too dangerous to drive talking about Ben's death." Pete drove into the Premium Outlets on Route 50 in Queenstown, Maryland.

"What else do you know?"

"Ralph Summers from the Washington Reporter just called me. He asked me if I had any comments on Ben's death. I said no."

"Good. If you said you're glad or sad he would publish your response and twist your words so you'd appear guilty."

"He asked me if I wanted to respond to any of the allegations printed in the three articles. I told him his source was wrong and denied ever asking Ben for confidential information related to the DOE bid."

"Good, I hope he quotes you."

"He said he would."

"Great. I meet with Shafer tomorrow at nine to discuss CIN Inc.'s next steps. I'm sure this will change our strategy. Call Art and Tim, and ask them to meet us in my office at ten. Thanks for calling. I'll drive home smiling."

Pete woke up early and waited for the newspaper. He sipped his coffee and picked at his bacon and eggs impatiently until he heard the paper slam against his door. The article reported Amy's denial of all the allegations, but he cringed when he read the last section speculating whether the FBI could continue the investigation in spite of Ben's suicide.

Pete walked into Shafer's office Monday morning to find him smiling.

"Good morning? Our meeting will be short. I met with my boss at eight o'clock, and we have decided to fight for the contract regardless of DOE plans. If DOE issues a stop work order we'll take them to court. Since DOE gave us an excellent performance rating, they shouldn't want to cancel, except for believing a lying, cheating contracting officer, who has committed suicide. Tell the DOE contract team not to worry; their jobs are secure."

Pete's staff relaxed at the contract management meeting when Pete told them of Shafer's assurances on their jobs, and that CIN Inc. had committed to defending any stop work order in court.

"Our stock price has crashed from twenty-six to nineteen because of the articles. You may be concerned how the crash will affect your stock options and your ultimate retirement—but except for Art, who has a federal pension—you're young and the stock price should recover, so you'll have a great retirement."

Pete thought I've already lost two million. The price better increase or I'll be forced to postpone my retirement again.

"It's not over yet. Since the FBI found Ben's body, we can assume they may continue their investigation until they absolve CIN Inc. Since Ben's dead, he cannot lie about Amy or CIN Inc. Last week, the situation had to be resolved in the courts, unless DOE or the FBI thought Ben's whistle-blower lied. Now Ben doesn't have to defend himself against the accusations, and unless the whistle-blower has proof, the investigation should end."

While not telling his staff, Pete feared the FBI would doggedly continue their investigation, even with Ben dead, and discover CIN Inc.'s efficient information-collecting procedures.

"Art, how are we performing at DOE? Is Roger Meeks still supporting us?"

"Still the same as Roger Meeks promised earlier. DOE's technical staff didn't like the way Ben treated them, so maybe we'll be OK."

Ben's death initially relieved Amy of fearing prosecution, but it made her wonder if she caused it. He took the pills, but did she send him to the medicine cabinet to get them? Her guilty feeling increased throughout Monday.

Pete's reference to the FBI investigation revived her fear of prosecution. While never planning to use the video, she assumed the FBI would question her and wondered if she had the strength to keep to her story.

Steve's absence tormented Amy. She missed not being in his arms. He didn't know of her new assignment to market his contract, and now it didn't matter. She considered her future at CIN Inc. with Steve over, and had been contemplating a new life since the articles appeared.

Amy called Pete. "I need to talk to you. Can you walk me to Starbucks?"

"Of course. I'm doing something now, but I'll meet you at the elevator at noon."

When they met, Pete said, "Would you like to get lunch?"

"No, I'm not hungry."

"What's bothering you, Amy?"

"I've decided to resign."

"Why?"

"Several reasons: the article and its personal attacks on me; Ben's suicide, the FBI investigation; Steve Gardner has stopped seeing me because of the articles, so my new marketing goal can never be achieved; and I'm burned out. I've enough money to live without working for a while."

"Amy, you think you have enough money, but you don't, if you live over thirty more years. If you leave CIN Inc. you will be leaving a four-year annual bonus of four hundred thousand.

"I'm sorry about Steve. You did great work analyzing the opportunity. I'll assign another marketing person to Social Security. Now that Ben's gone, you can go back to doing the QA on the DOE support contract until we find you an opportunity," Pete said, not wanting to lose Amy's skills.

"Pete, I'm sick of the marketing procedures we used. While I liked the sex, trading it for information caused Ben's suicide."

"No. He was a sexual predator, and if it wasn't you, he'd have found someone else. Don't blame yourself for his actions. You could see from the article, you're not the first one he sexually exploited. You didn't entrap him, he entrapped you."

"I'm afraid of going to jail. The FBI might be more efficient than we think. I'm worried I'll tell them something I'll regret under questioning."

"Amy, if you leave CIN Inc. you'll be admitting your guilt. If you stay, you'll have a lawyer to protect you during the questioning—if it occurs. I'm not going to accept your resignation. You're upset now, but if you leave, you'll be defenseless and it will be hard for you to get another job under the cloud of the articles and Ben's suicide. I'm your friend. Trust me. Don't talk of resignation until the investigation ends."

Amy, who had been completely sure of herself before they talked, began to have other fears: no job, no income, alone and defenseless against the FBI, the loss of $1.6 million, and no lover.

"I'll give the job one more month, and then we'll see what happens."

"You won't regret your decision."

Art left the Monday morning meeting reassured Ben's death saved his job. He wondered why Ben committed suicide, and he planned to ask Joan for her opinion that evening at dinner at his condo.

After Amy entered his condo and kissed him, Art said, "Let me tell you what Pete told us today at our staff meeting, and then I want you to tell me what you think happened to change Shafer's mind."

"Can we cook while you talk?"

"Yes. I'll prepare the swordfish and the risotto."

"Good, I'll make the salad after I pour us a glass of Chardonnay."

"Pete said that Ben's suicide changed everything. That with Ben dead, the problem should go away. That's Pete playing lawyer. I just wonder what actually happened."

"I don't know, and since Amy is my best friend, I'm not going to ask her. Ben's behavior toward women dependent on his approval for their income was deplorable. I've been in marketing for fourteen years, and I've never experienced his type of sexual pressure. He might have tried it with Amy and failed. I assume the whistle-blower is a woman he screwed in the past as part of her contract duties, and she became pissed off when he dropped her for another woman. I'm going to let it go. Since DOE loves you, and CIN Inc. is delivering, don't worry. I'm not going to talk to Amy, and I hope you don't."

"You're right. No matter what happened, it doesn't concern me. I'll let it go."

Chapter 21 FBI's Decision on Continuing the Investigation

The FBI team returned to headquarters on Pennsylvania Avenue Saturday evening, after searching Ben Kaiser's home, to plan the future of the investigation.

"Ben's suicide is a problem, since he's the main target for an indictment. With him dead, who do we go after? Both the article and the DOE report stated he acted alone in his criminal endeavors. I don't think CIN Inc. as a corporation conspired with Ben to win the contract. Amy Ericson is the only other target, and like the other women Ben was involved with, he probably manipulated her in spite of what the article stated. It's noteworthy, that all the accusations in the article, except the CIN Inc. allegations, cited an individual who made them," Jack said.

"I agree; it may not be worth our while. But I want to spend one more week investigating potential Ben Kaiser-CIN Inc. corporate corruption. I'm going to get the cell phone and laptop examined for any relationship between Kaiser, Amy, and CIN Inc.," Jennifer said.

"Are you sure you want to work a week more on this case?"

"Yes. Without reading the official autopsy or the DC police crime report, we're just assuming it's a suicide."

"You win. If it's ruled a suicide, or you don't find a major conspiracy at CIN Inc., you'll end it."

"Agreed."

"I'll call the DC medical examiner to expedite the autopsy," Jack said.

"I'll interview Ralph Summers, the Washington

Reporter writer, and follow that with talking to those named in his articles. I'll interview the CIN Inc. staff last."

"Good. Keep me informed."

Jennifer Tompkins met Ralph Summers at the FBI on Monday afternoon after reading the last article. She offered to visit his office, but as a curious reporter, who had never been to the FBI building, he chose to visit her.

"Thanks for coming, Mr. Summers."

"You're welcome. I've read your articles with interest, since they involve accusations of fraud in federal contracting at the Department of Energy. DOE has asked the FBI to investigate the allegations. Of course, the death of Mr. Kaiser has complicated this task."

"The article speaks for itself. Why did you say death and not suicide?"

"That's just a legal definition. We're waiting for the DC medical examiner's autopsy report before we can state how he died."

"Interesting. I thought the story ended with Kaiser's death."

"Not necessarily. There's still the matter of the CIN Inc. and DOE fraud in contracting allegations. You mentioned several sources in your article. Do you think they will testify in court?"

"Yes, they want to testify. Although, I recommend giving them immunity so they won't be implicated, or they may decline."

"Good. I plan to interview them. You made direct allegations that Ben Kaiser accepted sexual bribes in exchange for confidential information for the DOE IT bid, but you didn't mention the name of your source. Can you name them, since their testimony is the key to allegations of the Kaiser-CIN Inc. conspiracy?"

"I wish I could, since fraud should be prosecuted where ever it occurs, but the source asked me not to reveal their name. As a member of the press, I must protect their wishes. If I didn't, whistle-blowing sources may be less willing to provide us confidential information. Freedom of the press is critical in keeping government honest."

"Without that information it may be difficult to continue with the case. The FBI could always subpoena their name."

"We both know that would fail in DC, since sources are protected by the DC reporter shield law."

"Well, thanks for your help. I might get back to you. If your source changes their mind, call me."

"If Kaiser's death isn't a suicide, there will be another article. I'll ask my source to reconsider, and if they do, I'll tell you."

Ralph never called Laura.

Jennifer called and scheduled meetings for the names mentioned in the newspaper articles. Unlike Ralph, they preferred not to go to the FBI building. She learned nothing new from what the articles reported, except more details to confirm the original allegations. The witnesses could only be used to describe Ben's illegal behavior and could not implicate CIN Inc., since their events occurred before CIN Inc.'s bid on the contract.

Jennifer hoped for better results on Wednesday when she received the analysis report of Ben's cell phone and laptop use, after she completed the scheduled interviews with three CIN Inc. staff: Pete, Amy, and Art.

Pete's administrative assistant escorted Jennifer into Pete's office. She was surprised to see two men in the office; she expected to meet only Pete, who talked first.

"Hi, you must be Jennifer Tompkins from the FBI. I'm Pete Taylor. I'd like to introduce you to our corporate legal counsel, Paul Saunders. While we want to cooperate in your investigation, our corporate policy requires that counsel be present at all interviews by legal authorities to protect both CIN Inc. and its staff from incriminating themselves. I'm sure you understand.

"Yes. These questions will not take long."

"Can we get you coffee or something to drink?" Pete asked.

"No. I'm fine. Mr. Taylor, how long had you known Ben Kaiser?"

"I didn't know him that well. I first met him at Rehoboth Beach ten years ago. At that time he drank heavily, and one night he insulted one of my future employees, Amy Ericson—mentioned in the Reporter article—and we got into an altercation. I suggested he leave the beach and never return. He complied.

"I next saw him at the bidder's conference for the DOE IT opportunity six years later. The auditorium was full with several hundred contractors, so he might never have seen me. We met at our kickoff meeting after we won the contract. I'd meet with him occasionally at his office on contract-related business."

"At any time did you offer him a bribe to obtain DOE confidential information related to the bid?"

"No, of course not."

"Did you encourage any of your employees, specifically Amy Ericson, to try to obtain DOE confidential information?"

"No. Amy was the lead marketing executive for CIN Inc. on the opportunity, and her job was to obtain nonconfidential intelligence. She knew of CIN Inc.'s policy against obtaining illegal information, and that she'd be fired if we discovered she violated that rule."

Jennifer continued asking questions to confirm information printed in the paper and those in the DOE-provided files. When she finished, she asked to talk to Art Mitchell.

"I'll call him. You can talk to him in my conference room. Paul, of course, will be present."

"Thanks. Please show me to a restroom. I'll have that coffee now, if it's still available."

Jennifer asked Art the same questions she asked Pete and received similar answers.

"Mr. Mitchell, what can you tell me about Amy and Ben's relationship?"

"That question is too open-ended. Please ask a more specific question," Paul Saunders, the lawyer, interjected.

"Do you know if Amy and Ben had a romantic relationship in addition to their regular business relationship?"

"I have no knowledge of a romantic relationship."

"I assume that Amy briefed you on her meetings with Ben and the intelligence she gathered on the DOE IT contract. Is that correct?"

"Yes, our capture group had weekly meetings as the date for the release of the RFP approached."

"Did Amy provide you or the group with DOE confidential information, not available to the public?"

"No."

"How did you know the information was not confidential?"

"Amy always referenced her sources: DOE documents or websites, third-party references, or marketing meetings with Ben and CIN Inc. staff. I attended many of those marketing meetings with Amy."

Jennifer had finished her questioning.

"Thanks, Mr. Mitchell."

She turned to Paul. "Ask Amy Ericson to come for an interview."

"I'll call her."

Amy, looking stoic, but feeling nervous, entered the room and said, "Hi, I'm Amy Ericson. You're Jennifer Tomkins from the FBI."

"Yes, I am. I'm going to ask you a few questions related to the DOE IT contract and the articles in the Washington Reporter."

"Go ahead."

Jennifer repeated many of the questions she had asked Pete and Art and received consistent answers. She asked critical personal questions after fifteen minutes of routine questioning.

"Ms. Ericson, were you and Ben Kaiser dating?"

"I'm going to ask Ms. Ericson not to answer that question, because it violates her privacy," Paul said.

"OK. I'll ask another question related to the allegations in the newspaper articles. Ms. Ericson, did you trade sex for confidential information on the DOE bid?"

"No, I didn't trade sex for information. Furthermore, I assumed what Ben Kaiser told me wasn't confidential," Amy said, looking straight into Jennifer's eyes.

"Thank you, Ms. Ericson. I have no further questions."

Pete joined Paul in his office after Amy's interview concluded.

"Paul, how do you think the interviews went?"

"Fine. No one said anything that could implicate CIN Inc. and Amy in fraud connected with Ben Kaiser. I don't think DOE will be able to justify ending the DOE contract."

"Good. Tell Shafer what you heard."

While Pete exhibited a calm exterior demeanor, inside he trembled. He knew if the FBI continued their investigation, they would discover more details of Amy and Ben's relationship, and perhaps his use of George Steen to illegally collect information related to the DOE contract and other opportunities. As the leader of a large long-term conspiracy to defraud the federal government, he feared an indictment by the FBI.

Jennifer returned to her office Wednesday afternoon to find a report on her desk with the analysis of Ben's cell phone and laptop.

Jennifer and her boss, Jack, met on Thursday

morning to review Jennifer's progress, and the DC autopsy report.

Jack spoke first. "The examination of Ben's home laptop and cell phone finds contact with Amy ended at least thirty days before the release of the RFP. The e-mails between Ben and Amy were always professional. DOE let us examine Ben's office PC. We found nothing more showing a Ben Kaiser-Amy Ericson relationship. The DC medical examiner called me this morning. He told me they found no signs of forced entry or of other individuals in the room when Ben died. The police found only Ben's fingerprints on the glass he drank from and on his pill bottles. Thus, the DC police concluded, Ben committed suicide. What have you discovered?"

"Nothing new. Ralph Summers won't tell us the source of the allegations against CIN Inc. Amy Ericson looked me in the eye and repeated her statements that appeared in the Summers' articles—that she never asked Ben Kaiser for confidential information related to the DOE bid. Since Kaiser's dead, there's no way to contest her statements, especially after your negative findings on his laptop and cell phone. I tend to believe her. I'm willing to stop working on the investigation."

"That a good decision. Rather than close the investigation, since something might come up later, I'd like to keep it open and not release our findings to the public."

"I guess you'll assign me another project."

"I will, but not right now. Go home and relax, you worked hard enough the last week. I'll talk to you tomorrow."

No one told Pete and Amy that the investigation had ended. They drove to Rehoboth Beach to enjoy the tuxedo party and the alcohol-filled July 4 weekend—fearing an arrest at any time.

Chapter 22 Pete Taylor's Fate

Art and Amy stood over Pete waiting for the ambulance to arrive. Pete had stopped shaking, but he kept breathing. The ambulance took thirty minutes to transverse the seven miles of crowded July Fourth Route 1 and Rehoboth Avenue, from Beebe Medical Center in Lewes, Delaware, to downtown Rehoboth. The medics attended to Pete, providing him oxygen after they had diagnosed a heart attack as the likely clause of his collapse.

The ambulance driver asked Art, "Did you place the 911 call?"

"Yes."

"What's the patient's name. Tell me if you know their address, next of kin and any other identification information. What happened before he collapsed?"

Art answered the driver's questions, as the EMS staff continued working on Pete. They placed him on a stretcher and loaded him into the ambulance. The driver ended the conversation with Art, saying, "We are taking him to the emergency room at Beebe, where he'll be transferred to cardiac care. Follow us to the emergency room to learn about his condition. However, it may take several hours before he's stabilized and you can talk to him."

Amy and Art watched the ambulance leave. Amy looked at Art. "Are you in any shape to drive?"

"Yes. My car's at the beach house. Let's walk there since the Jolly Trolley will be too slow and crowded tonight."

They reached the car twenty-minutes later and didn't talk on the hour drive on congested Route 1. Amy spoke as they entered the hospital. "Pete has made me a rich woman, even though my career in government marketing may have ended. I hope my future is as exciting as the years since my divorce, when I had no idea what to do."

"You both introduced me to a new more exciting world than being a DOE bureaucrat after my retirement. While my original retirement income allowed me to survive, I now have real money, a vivacious, beautiful girlfriend, access to a summer beach house, and a detailed view of how government contractors operate. I can't ever go back to my former quiet, innocent life now that my wife has been dead for six years. I hope Pete's OK."

"So do I, but a heart attack at his age, weight, and lifestyle is not a minor event."

"You're right."

At the emergency room's receiving desk Art said, "My name is Art Mitchell. I made a 911 call for a friend, Pete Taylor, who had a heart attack in Rehoboth. Your EMS staff took him here and told us to come here to find out about his condition."

"Just a second." The receptionist accessed her computer and retrieved Pete's medical records.

"Are either of you a relative of the patient?"

"No. Both of us work with him."

"Do you know how to contact his relatives?"

"I have his oldest daughter's contact information on my phone. He said to call her in case of an emergency. Why?" Amy replied.

"We always notify the patient's relatives when a patient is brought into the Beebe emergency room. He's unconscious and couldn't provide us next-of-kin information. I was hoping you would."

Amy provided her the name and phone number. "What's his condition? When can we talk to him?"

"We moved him to the cardiac care unit, and his doctor has classified him in critical condition. You can't talk to him until he regains consciousness and his condition is upgraded from critical. I doubt that will happen tonight. I suggest you go home or to your hotel and call back tomorrow morning."

"The roads are jammed. We'll wait here a few hours until they clear. Hopefully Pete's condition will improve," Art replied.

"Take a seat here. If anything changes, I'll tell you."

Amy and Art sat down, and Art said, "I'm surprised you had Pete's daughter's contact information."

"Pete knew he had stress problems and feared losing his retirement funds. He gave me the contact information."

They both reminisced about their relationship with Pete, both the good and recent bad times. They wondered what the impact on their future would be if Pete died. Amy fell asleep at midnight, followed by Art fifteen minutes later.

The receptionist woke Art at 3:15 a.m. "I'm sorry. Your friend never regained consciousness, and his heart failed. The cardiac staff could not revive him. He died fifteen minutes ago. We contacted his daughter last night. She will be driving to Lewes early this morning. We haven't told her of his death, and we suggest you shouldn't either. We don't want to upset her while she's driving."

Amy woke up halfway through the conversation and heard Pete had died.

Thank you for reading *The Opportunity*. If you liked the book, or my other books, please write an Amazon review to inform other potential readers they would enjoy the book. Please open my Amazon author page to access the forms to write your review.

https://www.amazon.com/Frank-E.-Hopkins/e/B0028AR904

Chick on the book cover of the book you want to review and the review option will appear toward the bottom of the page.

About the Author

Frank E Hopkins attended Hofstra University in the 1960s. He became involved in writing while earning his Ph.D. in economics from the University of Maryland. He held the position of associate professor at the State University of New York at Binghamton in the 1970s, where he published numerous refereed journal articles and a monograph on industrial location. He continued technical writing while working at the Department of Energy in the late 1970s and as a government and business development consultant since 1980. While at the Department of Energy he started the publication, *Short-Term Energy Outlook,* which is still published by DOE. He moved to Ocean View, Delaware, in 2001 where, as a consultant, he managed or participated in writing large winning proposals in response to federal government solicitations.

The Opportunity is Frank's second novel. *Unplanned Choices,* Frank's first novel, is a historical romantic drama set in the late 1960s and early 1970s in New York City and Long Island during the turbulent period of the Vietnam War, the sexual revolution, the women's movement, and the struggle for legalizing abortion. Frank's collection ten of short stories, *First Time,* is set in East Coast locations he visited that inspired the book's stories.

Frank is active in the Rehoboth Beach Writers Guild and the Eastern Shore Writers Association, where he participates in writers critique groups. He is also a member of the Maryland Writers Association. His website address is http://www.frankehopkins.com.

In addition to writing, he plays golf and tennis, sails on the Chesapeake Bay, and enjoys the ocean and inland bays of southern Delaware.

Unplanned Choices by Frank E. Hopkins

Unplanned Choices, a coming-of-age romantic historical drama, is set in the late 1960s and early 1970s in New York City and Long Island during the turbulent period of the Vietnam War, the Civil Rights struggle, the sexual revolution, the women's movement, and the struggle for legalizing abortion.

The novel is the story of Steve Lynch and his first love, Anna Marino. Both Anna and Steve are raised in the Roman Catholic faith and struggle with the church's prohibition of sexual activity and their growing sexual drives. They both meet in college after abandoning the church. Anna became pregnant and died during an abortion, before abortion on demand became legal in New York. The novel describes the impact of the abortion on Steve, the abortionist, Anna's family and friends, and one NYPD investigator who commits murder.

If Anna could have legally had an abortion, she would not have died and the impact on the other characters in the novel would not have been as tragic.

Situations similar to that portrayed in *Unplanned Choices* could be replicated hundreds of thousands of times in the future if abortion becomes illegal or heavily restricted in the United States.

What Readers Say about *Unplanned Choices*

Couldn't put it down.
Incredible. A historical novel that outlines the never-spoken-about sexual revolution and restrictions of women's reproductive rights. The book was so realistic, the characters the same. Easy to get to know them. I wanted to read more and more since I too grew up in that era. *By Lou October 5, 2019.*

Unplanned Choices Explores Sexuality, Religion, Abortion and Culture in a Stimulating, Gripping Manner

UNPLANNED CHOICES

Unplanned Choices explores sexuality, religion, abortion, and culture in a stimulating, gripping manner. *Unplanned Choices* is a gripping book. I read it whenever I could until it ended. I want more from it, and I want more of it. *By Robert J. Anderson on December 1, 2013.*

I could not put it down it left such an impression.
I had to reread it again. I encourage everyone to read to see how far we have come with our rights as women. Please don't let them take it away from us. I was impressed that a man could write so openly and honestly with such insight on the issue of abortion. I will definitely put Mr. Hopkins books on my reading list. *By an Amazon Customer on December 9, 2015*

It's a page turner from page 1.
I really enjoyed this book and found it hard to put down… The story line was fascinating and the relationship it has to our present political climate is frightening. Every congressman and senator should read it along with every justice sitting on the Supreme Court. The thought that Roe v. Wade is even a matter for discussion let alone reversal is archaic and barbaric. They need to read this book for an accounting of what could happen if a woman's right to choose is taken away. I loved the courageous spirit of the women (and men) in this book. I think that style lends itself to a fast read and one that keeps you on your toes. It is now making its way around our office. I will definitely purchase this writer's second book. *By a verified Amazon Customer on January 12, 2016*

Because its subject is one that needs more attention
I applaud this author for taking on this difficult subject. Young people face these issues more than we could ever think, and there is very little guidance regarding all the various outcomes of these decisions. *By Norma on September 7, 2015.*

Awesome Read
I can relate to this book, as a young teenager and young adult in this era when abortion was illegal.
The book shows the doubt of a young woman back in the 60's who did not have a lot of choices in having to deal with a unplanned pregnancy. They had nowhere to turn except to find someone to help in their turmoil who did not have the skills of a professional physician. Some paid with their life as so well portrayed in this book. *By Judith L. Kirlan on October 10, 2016.*

Read this book for a wonderful perspective of a time gone bye but still relevant …
While reading *Unplanned Choices* I was transported to my youth and the

era of secret relationships. Many memories of the pressure of feeling guilty about natural impulses were resurrected. The characters are clearly defined and draw the reader into the story with enough tension to hold interest. Read this book for a wonderful perspective of a time gone bye but still relevant to today's social, political, and psychological issues. *By Amazon Customer on June 11, 2016*

Compelling and Informative

I recently experienced the pleasure of reading Frank Hopkins first book "unplanned choices ".it proved to be quite provocative, a real "page turner," always educating while inspiring serious thought. Hopkins probes abortion through the lens of Catholicism, re-introducing us to Margaret Sanger an early feminist, women's rights activist and nurse who coined the term "birth control," ultimately opening the first clinic in the United States. Additionally, he explores civil liberties and the Vietnam War. The narrative flows developing the characters while analyzing their choices. I would highly recommend this book. *By Linda D. on June 6, 2017*

First Time by Frank E Hopkins

The Delaware Press Association has awarded *First Time* second place for the best collection of short stories by a single author in their 2017 Communications Contest.

First Time is a collection of ten short stories. While each story has separate characters they are linked by the theme that each story exposes the main character to the first time they experience an event participated in by all.

The stories include anticipation of the happiness they expect; the dismay and wonder they feel during the event; and the surprising ending. The stories cover a wide range of events in childhood, coming of age, romance, recovery from divorce, and the declining years.

What readers think of *First Time*

There is something for everyone here *First Time* contains a variety of stories beginning with four dopey college students driving to Florida for spring break and ending with my favorite, a touching story of a widower re-tracing the last vacation he took with his beloved wife, Anne. It's a good collection and an excellent way to get to know the author, Frank Hopkins. *R. E. Reece on August 15, 2016*

...book of short stories entwining each one together...I enjoyed reading how you can relate to past experiences in some way to your own life...I certainly could especially...Santa Claus Stories and My Trip Alone...these stood out for me. *Judith L. Kirlan July 29, 2016*

First Time **is nostalgia at its best**. The variety of stories touch on some part of a reader's own life, from a spring break trip to an exotic love. Frank E. Hopkins does a fine job of weaving the stories that, at first seem to stand on their own, but then all come together. Each story taps into the emotions of events throughout life in a way the reader can relate. All-together, *First Time* makes a great beach read with each story taking just a little of your time. *Jack Coppley June 13, 2016*

First Time **is a witty, eclectic, entertaining collection of memorable times** Author Frank Hopkins' creation "First Time" is a ... collection of memorable times in the lives of ten individuals. First impressions are always the lasting impressions "First Time" will make a pleasant dent in your enjoyment psyche. *Amazon Customer May 17, 2016*

THE OPPORTUNITY

UNPLANNED CHOICES

Made in the USA
Columbia, SC
17 August 2024

40174279R00150